MOUNTING
EVIDENCE

By the Author

Harmony

Worth the Risk

Sea Glass Inn

Improvisation

Mounting Danger

Wingspan

Blindsided

Mounting Evidence

MOUNTING EVIDENCE

by

Karis Walsh

2015

MOUNTING EVIDENCE

ISBN 13: 978-1-62639-343-1

This Trade Paperback Original Is Published By
Bold Strokes Books, Inc.
P.O. Box 249
Valley Falls, NY 12185

First Edition: July 2015

Credits
Editor: Ruth Sternglantz
Production Design: Stacia Seaman
Cover Design by Sheri (graphicartist2020@hotmail.com)

Acknowledgments

I'd like to acknowledge and praise the years of hard work my mom, Maureen, has dedicated to protecting the wetlands in Tacoma. I got my love of nature from her and my dad, and I appreciate the gift.

As always, I have to give credit to the wonderful staff at Bold Strokes Books. Thank you to my editor, Ruth, because she understands my process of writing and is unfailingly patient with me. And to Sandy, who is a constant source of help and advice. To Cindy, Toni, and Connie, as well as the super-talented BSB proofreaders. And to Sheri for this lovely cover. I'm grateful to Radclyffe and the stellar team she has assembled.

Lastly—and most lovingly—thank you to my Cindy for supporting me from start to finish with this book and keeping me supplied with plenty of M&Ms to get through the long hours of writing and editing. My world is richer and brighter because of her.

To Cindy
As always, with love.

CHAPTER ONE

Lieutenant Abigail Hargrove tugged on the shirt of her unfamiliar uniform. The top and pants were skintight—suitable for riding a horse, but awkward while walking through a crowd and feeling too many eyes on her. Even though Abby was no stranger to close-fitting clothes during her off time, when she was on duty she was accustomed to the androgynous polyester-and-wool blend outfit that made her look like every other cop, regardless of how different she felt inside. Pockets bulging with notebooks and pens, a thickly laden duty belt hanging heavy on her hip bones, and the stiff outline of her Kevlar vest. Instead, she had on a snug, short-sleeved blue top with buttons revealing a deeper V than she'd have chosen for herself. Her snug pants had a slimming gold stripe down the side, and her polished black boots looked more stylish than her usual clunky black military ones. Admittedly, most of the glances she received seemed to be complimentary, but she'd prefer anonymity to flattering notice.

Even though her uniform was drawing some looks, her surroundings were doing their utmost to deflect focus away from her. The garish lights and sounds of the Washington State Fair jealously clamored for attention, and Abby skirted long lines of people waiting for fried food or a turn on one of the flashing, whirling rides. The colors were bright and primal, urging fairgoers to stop and spend. No subterfuge or subtlety. The fair in Puyallup was one of the few childhood pleasures Abby still enjoyed.

She paused near her favorite concession stand, briefly tempted by the thought of a cheeseburger topped with a heap of grilled Walla

Walla sweet onions—one of the iconic Washington fair foods—but she ignored her rumbling stomach for the moment and walked on. She'd save the treat for later. The only thing worse than wearing the revealing Lycra uniform in public would be wearing it with a big ketchup or grease stain down the front. She shifted the strap of her navy gym bag, readjusting the comforting weight of street clothes and shoes that it held. She'd perform her duties for the mounted police unit, filling in for a missing officer at this high-profile publicity event, and then she'd become just Abby again. Part of the crowd.

Like many other local officers, she used two weeks of vacation in the fall and spent them doing off-duty work at the fair. It paid well, but that wasn't her reason for giving up her personal time. She had visited the fair as a civilian since she was a kid—screaming on the rides with her friends and trying to beat the suspiciously easy-looking games—and she felt the same rush of anticipation coming here as a working adult. Cool, foggy mornings. Leaves shifting to red-gold. Autumn wasn't autumn unless she came to Puyallup and walked through the barns and exhibit halls, munching on an ear of corn dripping with butter. But aside from the food and memories, the best part of the fair was being assigned to work with officers from other departments. Occasionally she found one who didn't know her family name and reputation.

Abby stopped yet again, pulled by the smell of cinnamon emanating from the elephant ear stand. She licked her lips at the thought of fried dough covered with sugar and spice. Yum. She really should have eaten something before coming to work, but she had been too edgy to feel hunger. Until now, when the aromas seemed amplified by the environment. She was about to resist the call and continue her walk to the barns when a familiar voice called her.

"Hey, Hargrove." Officer Harvey Wayne waded through the crowds and to her side. "Is this where we get kickbacks? Free elephant ears if we promise not to check for clean grease traps?"

Abby forced a smile, although it felt more like a grimace. Some of the older officers on the force, especially those who had served alongside her grandfather, seemed to feel obligated to make jokes about her integrity every time they met. She carefully avoided any suggestion of impropriety in her own conduct, but the name Hargrove had been blackened enough that her efforts were futile.

"I was just deciding where to buy my lunch," Abby said, her voice even and quiet.

Harvey laughed and waved his hand. "I kid, of course. Nice uniform, by the way. You must be riding with your team instead of foot patrol with the rest of us schmucks."

He checked out her shape from her neck to her toes with all the tact of a charging rhinoceros. Abby wanted to cover herself with hands and gym bag but she resisted and forced her expression to remain neutral. His partner for the day—a woman Abby didn't recognize from Orting PD—seemed to be appreciative as well, but in a less obvious way. She was tall and muscular, with a blond heartiness that lived up to the Scandinavian name on her badge. Officer Jorgensen. She looked unbreakable. *Hers* was the kind of notice Abby would normally encourage, but not today. Not in uniform, whether mounted or patrol.

"Yes, I'm filling in for Jensen while he's on leave."

Harvey turned to his partner. "The lieutenant here managed to get approval from the chief and the city for a mounted unit. And in a department that's always facing budget cuts and layoffs." He looked at Abby again. "I don't know how you did it, Hargrove, but I'm impressed."

Liar. Abby heard the criticism in his voice even as he pretended to compliment her in front of his beautiful partner. He was the one trying to impress, but Abby guessed that his target would be more interested in her figure than in his portly male one. Not for long, though, because she was sure Wayne would elaborate on his poorly veiled insinuations once they left Abby's earshot. What would he claim she had used to get approval for her special unit? Bribery? Blackmail? Some form of corruption, because that's what a Hargrove would do.

The real reason she had been able to convince her superiors to grant her request wasn't common knowledge, even in the gossipy

Tacoma department. Abby and her riders had been expected to fail—and miserably—so the city manager could arrange for their rezoned stable area to become a lot full of pricey condos. Funny that a Hargrove had been the innocent one for once, duped by a corrupt scheme. But she didn't let herself rise to the bait Wayne was dangling in front of her. She didn't attempt to defend her indefensible family. No one, no matter how insulting or vindictive, had ever made her lose her cool enough to do so. She had her own way of handling her family's past transgressions, but that took place behind the scenes. In front of an audience, she was solid ice.

"I'd love to see your horses perform," Officer Jorgensen said, with a smile that promised a more intimate kind of performance if Abby was willing. "What time do you ride?"

"We do demonstrations at one and three, by the Pavilion. After that, we'll patrol the midway until the fair closes." Abby might be unemotional on the surface, but her insides were in turmoil. She wanted to ball her hands into fists and look away. Instead, she tried to detach her mind from the conversation, keeping her hands relaxed at her sides while her stomach clenched in their place. Jorgensen would be all too aware of the Hargrove reputation long before one o'clock. Abby felt the loss already. Not of a potential lover—yes, Jorgensen was her type, but Abby's few partners in bed *never* had connections to police work—but the loss of another battle in the never-ending war to somehow get beyond the reach of her family name. Somehow.

"We'll try to stop by," Harvey said. "See those Tacoma tax dollars at work."

"Maybe I'll see you later, then," Abby said, hoping she wouldn't. She walked a few yards before turning back to look at the pair. Wayne leaned close to his partner and gestured toward Abby as he spoke. She shook her head and continued on her way, wondering what stories he was telling. Even she didn't know the true extent of the infractions her grandfather had committed. She had heard some rumors, of course—cash and drugs that never made it to evidence lockers, kickbacks and bribes, even a hint of a sex-ring scandal with a former chief—but she and her family had a firm don't ask, don't tell policy in place. She did her personal research through the department archives, slowly uncovering suspicious reports and doing her best to make things right in a private way. But she had to wade through so many calls and case files, always in secret, and she knew she'd never be able to fix them all. Still, one by one she made the effort.

Abby followed a stripe of green paint on the ground, leading her to the same-colored gate in the southwest corner of the fairgrounds. She could have entered that way and saved some walking, but she had come through the red gate out of habit. She had been entering the fair the same way for over thirty years, and she didn't care to change the familiar ritual. She stopped and looked at the four red barns with bright white trim before her. Brightly colored banners with horse silhouettes identified them as the equine stabling areas. Draft horses, 4-H horses. Another familiar sight from her earliest fair days. The old-fashioned farm aspect of the fair was still alive in the livestock barns and grange exhibits. Goats, cows, and other animals were housed in the center of the fairgrounds, side-by-side with sellers hawking everything from miracle mops to hot tubs. The horses, however, claimed the quieter edge of the fairgrounds. Behind the barns were areas for schooling and safe travel between the stalls and the riding arena. All of the fair barns were kept clean and swept, but the smell of horses and hay still managed to infiltrate the heavier odors of barbecue and pizza.

She sighed with relief when she stepped into the draft horse barn. The crowds were jammed as tightly in here as on the midway since these huge and gentle animals were always a popular draw, but the atmosphere changed somehow. The gaudily colored souvenirs and attractions were replaced by the muted tones of chestnut, gray, and bay. Shrieks and blaring pop music faded behind the sound of rustling straw and an occasional neigh. She walked down the aisle and felt more relaxed just looking at the horses. Tied in straight stalls, they calmly ate hay while their grooms brushed and braided them for the afternoon driving exhibitions. Clydesdales, Percherons, ponies, and draft mules. This had been one of her favorite parts of the fair since childhood, and the massive animals helped pull her back to a more innocent time, when she had been horse crazy and carefree, unaware of how her parents were able to afford her riding lessons and new tack.

She stopped to watch one of the handlers as he lifted an enormous collar over a patient Belgian's head. The leather was polished to a glossy black shine, and the silver embellishments sparkled in the muted sunlight coming from the far door. Abby had been determined to have a career with horses, as a vet or a trainer, before she learned the true price of her riding hobby. She had been twenty-one, nearly half a lifetime away from her current thirty-six, when she overheard her grandfather laughing about some jewelry that had gone missing when he was on a burglary call. *Thank God for senile old women*, her father had said. *That new saddle Abby wants costs a fortune.*

Abby spun around quickly, with a muttered apology for bumping into the young couple behind her, and hurried out the back door of the barn. She leaned against the wall and angled her face so the September sun warmed her closed eyelids and cheeks. Riding had never been the same after that. She had sold her competition horse and changed her major from biology to sociology at Tacoma's University of Puget Sound. She quit spending her time at the barn and took on two jobs and a student loan to pay for her own education. Her eavesdropping was never discussed, but the tenor of her relationship with her family shifted in a heartbeat. If her father wondered what had made Daddy's Little Girl turn into a civil but cold acquaintance, he never tried to find out her reasons. As far as she could tell, he hadn't been personally involved in illegal activities while he was a cop, but he had knowingly benefited from his dad's corruption. In Abby's opinion, his passive acceptance made him even more cowardly than if he'd done the deeds himself. He had retired soon after she was first promoted. The grandfather she had adored passed away mere months after his own retirement and before Abby joined the force herself, but his legacy lived on.

She opened her eyes and brought herself back to the present. She still had horses in her life, at least, even if indirectly. Until recently, she'd had the mare she had just begun training way back when her world had fallen apart. Now, she had her mounted unit. Usually she was a spectator and backstage operator for the team—overseeing budget and schedule, hunting for grant money to keep the horses in oats and shoes. For the next two weeks, though, she'd be a participant, riding after so many months without a horse. She might not be as fit as the riders in her unit, or as skilled as her sergeant Rachel Bryce, but she ought to be able to hold her own. Stay on without making a fool of herself. Keep her composure even though the thought of riding here of all places made too many memories and too much shame resurface.

She looked to her right. A few spectators wandered in the paved area behind the barn, but mainly it was claimed by 4-H kids and their horses who had qualified to participate in the state finals at the fair. A few were walking their animals back and forth between the stabling area and the schooling ring. Several others were bathing their mounts at the wash racks, chatting with friends as they soaped and rinsed their horses. Abby had been one of them, qualifying every year she had been eligible because she'd had the best instruction, horses, and show clothes that dirty money could buy.

Later in the week, when she felt ready for the memories, she'd walk through the 4-H barns and visit with the horses. Until then, she'd slip through the draft barn and behind the main stables to get to the four stalls she'd reserved in a private back corner of the last aisle. She spotted Rachel near the wash racks. Her sergeant—never one to back away from the nitty-gritty details of horse care—was resting on one knee with her back to Abby while she scrubbed a navy blue water bucket. As if aware of Abby's notice, Rachel looked over her shoulder.

"Hello, Lieutenant," she called. "Good to see you ready to ride."

"Thanks, Bryce. I'm glad to be here." Not a complete fabrication, but not absolutely honest, either. Abby walked past the first 4-H barn, refusing to peek through the wide-open door. "Have Billie and Don arrived yet?"

A shrill neigh blocked out Rachel's answer. Abby heard the clatter of shod hooves on cement and she reflexively moved to block the aisle.

"Shit. Nirvana, come back here," a woman shouted from behind the loose horse.

The dark bay mare trotted out of the barn and directly to Abby. She reached for the dangling lead rope although the horse seemed more inclined to stay and nuzzle her than to run any farther. Abby ran her hand over the horse's satiny neck.

Shit was right.

CHAPTER TWO

Abby knew Kira Lovell by name but she had never met—or planned to meet—her. Kira's vitals had been on the report Abby had read almost a year ago, and given the matching attributes combined with her connection to this horse, Abby had no doubt about the identity of the woman coming toward her. The small boxes on the report form had been filled out with Kira's information, but the contrast between black-and-white data and the live version was startling. *Brown hair* didn't do justice to the highlights and lowlights of gold and chocolate in the delicate wisps of hair pulling loose from Kira's ponytail and framing her face. *Blue eyes* had little in common with the mosaic of aquas and greens in Kira's eyes. She wore a red, navy, and white plaid shirt with the sleeves rolled up to reveal tan forearms and the tails knotted at her small waist. Faded jeans and bright red sneakers gave her a youthful air. *Five foot six* and *125 pounds* meant nothing until Kira's curves and the long line of her legs filled it out and gave the numbers dimension and depth.

Even the report itself had been a conflicting mix of fact and not-quite-the-truth. Kira had called the cops to her house on a domestic call, alleging her girlfriend Dale had abused her, but the responding officer—Abby's brother, Rick—had written that the claim of abuse was not only unfounded, but recanted by Kira. Abby's research had led her to believe otherwise. She couldn't prove it, but she didn't believe justice had been administered on the scene, so she had taken matters into her own hands. Secretly and anonymously. That was how it was meant to stay.

Her brother's indiscretions were more difficult to conclusively identify than her grandfather's clumsy and overt corruption. She'd been collecting hints of mishandled calls and suspiciously self-serving decision making, and her cherished hope was that she'd learn enough to convince him to change. Or blackmail him into becoming a better man and officer. If she couldn't, and if she found out he was traveling the same road her grandfather had paved before them, then she'd have no choice but to turn him in.

She'd do whatever it took, within her ethical boundaries, to avoid that, but Kira was a concrete reminder of her fears for her brother. And Nirvana bound them all together. Abby waved off Rachel who had been about to come help catch the horse, and her sergeant waved back before returning to the bucket she'd left behind. Abby clenched her fingers around the hot-pink nylon lead rope, and then relaxed them before holding the lead out for Kira to take. "This is your horse, I assume?"

"My daughter's," Kira said. She reached for the rope with one hand and tucked the other in her back pocket. Abby felt her slight tremble as their fingers briefly touched, and she understood how worried Kira must have been when the horse escaped. The vibration traveled through Abby and echoed inside after their contact ended. It was only the aftershock from the collision between her secret life and warm, pulsating reality. Would she have reacted to Kira the same way if they'd met beyond the context of Abby's job? She rubbed her palm with her thumb, trying to erase the lingering effect of Kira. *Yes.*

"Thank you for catching her," Kira said. Her voice was low and well-modulated, like Abby would expect from someone who was an actress or a public speaker. She was disconcerted by Kira, who was thoroughly a surprise. And by her own equally unexpected responses. Abby had formed opinions based on the details she'd read in the report, but Kira wasn't the fragile, helpless woman she'd imagined. Like someone with a family history of addiction who swore off alcohol, Abby never got involved socially—whether as friends or potential love interests—with people who were connected to her or her family by work, but she found herself wishing she didn't have to keep such tight control over the barriers between her public and private worlds.

"No problem. I'm glad I was able to stop her," Abby said. Even though Kira held her rope, the mare stayed close to Abby, sniffing every pocket before pressing her forehead against Abby's chest with a deep sigh. She should walk away, leaving both of them behind, but she couldn't resist smoothing the horse's cheeks with her hands, reaching under her chin to scratch the itchy spots she knew so well. Muscles, tendons, pulse, warmth. The feel of the horse grounded Abby in the past for a brief time. Kira and Nirvana both embodied something earthy and pure, and Abby longed to trade her insubstantial life of guilt and atonement for the physical reality of Kira's world. But Kira had already been bruised by contact with the Hargroves. Being with Abby might immerse Kira fully in their lives instead of releasing Abby into hers.

"She seems to like you," Kira said. Her voice held a hint of something. Confusion? Suspicion? No. Abby was ascribing her own tendencies to Kira. Kira was just making a comment.

"She must know I like horses," Abby said. She smiled and gave the mare a pat on the forehead. "I'm riding with the Tacoma Police Department's mounted unit."

"Yes, I saw the uniform."

Did Abby detect a hint of disdain in Kira's voice? Or was she hearing it because she was expecting it? She was getting uncomfortable with the subtext in their interchange. It might only be on her side and Kira might be innocently carrying on a casual conversation, but Abby was confused by the constant second-guessing.

"It was more than sensing a horse person, though," Kira continued before Abby could make an excuse and get away. "She heard your voice and pulled the lead rope out of my hands. She's never done anything like that before. And then she ran right to you. Why?"

Abby stepped back, breaking contact with the mare. She needed to leave. Now. "How would I know why your horse ran away from you? She's at a new place, with unfamiliar noises and crowds, so it's only natural that her behavior would be—"

"Hargrove?" Kira asked.

Startled out of her rambling explanation of the horse's actions, complete with gestures at the horses and people around them, Abby looked at Kira and saw her staring at the small brass name badge that had been hidden from view by the mare's head only moments ago. In another time and situation, Kira's pointed focus on her chest would be welcome. Abby felt a shiver of arousal even though she knew Kira's attention was due to Abby's damned name and not her body. Her own desires were superseded yet again.

"Um, yes."

"And you're related to the other Officer Hargrove...how?"

"He's my brother."

Abby didn't offer any more than her terse statement. She had been prepared to deflect attention and keep her identity from Kira, but she wouldn't lie. She wouldn't defend or apologize. She remained silent and watched Kira clearly struggle to figure out what question to ask next.

"Hey, Mom, I've been looking all over for you. Why'd you bring Nirvana out here?"

A tinier version of Kira walked over to them. The same wavy hair as her mother, but longer and closer to blond in color. Similar features, but seemingly more prone to lightness and smiles. After one glance, anyone would be able to identify the two as mother and daughter.

"Wow, are you one of the mounted police riders? That is so cool! Have you ever shot anyone from horseback?"

"Julie!" Kira sounded shocked at the girl's question, but Abby wanted to laugh out loud in relief as Julie managed to break the tension that had been building between the two adults. Kira was rapidly putting together the puzzle pieces Abby spent her life trying to scatter, yet she perversely kept giving Kira clues. She wasn't used to having sexual attraction interfere with her mission in life, and the more Kira knew about her, the more she'd want to avoid Abby. Abby needed to drive Kira away for her own well-being.

"No, I haven't, but I usually have more of a supervisory role with the unit. You can ask the other officers about the police work they've done. None of them has shot someone, but they've each caught their share of criminals."

"I'd love to talk to them. Angie and I tried to see your horses, but that whole end of the barn is closed off."

Abby couldn't stop her smile at the obvious request, complete with dramatic sigh. "Stop by anytime and we'll let you in so you can meet them," she said, feeling helpless to keep herself from making the offer.

"That's very generous of Officer Hargrove," Kira said to her daughter, saying the name as if it tasted bitter in her mouth. "But I'm sure she has more important things to do with her time."

"She offered, Mom. I didn't ask."

"You hinted. That's the same thing."

Abby smiled as she watched mother and daughter face off in what sounded like a laid-back argument they'd had many times before. This pair could prove to be dangerous for her. Julie was frank and chatty, making Abby feel uncharacteristically at ease. Kira made her feel things, too, with her subtle strength and effortless beauty and the scent of gardenias when she came close.

"I'll tell my sergeant, Rachel Bryce, to watch for you if I'm not there," she said, striking a compromise. She'd be able to grant Julie access to the police stable, while reassuring Kira that she wouldn't be around. She didn't think Kira would want anything to do with the police in any fashion, but a visit to the stable might be less unpalatable if Abby herself wasn't involved.

"That'd be awesome! Thanks, Officer Hargrove."

Kira cringed when she heard her daughter say that name. She had spoken it herself, about a year ago. *Please help me, Officer Hargrove.* Spoken to a different person, in a very different kind of plea, but the memory was tied to her, body and soul. Tension, anger, helplessness—they arose automatically at the sound of that name. They were feelings she never wanted Julie to experience, but Julie wasn't in the same situation. Kira might feel as if she'd been transported back in time, back into the midst of pain and helplessness, but Julie was in the present. Cheerful and at ease as she and this other Hargrove talked about a book they'd both read on using mounted police techniques for training a spooky horse. Kira closed her eyes briefly as she struggled to get her mind, her body, and her reactions back to now.

"I can't wait to see your demonstration today so I can get some training tips for working with Nirvana. Are you actually riding, Officer, or do you just supervise the demos?"

"You can call me Abby, please. And yes, I'll be trading in my desk chair for a horse during the fair."

Kira opened her eyes when Hargrove laughed. Abby. Her laugh had a musical quality and made her sound more dimensional than her polished exterior implied. Her light makeup and controlled expression gave her an airbrushed quality, as if she had applied a mask over a human face. Kira focused on what she could clearly see in Abby, like her perfectly upswept auburn hair, her aloof demeanor, and the pressed and spotless uniform that set her apart as an authority figure. The gun strapped casually on her hip. Kira tried not to see the cracks that appeared for brief moments. The warm, almost childlike smile when Julie's charisma charmed her. The haunted look in Abby's eyes when she touched Julie's horse. Kira had been around enough dominant personality types in her lifetime. Far too many. She didn't need anything to distract her from the resolve to stay far away from the kind of personality that could make her feel helpless ever again.

Of course, Abby wasn't her brother. Whatever issues Kira had with him, his sister hadn't been on the call that night. She hadn't been the one to abandon Kira when she most needed help. She wasn't involved. But the similarities between the two siblings were hard for Kira to ignore. There was a resemblance in appearance, once Kira started looking for it, but Kira didn't care about that. What set off the alarms in her head was the way Abby wore her uniform. Proudly, as if she had been born to carry the weight of responsibility and power that the simple material conveyed. Of course, the fit of Abby's was more distracting. Kira had to work hard to keep her gaze from dropping below Abby's waist and down to those snug navy pants. But her attraction had to be tempered by reason. Abby's brother had flaunted the control his more generic uniform gave him. Abby's alpha streak seemed less overt, but no less present.

"You'll want to watch the rest of my team closely, and not me," Abby said. "They've been working with their horses for almost a year now, and I think you'll be impressed by their level of training. I'll look like an amateur in comparison, but I'm sure you'll pick up some great training ideas if you study Sergeant Bryce and the others."

"But you *do* know how to ride, don't you?"

Kira heard the wistful note in Julie's voice. Her daughter had found someone to worship, but Abby would be dropped like a disgraced idol if she couldn't stay on a horse with some degree of skill. Kira would be happy to have that happen, but Abby wasn't cooperating.

"I do. I even competed here at the fair when I was about your age. But being a lieutenant means I don't have time to ride like I used to. These two weeks will be a sort of vacation for me, but I'm sure I'll end up with saddle sores and aching muscles."

Kira sighed. So much for Abby's inability to ride quashing Julie's adoration. Kira hadn't been too optimistic, though. She saw how Abby moved and how natural she looked in the equestrian uniform. Kira imagined her looking equally graceful on the back of a horse, drawing the attention of every woman in the crowd as they applauded her skill and drove her ego even higher. Besides, she had recognized Abby as a horsewoman the moment she saw Nirvana run straight to her side…

"Do you have a horse of your own, Lieutenant?" Kira interrupted their conversation.

She watched as Abby hesitated before answering. "I did. But not anymore."

"Until how long ago?"

"About a year ago."

Again the brief pause. Kira almost stopped her line of questioning when she realized Abby didn't want to give her any more information, even though she seemed compelled to tell the truth. Kira had lived with so many lies and half-truths, she couldn't believe someone with such integrity really existed. Julie stepped in and unknowingly pieced together the suspicion that had been forming in Kira's mind.

"Hey, that's when I got Nirvana! I entered an essay contest for 4-H members, and I won her. It was the best day of my life."

"I'm glad it was. She seems like a special horse, and I'll bet you've given her a great home."

Abby's eyes didn't leave Kira's while she spoke. There was something Kira couldn't define in Abby's expression. Sadness and loss, but also a sense of relief at Julie's obvious happiness.

"We've often wished we knew who the anonymous donor was," Kira said, "so we could thank her…or him for this gift."

Kira's mind faltered as she tried to figure out the web of connection between her and Abby. She'd thought her bewildering night with Hargrove had been over the moment he turned away from her pleas and walked out of her life. For some reason, Abby had reached out to her by giving Julie Nirvana. Abby seemed as disconcerted by this meeting as Kira was, so why had she insinuated herself into Kira and Julie's life? What was her motivation? Kira had to override the instincts attracting her to Abby and rely on logic and lessons learned instead, although she couldn't reconcile the wonderful gift of Nirvana with the obvious indications of a deeper relationship than she'd been aware of between her and the Hargroves.

"I don't know how anyone could want to give her away," Julie said, hugging the patient mare's neck. "But I'm very grateful."

"Yes, I also wonder why her previous owner gave her away." She really had been curious about Nirvana's past, but it had never once crossed her mind that the mysterious gift might have remotely sinister intentions behind it. She watched Abby closely, trying to discern any sign of malice in her eyes, but what she saw was a forthrightness that was hard to reconcile with her obvious subterfuge, and a sensual appeal impossible to harmonize with Kira's driving need for caution and self-protection.

Abby shrugged. "Who knows? At least it worked out well in the end. That's all that matters. Look, I need to get to work. Good luck in your classes, Julie. Be sure to stop by and see the horses anytime you want. Kira, it was a pleasure meeting you."

Kira shook the offered hand. Abby's face didn't really register pleasure, but something much more complicated. The whole interchange had been odd, and the only thing Kira knew for certain was how strong and comfortable Abby's hand felt when it gripped hers. Dangerously right.

"Nice to meet you, too," she said quietly as Abby patted Nirvana's neck one more time and walked away from them.

CHAPTER THREE

Kira followed Julie and Nirvana down the aisle and back to their assigned stall. 4-H riders were everywhere and constantly on the move as they either cleaned or prepared for the upcoming show. Some kids were sweeping the aisleways or pushing wheelbarrows full of shavings, while others were grooming their horses. Kira stepped around a freshly swept pile of shavings, but she felt disconnected from the noise and crowds surrounding her. Julie was still talking about Abby Hargrove, and Kira barely registered the words she was saying. She was more concerned with her own questions about Abby. Was she a good role model for twelve-year-old Julie, or was she too much like her brother? Kira couldn't believe that one sibling could be so uncaring and cold while the other wasn't, but she had no basis for judging Abby yet. After all, Abby had given Julie her wonderful horse, but was she planning to take her back now that she'd seen her again? Now that she needed horses for her mounted unit? The loss would be painful for Julie, and Kira couldn't bear to have her daughter's heart broken.

She had to protect her own heart, too. Why did she fall for the bad girls? Abby had the presence and confidence that, in her experience, went hand-in-hand with arrogance. Yet Kira still couldn't stop herself from being attracted to Abby. What she *could* stop, however, was any more interaction between the two of them. True, Abby hadn't even admitted the horse was hers, let alone said or done anything to suggest she planned to reclaim her. But Kira needed to prepare for the worst. She'd fight Abby if she wanted to take Nirvana away from Julie, or she'd somehow manage to pay whatever it cost to buy her, but that would be the extent of their relationship. Kira would feel better, albeit poorer, if she owned the mare outright and didn't have to worry about her ever being taken from Julie.

Kira was so distracted she nearly bumped into the man standing by Nirvana's stall. He put out a hand to steady her, and Kira recoiled when he touched her shoulder. She took a step back and forced a smile.

"Sorry. I didn't see you there." She was too wrapped up in her thoughts—how had Abby managed to breach her defenses so quickly, especially when Kira saw all the red flags? She needed to get hold of herself, pay attention to where she was walking, and concentrate on her daughter.

"Mom, can you hand me the tail comb?"

Kira sifted through the tote holding Julie's grooming tools and handed her the comb. She realized uncomfortably that the man was still standing next to her. Too close. The heavy scent of his expensive aftershave made her nostrils burn. He leaned against the stall door and smiled down at her. Kira made a concerted effort to stay where she was and not look away. She had pulled away from him at first because she'd been startled out of her reverie. Now, she felt an even stronger urge to grab Julie and run away, but she remained still. She was too close to the edge these days, too ready to flee. She hadn't always been like this, but even though she hated the frightened part of herself—the part that made her thigh muscles tense as they got ready to propel her to safety and her shoulders hunch in a self-protective way—she could rationally understand what was happening. She saw threats everywhere, in everyone. She got that. The tough part was that she didn't trust her own instincts anymore. How could she recognize when the danger was real and when she was overreacting? First Abby, now this man. Either way, though, she had to control her impulse for flight. She was ready to stay and fight.

"Hi, and welcome to the 4-H barn." Julie took the comb from Kira's hand and introduced herself to the visitor like she had been taught to do as a 4-H member. The kids were supposed to act as ambassadors to the fairgoers who walked through the barns, but Kira had a hunch that Julie would have been just as friendly and welcoming even if she hadn't been told to do so. It was just her nature. "I'm Julie and this is my horse, Nirvana. We're competing in showmanship today. If you have any questions, please let me know."

"Thank you, Julie, but I'm here to see your mom. We're friends from work."

"Really?" Julie asked, looking from her mom to the stranger and back again.

"Really?" Kira asked at the same time. She frowned as she tried to recall the man's face. He was taller than she was, with a slim build. Sandy brown hair and intense green eyes. Good-looking enough, but with a mean edge to his suave appearance. Kira wouldn't have forgotten a face like his. "I don't remember meeting you before."

"I'm Tad. Tad Milford. Does the name ring any bells?"

Crap. She should have trusted her instincts and run when she had the chance. She had been right that they hadn't officially met, but she'd recently spent a few afternoons outside of the Milford Corporation's offices, getting people to sign petitions to stop his new development.

"Your mother is trying to stop me from building houses on a piece of land I legally own," Tad said to Julie. "Now, you don't think that's fair of her, do you?"

"If Mom's involved, it must be because you want to destroy a wetland. That's not fair to the earth."

Kira was torn between pride in Julie's efforts to side with her and a fervent hope that her dramatic defense of the environment wouldn't continue. She stepped into the stall and stood between her daughter and Tad.

"Mr. Milford, my daughter is about to compete in a horse show and we need to get ready. This is neither the time nor the place to discuss business, but I'd be happy for you to schedule a meeting with our neighborhood coalition and we can debate our respective positions there."

"Your position is weak. You'll never be able to stop progress, and you have no right to tell me what the hell I can or can't build on *my* land. No fucking right."

The muscles that had only seconds before been poised and ready for flight were now aching to take a swing at Tad Milford's smug face. She stepped closer to him.

"Get out now. Or I'll have you thrown out."

He laughed. "What are you going to do? Beat me up? Or maybe you'll call your little cop friend." He reached out and dragged a finger across her right cheekbone. "But last time you tried calling on a Hargrove, you didn't get any help at all, did you?"

Kira felt a violent shiver ripple from her gut to her racing heart. He had touched the spot where she'd been cut and bleeding that night, when the cops had come and then left her behind. His finger reopened the memory of the painful wound as if it was a razor blade. She pressed the palm of her hand against her cheek, expecting the warmth of blood, but her skin was smooth and dry.

"No one can help you now, either. Mind your own business and stay out of mine. We wouldn't want you or your daughter to be hurt again."

She had to try twice, but she finally was able to get words past her constricted throat. Her voice sounded like an angry hiss to her own ears. "I don't like being threatened, Mr. Milford. If you lay one finger on my daughter, I will make you pay."

He shrugged. "It wasn't a threat. It was a statement of fact. You will stop your efforts to delay my construction schedule, and then we'll all be happy and safe."

Kira saw his property in her mind, followed the twisting trails leading around the edge of the water. She had spent hours in the marsh, searching for sedges and cattails, watching the patterned visits of ducks and songbirds. The tract of land might look like an insignificant few acres of soggy ground to most people, but Kira saw the intricate interplay of flora and fauna as different species came together and thrived in their unique community. She had been drawn to wetlands specifically because they were so undervalued and unappreciated. Milford's proposed building site was part of a larger watershed area stretching through Puget Sound. A few areas were preserved—thanks mostly to small grassroots organizations. She used her degree and expertise to help them, to elevate their neighborhood-based efforts and give them credibility. To protect the endangered and misunderstood underdog of an ecosystem. She kept her voice impersonal when she spoke to businesspeople and government officials about saving wetlands, but her vocation was deeply personal.

How dare Tad Milford bring his greedy, grasping threats into her family life? He might make a small fortune on the development, given Tacoma's thriving housing market, but he had no right to destroy the city's natural resources in the process. She'd seen too many wetland areas get eaten away by too-narrow buffer zones and too-closely encroaching homes. He might have money and influence over the city council, but she wouldn't let him buy his way out of his obligation to the environment without a fight.

"*You* will stop your efforts to intimidate me outside of work," she said. She wanted to add an *or else*, but she couldn't think of one. Or else she'd get a restraining order? She didn't think the police were likely to be of any help to her, especially since he seemed to have connections there. Or else she'd beat him up? She didn't want to make him laugh at her. She had to fight back the only way she knew how, as if she were arguing a case in front of the council and not pleading to be left alone. He was pushing his way into her life, into Julie's world, and he needed to be shoved out. "Given my record with cases like yours, you might want to back out of the fight now. If you don't respect my request for you to stop bothering us, I will make it my life's mission to see that you're never permitted to build so much as a doghouse on the property. If you are willing to be civil and confine our interactions to the workplace, then I'm sure we can reach a compromise that will be beneficial both to you and to the environment."

Tad smiled. "The decision we reach will benefit me, not that damned swamp. Trust me, it will be drained and covered with houses before the year is out." He turned away from her and nodded with insulting formality to her daughter. "Good luck in your class, Julie."

Kira watched him walk down the aisle. Her fists were balled in helpless rage, and her entire world seemed to shrink down to fit on the retreating form of Tad's back. Julie's trembling voice broke her out of her hyperfocused state.

"Mom? Is he really going to hurt us?"

Kira spun around and pulled Julie close to her in a tight hug. She felt tremors but wasn't sure which one of them was shaking the most. "No, baby. We're fine. He's just a mean businessman who's accustomed to getting his own way. He can't use money to buy his way out of this, so he's using empty threats instead."

"Are you sure?" Julie mumbled against her neck.

Kira put her hands on Julie's shoulders and held her away so she could look directly in her daughter's eyes. "Yes. I will protect you from *any* threat. Look around us. There are people everywhere, so what can he do?"

Even as she saw Julie look around as if surprised to see so many people, the sounds of kids talking and horses stomping the ground finally filtered back into Kira's consciousness as well. She had felt isolated because he had scared her, but she wasn't. She had given him power over her mind, and she hated how easily confidence had slipped from her grasp. But she couldn't let Julie see how frightened she really was.

"You need to forget all about that creep. Showmanship is your best class, and he doesn't have the right to intimidate you and keep you from doing well. Okay?"

Julie nodded. "Okay."

Julie returned to her task of grooming Nirvana until she glistened under the fluorescent lights of the barn. Julie had been shaken, but she slowly bounced back to her usual bubbly self as she brushed her mare. Kira envied her resiliency. She would denounce Tad's words with confidence and she'd protect Julie with her life, but inside she was ragged and raw. She kept smiling until she watched Julie walk toward the show ring with her usual lighthearted step. Kira went into the far side of the Paulhamus Arena, where the stands were nearly empty, and she climbed to the top of the bleachers. There, finally alone, she allowed herself to sag in despair. Tears threatened, but she blinked them away. She wouldn't back down and she wouldn't cry, but she wondered if she'd always feel so helpless in the face of someone else's strength. Tad Milford scared the shit out of her. He looked every inch as mean as his words sounded, and he'd seemed aware of the details surrounding her run-in with Officer Hargrove. How could he know about that night? Even more perplexing was Abby's connection to all of this. Her brother had been in Kira's house, and now Julie was walking into the ring leading Abby's horse. How the hell had Abby gotten tangled in Kira's life? And how could Kira extricate herself without getting burned by the heat Abby generated inside her?

CHAPTER FOUR

A bby watched Kira and Julie disappear into the crowded 4-H aisle. She was tempted to go after them, if only to keep talking to Kira. She hadn't felt connected to others so deeply for a long time. She had been training the then two year-old Nirvana when she had realized her dad was using her grandfather's filthy money to pay for her hobby. She had sold the older horse her parents had bought her, but she kept Nirvana because the horse had been *hers*. Bought with money she had saved for years. Exercising horses, braiding manes and tails at shows, doing any odd job she could find. She had been fervent about counting and hoarding her growing funds— perhaps she had always guessed that something was going on beneath the surface of her grandfather's career. Or maybe part of her had recognized they were living beyond the means of a legitimate patrol officer's income. Whatever the reason, she had managed to purchase the promising young mare, and she had been doing all of the training on her own.

And she'd finished the training without help, after she'd broken emotional ties with her family. Nirvana had been a source of comfort and a reminder of loss since that time. Abby had never managed to fully commit to riding as she had in the innocent past, but she had been unable to part with the mare until she had read Kira's report and had learned about her horse-crazy daughter. Abby had given Nirvana to Kira and Julie, and then had maintained a connection to horses by establishing a mounted unit. She had missed her own horse over the past year, but she felt a sense of rightness after seeing the now seventeen-year-old horse again. Julie loved her with unfiltered joy, without any of the guilt or ambivalence that Abby carried in her heart.

Abby turned away from the 4-H barn and walked toward the police horse stabling. She might be connected to Kira by tendrils—her horse, her brother, Kira's past—but she was still on the outside. She had made some changes in Kira's and Julie's lives, hopefully for the better, but now it was time to regain some distance.

As Abby came through the door of the far red barn, she saw Callan Lanford in the first stall, standing next to Rachel's liver-chestnut gelding, Bandit. First hired to train the mounted police unit and now Rachel's lover, Cal looked as comfortable in her riding clothes as Abby felt awkward in hers. Her fitted white polo shirt and tan breeches were as impeccable as always, and her shimmering gold hair was fastened in a tight knot so it would fit under a riding helmet. Abby couldn't see Cal's feet where she stood behind the wall of the stall, but she would bet her meager retirement fund that Cal had on brightly polished tall black boots. She was born to play polo and had the championship trophies to prove it.

Abby was about to greet Cal when Rachel came around the other side of the horse.

"So that's where you were when you told me you had to work late?" Cal asked, her hands on her hips. "You went to see *her*?"

"I never actually said I had to work late, I just implied it." Rachel seemed as relaxed and casual as Cal looked unyielding and elegant. Rachel's mounted uniform was as neatly pressed and cleaned as Abby's, but she projected a different aura than either Cal or Abby. She had a more earthy grace about her and always appeared in tune with her horses and surroundings. When Abby had first brought Rachel on as the leader of the mounted unit, she had fully expected to be disappointed in the sergeant the brass had imposed on her. Rachel had been angry and ostracized, battling both a bad reputation and a stubborn nature, but she had proven herself to be the ideal candidate for the job. She had managed to turn a mismatched group of horses and riders into an effective and capable team. Abby had been surprised by Rachel's metamorphosis into a true leader, despite the people determined to hold her back—including Abby herself. But she had developed a deep respect for Rachel, as well as admiration for the strong partnership she had formed with Cal. They usually seemed to make an ideal couple, but not today.

"You *lied* to me?" Cal asked.

"Fudged the truth," Rachel said in her composed voice. "I didn't want to fight you for her and I saw her first."

"That's not fair. I would never have tried to keep her from… well, you don't need her like I do."

"Find your own—"

"Sergeant, Cal, please lower your voices." Abby wasn't sure who had prompted the heated exchange between the two women, but she had to stop it. "This isn't the time or place to discuss your personal—"

"Hey, Lieutenant," Rachel said with a calm smile. "Why don't we let you decide this for us."

Cal crossed her arms over her chest. "Right. Ask Hard-Ass Hargrove. Of course she'll side with you."

Abby couldn't keep from smiling at Cal's petulant use of her nickname. She'd been called that name since her first promotion—always behind her back, but loud enough for her to hear. She had hated it, even though she never altered her cool and rigid leadership style. She wasn't on the job to make friends or for personal fulfillment. She was there to make amends and to prove that a Hargrove could have both power and integrity at the same time. Cal had taken to calling her by the taboo name, and somehow the constant and humorous use of it directly to her face had taken away most of its sting.

Abby leaned her elbows on the stall divider. "Who is this mystery woman causing trouble in paradise?"

Rachel and Cal looked at each other before breaking into laughter. "She's a horse, of course," Rachel said. "Come see her."

They came out of the stall, pushing and joking playfully with each other, and Abby followed them across the aisle and into another stall. She enjoyed being around the two, even as she maintained a careful distance. Rachel and Cal were the type of women she could see as friends, but she had to maintain the professional demeanor her rank and her own needs imposed. Rachel seemed to easily balance her relationship with her leadership duties, even though Cal was part of her work life as well as her personal one, but Abby wouldn't do the same. She stayed on the outside of the mounted unit, separate but still close enough to lead them and to observe the interplay between Rachel, Cal, and the other riders. She was accepted as part of the unit since she had helped them overcome the threat from Tacoma's corrupt city manager who was trying to destroy them, but she didn't allow herself to *feel* like a member of the team.

"Lieutenant, meet Elegant Action, aka Legs, our new trainee." Rachel slid the stall door open and walked inside. A tall, steel-gray mare walked over to sniff at Rachel's hand and Abby gave a low wolf whistle. Rachel laughed. "I know, right? She's stunning. I've only been working with her a few days, but she seems to have the perfect temperament for the job."

"Which would also make her an ideal polo pony, not to mention her great bone structure. You should see her move, Hard-Ass…I mean, Abby. Her talent will be wasted on the streets of Tacoma."

"Nonsense," Rachel said. She bent over and ran her hand down the mare's foreleg. "Her good bones will keep her sound and make her comfortable to ride. Besides, she's intelligent and needs a job to do. Something challenging."

"As opposed to the simple sport of high-goal polo?"

"Exactly," Rachel said as she stood upright again.

Abby circled the mare slowly while the two traded jibes. She was beautifully put together and had a soft expression on her face. "Is she a Thoroughbred?" she asked, interrupting Cal's monologue about her need for a new horse. Abby had seen Cal's barn and her well-bred, well-trained string of horses. There was no way she was getting this one.

"Yes," Rachel said. "Good eye. She's from a rescue center that rehomes ex-racehorses. They have a lot of good horses available, in case someone desperately needs yet one more polo pony, even though someone already has seven."

"Just you wait and see," Cal said as she let herself out of the stall. "I'll find one even better than Legs, and you'll be jealous."

"Is she really that good?" Abby asked as she ran her hand along the mare's back. She had found grant money for Rachel to add a fifth horse to their string—first as a reserve mount, but hopefully soon as a horse for yet another team officer. She felt a tingle of excitement. The mounted unit had been a dream for so long, and now it was a growing presence in the city. She saw her own pride reflected in Rachel's face as she looked at the horse.

"Yes, she is. She's been on the racetrack, so she's used to crowds and close quarters. She's easy to ride and not spooky at all, plus she's friendly with people. I thought you could ride her during the fair, if you want, since Sitka doesn't need the exposure."

Abby had been called up to take Clark's place and she had expected to ride his bay gelding, but she wasn't about to give up a chance to swap him for the Thoroughbred. Hell, she was considering this a vacation, a trip down memory lane. She might as well have a striking mount while she was at it.

"Sounds good to me," she said.

"Great. Her grooming kit is hanging on the door. I'll get your tack out of the trailer." Rachel turned to leave, but Abby called her back.

"You've done a great job with this unit, Bryce," she said, her eyes never leaving the horse. "You've made me proud."

"Thank you, Abby," Rachel said quietly, using her given name for the first time that Abby could remember. Cal used it occasionally, but she didn't seem to have the same boundaries and respect for rank as Abby and Rachel did.

Abby hummed to herself as she groomed the patient mare. The shrill sounds of a crowded fair receded into the background here in their isolated aisle, as they did in all the animal barns, giving the people in them a sense of stepping back in time. Abby couldn't remember the last time she'd felt a sense of peace like this, but she could trace her present emotion back to the moment when her hand touched Kira's. She still felt the residual energy Kira had imparted to her through trembling fingers. Abby had been worried about being revealed as Nirvana's donor, Rick's sister, and someone tainted by association with corruption, but she had—for a short time—been more physically present in her own skin than usual. Kira was intelligent, yes. Sexy? God, yes. Yet as attractive as she was on her own, Abby admired what Kira had created with Julie and Nirvana. A mother and daughter at a show, simple as that, but it was everything good a family should be. Together and strong. Supporting and experiencing life together. Everything real and honest that Abby had been missing from her own family.

Abby's enraptured state would most likely disappear once she was riding in front of a crowd, though. TPD officers like Wayne would see her and whisper to their partners from other departments. But here, in the muted atmosphere on the fringe of the fairgrounds, Abby felt a moment's respite from her need to maintain an aura of calm untouchability.

"Your friend's daughter just headed over to the competition ring," Rachel said from the doorway. She settled a black all-purpose English saddle on a rack and fidgeted with the stirrups. "We'll be schooling the horses next to the arena, so you can watch her if you hurry."

"My friend's…what?" Abby asked, startled out of her Zen moment.

Rachel shrugged. "That pretty woman you were talking to outside of the 4-H barn, after you so gallantly rescued her horse. You seemed to know each other, so I thought maybe she was your, um, friend?"

Abby stopped brushing the mare's mane. "Are you fishing for something, Sergeant?" she asked in her most threatening cop voice.

"Well, if I were, I think your defensive tone would have given me the information I was seeking. Like I said, you might want to stop dawdling or you'll miss her class." Rachel walked away before Abby could respond.

"Insubordinate, wannabe detective," Abby muttered as she returned to her job. Bryce was getting too close. Calling her Abby, teasing her about Kira. Insinuating that she had some connection to a woman she had just met. Disorienting Abby because her fantasies had driven her unresistingly into Kira's reality. Still, Abby felt a growing impatience as she hurried to clean her horse's hooves and put on her tack. Only because she was interested in seeing Nirvana perform in the ring. Not because she cared about Julie and Kira beyond the single act of atonement she had made in an attempt to right her brother's wrong. Ha.

Abby led Legs out of the barn and into the bright sunlight. No more hiding. She had to try twice before she was able to stretch far enough to get her foot in the stirrup and swing herself onto Legs's back. She dutifully jogged every morning and worked out in the gym three times a week, but she hadn't been on a horse for over a year and she was out of shape for riding. She was strong and fit, but her flexibility had taken a hit lately. She spent more time sitting in her office than being active outside, and even her weekends were devoted to the sedentary acts of researching old reports and calls.

"Ready?" Cal asked her. She was sitting on Billie Mitchell's large chestnut, Ranger, and she managed to give the impression of skill and confidence even when she was standing still on a horse.

"I guess so," Abby said. She shifted in the bulky saddle, trying to get comfortable. She knew the deep seat and leather blocks were designed to give a rider more security than a simpler, lighter saddle, but she felt awkward. She was accustomed to hacking around for pleasure, not chasing perps from horseback. She untwisted the reins of the double bridle and closed her hands over the heavy leather. She'd read all of Rachel's notes on the horses and equipment, so she knew the double bridles were important to have in case the team was in a dangerous situation and needed extra stopping power, but Legs felt light and responsive enough to be controlled with only a simple snaffle bit.

"Here, hold the reins like this." Cal sidestepped until Ranger was close enough for her to reach over and move Abby's hands. "Then you can move your fingers and get more stop if you need it, but most of the time your contact will be light. Hey, Cowgirl, are you all set?"

Rachel led Don's pinto mare, inaptly called Fancy, toward

them. "I suppose," she said as she swung into the saddle with one smooth motion. "Let's get this over with."

Abby smiled at Rachel's grimace. Don's mare was a far cry from beautiful, and Abby had heard complaints from everyone who rode her about her rough gaits. She and Don gave the impression of a farmer and his old nag out for an evening stroll, but Abby had once seen them corner and subdue a fleeing bank robber. Their laid-back demeanor had vanished in an instant, and Don had suddenly shown he was a seasoned officer with a well-trained police horse. Still, she was relieved she was riding the more responsive, less jarring Thoroughbred. Don and Billie would be joining them for the afternoon's demonstration and their evening patrol duty, but she, Rachel, and Cal were giving the horses some exercise first. Rachel had said it was to get them accustomed to the fair noises and crowds, but Abby had a feeling Rachel mostly wanted to give Abby a chance to ride before she had to perform. She also guessed that Rachel was compensating for her lack of mounted patrol experience by giving her Legs to ride.

She had to admire Rachel for masking the allowances she was making so beautifully. Legs looked like a prize, but she was meant more as a baby-sitter than a status symbol. Abby wasn't about to complain. She had no street time with the unit, even though she was technically the boss, so she was happy to ride the quiet new horse and stay on the sidelines as more of a figurehead than an active patrol rider. Over the next two weeks, she'd put her ego aside and let Rachel and Cal take the lead. The idea of taking a short break from always needing to be in control and in charge was an appealing one.

Rachel and Cal broke away from her when they got to the small sand warm-up ring behind the large Paulhamus Arena. The indoor arena would host the 4-H equine events, the draft horse demos, and a nightly rodeo. This year, for the first time, Tacoma's mounted unit would demonstrate some of their training and riding exercises. There were too few of them—on their mismatched horses—to do a full-scale choreographed ride like the Canadian Mounties did, but they should still give the audience a good show. Abby stopped Legs in the holding area behind the arena and looked inside, letting her eyes adjust to the darker indoor lighting. Later today, she'd be riding in there. Right now, she saw a group of about fifteen 4-H kids, standing next to their horses as they were judged in the showmanship class.

Abby quickly found Nirvana and Julie in the lineup. The mare stood squarely with her ears perked. The class was judged only on the ability of the unmounted handlers to turn out and present the horses well as they led them through a pattern of cones and rails, not on the horse's looks, but Nirvana's quality conformation couldn't hurt her score. Abby had been there herself, oh, so long ago, and she remembered the jittery feeling in her stomach as she tried to keep her face and body serene. A picture of herself and her old competition horse—the one her dad had bought for her with tainted money—imposed itself over Nirvana and Julie as they left the lineup for their individual performance. Abby was right there with them as they trotted a figure eight and backed through a serpentine of cones. Julie's performance was steady and precise, and Abby dropped the reins on Legs's neck so she could join in the applause when they were finished. The image of herself out there disappeared.

She heard a whoop and loud clapping on the far side of the arena, and she saw Kira standing in the highest corner of the ring. She was far away from the cluster of 4-H kids and parents in the bleachers nearest Abby, but Kira didn't seem to be hiding as she cheered on her daughter. Abby forgot to watch the rest of the class and instead concentrated on Kira. She was beautiful and fiery. Intelligent, too, since she so quickly had figured out Abby's connection to Nirvana. Kira might not know exactly why Abby had given Julie the mare, and she never needed to know. Abby had concealed her gift under the guise of an essay contest so Kira hadn't had to feel obligated or pitied. Neither obligation nor pity fully explained why Abby had let a piece of her heart go to Julie.

But the sacrifice had been worth it. Abby stayed by the back gate long enough to congratulate Julie when she came out with a reserve championship ribbon fluttering on Nirvana's halter. The happiness on the girl's face, as well as her obvious good care of her horse, gave Abby an unaccustomed sense of pride.

"Good work, Julie," she said. "Your pattern was nicely done."

"Thank you. Is this your police horse?"

Hers for two weeks. "Yes. This is Legs. Her registered name is Elegant Action. The pinto over there is Fancy and the chestnut is Ranger."

Kira walked over and put an arm around her daughter's shoulders. She gave Abby a brief nod, but kept her attention on Julie. "Very well done. I'm proud of you."

"Thanks, Mom. I'm going to hurry and put Nirvana in her stall to eat lunch. I don't want to miss the police ride. See you later, Abby."

"Don't you dare hurt her," Kira said once Julie was out of earshot.

"I…what?"

"Don't ask for your horse back. I'll pay whatever it takes to—"

"I'm sure Julie earned the horse by writing an excellent essay and winning a contest. I'd never be so mean as to get in the way of that, even if it were in my power."

Kira looked at her with an unreadable expression. She looked wearier than she had only moments before. Did she get nervous watching the competition, or was she seriously afraid Abby would renege on a done deal?

"Are you okay?" Abby asked.

"I would do anything to protect her," Kira said before she followed the path Julie had taken.

"I have no doubt about that," Abby said out loud even though Kira was too far away to hear. She shook her head and turned Legs toward the schooling arena at a brisk trot. Kira confused her, but she had a feeling she was as much an enigma herself. She was related to the officer who had refused to help Kira on a domestic abuse call, and now Kira had discovered she had given them the horse in a rigged contest. Of course Kira was on edge around her. Abby would have liked to explain herself, to set Kira's mind at ease about her intentions, but that would mean revealing too much private information. Far from wanting to take Nirvana back, Abby had been envying the horse her chance to be part of Kira's family. She could quit her job and give up her battle against the sins of the past. Move in as Nirvana's groom? Or, better yet, Kira's sex slave?

Abby laughed at herself. She had to work off her unproductive energy and, barring sex, riding was her favorite way to do it. She nudged Legs into an extended trot around the arena. Her own legs felt like limp noodles as she rode, but her heart was still oddly light. She usually used money as a way to atone for the mishandled cases. Small anonymously funded scholarships and grants, even a used car or two. She bought items or gave donations to the victims—as much as she could afford—but this had been one of the rare times she had offered up such a personal gift. She was grateful to have the opportunity to see what pleasure one of her offerings had given to the recipient. This glimpse into a result from her actions increased her desire to keep going. To give more. Take back Nirvana? Kira was crazy. Beautiful, but crazy. Abby would never consider doing such a thing.

She might, however, be tempted to see the three of them again. The fair lasted over two weeks, and they were bound to run into each other again. Julie would most likely be at every riding demo she could attend, and hopefully she'd drag her mom along as well. Abby could manage to be by the arena when Julie and Nirvana were scheduled for a class. Kira would keep asking uncomfortable questions, and Abby would continue to give vague reasons for her actions, but the idea of being around Kira made the uneasiness seem like a bearable emotion. Not seeing Kira again? Not feeling the keen awareness of her presence and not sharing in Kira's satisfying family dynamic with Nirvana as her proxy? Abby wasn't willing to make those sacrifices. In time she'd have to do so, but not just yet.

Abby asked Legs to canter, and she relaxed into the smooth rhythm. This was much easier on her protesting thighs. She felt an unfamiliar sensation—was it hope?—that she might have a chance to talk to Kira some more. They had been connected by police work, by her family, but now the debt was settled and they were back on equal footing. She wouldn't actively seek Kira out, but then again she wouldn't mind if she and Kira happened to run into each other, if they got a chance to spend some time together. Her plan was passive, but it was all she was willing to permit. Action was only devoted to being a cop, and to fulfilling her life's mission. Nothing could stand in the way of that.

CHAPTER FIVE

Kira grabbed a handful of canes and hacked at the base of the clump with her machete. She felt the thick nubs of the jointed stems even through her thick gloves, and the bright green leaves waved in her face as she struggled to cut as close to the roots as she could get. Damn knotweed. The invasive plant would crowd out everything else in the wetland if she let it have its way. She occasionally had to resort to herbicides to control the dense thickets, but she preferred to avoid that method if possible. Consistent and aggressive pruning would eventually deplete the roots and kill the plants, but her muscles paid a heavy price.

She severed the last bits of connective fiber and landed on her rear with a thump when the canes gave way. While still sitting, she slid the ugly bouquet into a plastic garbage bag, careful to pick up every loose part of the plant to avoid sowing a new crop. She wiped sweat off her forehead with the back of her hand and took hold of the next group of stems.

After the weekend at the fair, she had needed to immerse herself deep in the heart of one of her preserved wetland areas. Mud and ferns and thick grasses replaced the metal and cement and overly bright lights of the midway. Mucky water and birdsong washed away some of the residual tension she felt after her run-ins with Abby and Tad.

Her feelings about Tad Milford were easy to understand. She was angry at him because he had threatened her and at herself for being scared. He had intruded where he didn't belong. She had spent the past few days fighting back in the best way she knew how—by redoubling her efforts to preserve the integrity of the wetland he owned. She had contacted all her regular supporters on the city council and in the Department of Ecology, and she'd finished work on three different proposals. Two were possible compromises, allowing him to build in restricted ways while using buffer zones and replacing some native species in the undeveloped areas. The third—her favorite by far—was a bid to buy the property with grant and city money. She was less hopeful about this option, but she had been successful with similar properties in the past.

Like this one. She finished cutting down the last of the knotweed and lugged the heavy bags back toward her car, stopping to pick up a few stray pieces of garbage along the way. Not the most glamorous side of her profession. Kira shoved an empty soda can and a candy-bar wrapper into one of the bags before she leaned against a cottonwood trunk and pulled off her gloves. She rubbed at the callouses near the base of her fingers. Even with protection, hours of chopping with the machete were brutal on her hands. Was there a glamorous side to her profession at all? Not really, but there were rewarding aspects to it, and they kept her going. Protecting what she saw as a beautiful and complex ecosystem from Tad Milford's greed would definitely be one of the perks.

Kira pushed away from the cottonwood and continued dragging the bags along the narrow path. Dirty and sweaty as it was, the physical exertion had been good for her. She felt some semblance of equilibrium returning. She'd spent most of her week in some wetland or another—not uncommon for her, but this time the reasons had been more personal than professional. She'd made a few forays onto Milford's property in an attempt to find any way possible to bolster the wetland's rating, to give it every chance of survival.

Kira opened the trunk of her car and put the bags inside. They barely fit, and a few snags of black plastic were visible on the edges of the trunk lid after she shoved it closed. A good day's work. She got in the car and sat for a few moments, drumming her fingers on the steering wheel. Her experience with Tad had been simplistic and easily converted into energy. Energy to fight against him and energy to burn off with some hard labor. Abby, on the other hand, had created a much different kind of tension inside her, and Kira hadn't been able to dissipate it nearly as well. Abby hadn't engendered fear in her, but she'd been disturbing just the same. She'd forced Kira to relive the night she'd met Abby's brother. Dale, the cut on her cheek, the shame of being caught in a situation she'd never expected to experience. How different would things have been if *this* Officer Hargrove had answered her call? Abby the white knight, Abby the mysterious horse donor. Kira had so many questions to ask, but instead of looking for an opportunity this week at the fair, she'd sought ways to avoid seeing Abby again.

Kira started her car with a rough twist of the key, and the engine revved loudly. She wasn't afraid of Dale anymore, or of her memories. She was free now and determined not to get ensnared by another alpha personality ever again. The only reason she'd been too cowardly to interrogate Abby further was because she was attracted to her, but she was strong enough to resist her body's reactions. She'd dealt with Tad by confronting their fight head-on, and she should do the same with Abby. Tonight when she and Julie went to the fair, she'd march right over to the police stables and…

Kira stopped at a red light and resumed tapping her fingers on the wheel. And…what? She pictured Abby standing in front of her wearing that sexy riding uniform, perfectly fitted to every curve. Abby, with her polished appearance and stern manner, but eyes so soft they almost seemed vulnerable…

The driver behind her honked, and Kira broke out of her daydream and accelerated through the green light. Vulnerable to what? Kira had no idea, but she knew her own vulnerabilities all too well. Abby—at least her type—was one of them. Kira sighed. Maybe she'd seek out Abby and question her tonight. Or maybe she'd wait until the weekend…

❖

Kira texted Julie as she walked across the fairgrounds, dodging other pedestrians as they moved in and out of her peripheral vision. She'd been close enough to Puyallup while working at her wetland on the south side of Tacoma to make it easy enough to stop by and check Nirvana. Julie had begged to be allowed to miss school for the entire two-week run of the fair. She'd debated the issue several times with Kira, injecting all the passion and angst a preteen could muster into her arguments. Nirvana wasn't used to being in a stall. She'd miss her pasture and wither away without Julie there to comfort her. Just think how much more Julie would learn about responsibility and hard work if she could only stay at the fair and take care of her horse...

Kira hadn't relented. Julie could miss a few days of school when it interfered with her riding classes, but no more than necessary. Kira had privately made one concession, though, and she stopped by the barn almost every afternoon, texting Julie pictures of a perfectly content Nirvana, who seemed quite happy to stand in her stall and eat expensive hay all day.

The shrill beep of a brightly colored motorized trolley interrupted Kira's texting. She jumped out of the way as a man in striped overalls drove past her with a tram full of fairgoers. She stayed on the side of the walkway and finished her text under the rhythmic shadows from the Skyride cars. She hit send and inhaled deeply. The air around her was smoky from a nearby barbecue pit, and her stomach growled in response to the honey-tinged scent of burning alder wood. Tempting, but if she was going to eat carnival food for lunch every day, she'd opt for one of the healthier options she'd found when she'd researched the nutrition information for the fair.

She passed by the log-cabin-style barbecue joint and glanced inside at the lucky patrons with plates of ribs and baked potatoes on the long tables in front of them. Her attention was caught by one woman in particular. She was even more tempting than the food, with her threadbare KISS T-shirt and wire-rimmed shades. Kira shook her head. Leave it to her to aim right for the badass rocker chick. At least her interest in another woman proved she wasn't as enthralled by Abby as she had thought.

Kira stopped and backed up a few paces. Damn. It *was* Abby. As if aware of her presence, Abby looked directly at her and sketched a wave with sauce-covered fingers. Yeah, that helped. Now all Kira could picture was licking them clean one by one. She'd been caught staring, so she had no choice but to enter the food booth and at least acknowledge Abby.

"Hey," she said when she got to Abby's spot in the back corner. "I barely recognized you without…with your hair…" She waved in the general direction of Abby's straight and glossy hair where it draped softly down to her shoulders, like expensive silk. "I didn't realize you could remove it from that bun without cracking it."

Abby grinned and ran her fingers down her center part, red-brown waves catching the filtered sunlight. "This is my off-duty look. I only wear the bulletproof bun when I'm working. Safety first."

Kira tried to smile back, but her lips felt tight and her mouth too dry to move. *Stop staring and get out of here.*

"Have a seat," Abby said. She wiped her fingers on a tattered napkin and pushed the chair across from her away from the table.

"Okay," Kira said. Only because her knees were feeling peculiarly weak at the moment. She'd sit for a while and *then* get out. "I have to ask you—"

Abby groaned. "I know you do. First let me get you some food, though. Are you hungry?"

She stood and Kira looked up at her. Tall and proud, with a precise bearing that shone through her bleach-marked, ratty clothes like a diamond wrapped in burlap. Yes, Kira was very hungry.

"Well, I was going to get a salad for lunch, but this smells awfully good."

"Be right back."

Kira perched on the edge of her plastic chair. This might not be her best idea, but maybe she'd get some real answers from Abby while she was here. She'd treat the lunch as a fact-finding mission. Research. Luckily Abby got back to the table within minutes because Kira was about to break off a chunk of her cornbread and eat it.

She took a bite of succulent ribs, barely needing to chew the tender meat. "Tell me about—oh God, that's good!—Nirvana and why you gave her to Julie."

Abby watched Kira lick the thick burgundy sauce off her fingers. She had to remind herself to breathe, let alone keep control over every word she said and every detail she either shared or kept hidden. She needed freedom from the ever-present need to hold up a heavy shield. One hour of pure selfishness? She'd take it.

"It's not unusual for 4-H alums to gift other riders with their horses. Especially when said alums have demanding jobs and too little time to spend on activities like riding." She held up her hand to stop Kira's follow-up questions. Her words were true, even though they didn't accurately explain her personal motivation. "No more. Julie has her horse and they're good for each other. You can't deny that. And now I'm really off duty. No topics more serious than food or carnival rides."

Kira seemed about to protest, but she eventually nodded and took a huge bite of her loaded baked potato. "Deal," she mumbled around the mouthful of food. She waved her fork. "So, talk about rides. What's your favorite kind?"

"Anything that goes fast," Abby said. She remembered her first visits to the fair once she was old enough to graduate from kiddie rides to the more grown-up versions. She and Rick had been fearless, spinning and twirling on rides until they were too dizzy to walk straight. "I like the feeling of air whipping around and through me, and I love vertical drops that make my stomach sink."

"I believe it," Kira said. She drizzled honey on a piece of cornbread and popped it in her mouth. "I'll bet you drive like a fiend, too."

Abby was momentarily distracted by the honey, imagining it dripping onto her own skin for Kira to lick. She took a drink of iced tea before she could speak again. "Guilty. Before I was old enough to get my license, I was an exercise rider at the track. I'd gallop Thoroughbreds for hours every weekend. That was a thrill."

Kira put down her fork and pointed her finger at Abby. "Do not tell Julie about that. She'll want to do it because you did, and I'm not going to sit in the bleachers and watch her barreling around a track on some barely controlled racehorse."

"I promise I won't tell," Abby said, but she liked the thought of Julie looking up to her and wanting to be like her. She'd never thought of herself as a role model for anyone, and she realized the responsibility of it. She'd been disappointed by the people she'd idolized—especially her grandfather—and she knew firsthand how painful the fall from grace was. "What about you? What rides do you like?"

"I don't care about fast, but I like to go upside down."

That can be arranged. Abby needed to get her imagination under control. Kira's words were inspiring some enticing visuals. "Why upside down?"

Kira put her elbows on the table and gave the question some thought. "I like getting a new perspective, I guess. Everything looks different when you see it from another angle. And I notice the pull of gravity more, even though I barely give it thought when I'm right-side up."

Abby smiled. She hadn't done this in ages. Talk about nothing in particular, share small pieces of herself with another person. A new perspective, and something so basic and everyday that she was startled by a feeling of profound intimacy. "Your turn," she said. "Pick a topic."

Kira looked around at the various booths and kiosks in this corner of the fair. "Aha! Okay, you're getting your caricature drawn. What's the one feature you secretly hope the artist won't choose to exaggerate because you really don't like it?"

"Good question," she said. She propped her chin in her hand and thought about her answer. Most of what she didn't like about herself was genetic and invisible. "My lips," she said. "I always thought they were unprofessional."

Kira raised her eyebrows, and Abby thought she saw a soft flush of pink on her cheeks, but the sunglasses made it difficult to tell. "Your lips are…unprofessional?"

"Yeah. If they were thinner I'd look more authoritative."

Kira gave a strangled sort of laugh and she reached across the table to lightly run her index finger over Abby's lower lip. "Trust me, they're perfect."

Abby caught Kira's hand before she could pull it away. She held it against her mouth for another moment before darting her tongue across trembling fingertips. Hints of wood smoke and something grasslike and delicious. Kira snatched her hand away.

"Hey, if you put it near my mouth I'm going to kiss it."

"I'll keep that in mind," Kira said. She was laughing along with Abby, but this time there was no doubt she was blushing.

"Your turn to answer," Abby said. "Please say you don't like your breasts so I can touch them and tell you they're perfect, like you did with my lips."

Kira shrieked and threw her sauce-stained napkin at Abby. She caught it easily and reveled in the lightness she felt as laughter moved through her without resistance—a rare and pleasant sensation, just like the feel of Kira's fingers had been.

"Hargrove? Jeez, I barely recognized you in that getup. Rock on!" Harvey Wayne stood next to their table. His arrival had gone unnoticed while Abby had been caught up in laughter, but the moment she saw him, her inescapable life burst the fragile bubble of make-believe she'd created.

He leered at Kira. "Who's your friend? I have to say, Hargrove, you sure manage to attract the lookers. What's your secret?"

Before she realized she was going to move, Abby was up and standing between Wayne and Kira. "We're having a private lunch," she said, but she felt Kira's hand on her upper arm.

"I have to go anyway, Abby," Kira said. "Julie will be home from school soon, and we'll have to get back here for the show. Thanks for lunch."

She left quickly, and Abby let her go, resigned as she'd been to the inevitable end to their off-duty truce.

"Was it something I said?" Harvey asked. Abby just shook her head and gathered up their empty plates. Even if he hadn't come along, her work life would have intruded eventually. She tossed her trash in the garbage and walked away.

CHAPTER SIX

Abby gritted her teeth and swung her leg over the back of the seventeen-hand-tall mare. Legs's shoulder was an inch higher than the top of Abby's head, and she would have been a challenge to mount even without tight and aching muscles. A week of unaccustomed riding had made the task nearly impossible, but no way was Abby going to use the fucking stool Cal had discreetly placed at the end of the aisle. A small group of onlookers hovered near the door to the barn while the officers prepared for their nightly patrol, and Abby wasn't going to look weak in front of them or the rest of her team.

"Don't be a hero, Lieutenant," Don said with a grin in her direction as he used the stool to climb on Fancy. "I remember the first few weeks of training with Rachel. My thighs hurt so bad I thought I'd be permanently bowlegged."

Abby adjusted her stirrups without looking at him. Her ankles were chafed raw from her tall boots and she had a series of small bruises on the insides of her calves and knees, but she wasn't going to admit it. "I appreciate your concern, Officer, but I'm doing fine. I've ridden before."

Yes, she'd ridden in the past, but this was completely different. Even busy horse-show days didn't compare to a few hours of patrol on the midway. The riders were always on alert, always surrounded by unpredictable crowds. Each evening, after their shift, she'd dropped to the ground from Legs's back and felt as if she was going to disintegrate at the first jarring contact with the pavement. She'd barely make it home to the relaxing comfort of a few beers and a bottle of foul-smelling horse liniment—another gift from Cal—and then she'd crawl out of bed to start over again the next morning.

Don laughed. "Must've been someone else I saw hobbling around the barn aisle. My mistake."

"That does it, Lindstrom." Abby glared at him while Billie came out of the barn and used the stool to mount Ranger. "You're on probation for insubordination. For your punishment you have to carry me out to my car tonight because I don't think I can walk that far."

"Another day or two and you'll be feeling better," Billie said. She moved Ranger into position on Abby's left side. "As long as you keep using Cal's liniment every night."

"Ugh," Don said. "She's using it, don't worry. I smelled it as soon as I got through the gate this afternoon."

Abby tried to glare at him, but she couldn't stop from joining in their laughter. He was exaggerating, of course, but not by much. Even with repeated showers, she smelled like someone who had recently been embalmed. Still, the liniment helped enough that she didn't care. Her muscles would heal—stronger than before—but her relationship with her team was changing, and she wasn't sure how she'd be able to return to her former aloof and authoritative position. She had to make it happen, she just wasn't sure how.

Abby's attention had been split between the police stables and the show-horse area, and she was finally rewarded when she saw Kira emerge from the 4-H barn, looking adorably like a teenager herself in dark khaki capris and white sleeveless T-shirt even though the evening was turning cool. Kira immediately looked to her right when she got outside and she gave what was probably supposed to be a casual wave, although it seemed anything but as she turned and darted back into the barn. Was she in the habit of looking for Abby, too? She had enjoyed lunch with Kira the other day. No Nirvana to remind Abby of her life-consuming familial obligations, and no uniform to force Kira to relive bad memories. It had been a brief moment for each of them to step out of their normal lives, and Abby treasured those rare opportunities whenever she found them. They were the exceptions, though, and never could be the rule.

Roles had always been clearly defined for Abby. She was the boss over her sergeant and the officers on her mounted team and she ruled strictly but fairly. She was deferential to her own bosses. Rules were followed, impropriety of any kind was scrupulously avoided. Lines were never crossed. Now, in the span of one week, everything had become blurred.

Rachel and Bandit came out of the barn and took the lead as the unit moved as one toward the midway. The original plan, Abby knew since she'd help draw it up with Rachel, was for them to patrol in pairs. Walkie-talkies would connect the four together, and police radios would tie them to the foot-patrol officers at the fair. Abby had expected them to make allowances for her since she wasn't familiar with their routines, but she hadn't anticipated the resulting change in dynamics. She'd envisioned herself as an observer, overseeing the troops as they worked. Instead, she'd been coddled and protected as if she was one of their grandmothers on a ride-along. Billie and Don on either side, and Rachel ahead. She wasn't so much bothered by the care her team was taking—after all, they were right to do so—but the close quarters led to close conversations. At first, Abby had tried not to join in, and she had remained nearly mute while the three others—bonded by long hours spent in each other's company— chatted and laughed. But how many jokes could she hear before she chimed in with a funny retort? Her resolve to stay distant had lasted less than an hour, and even though she occasionally made a new resolution, she was just as quick to break it.

Kira had challenged her as well. She brought up uncomfortable questions about Nirvana and Abby's brother, and she didn't seem satisfied with Abby's evasive answers. And though she'd spent her career determined never to mix her professional and personal lives, after five minutes spent with Kira and Julie, Abby had been ready to abandon that principle, too, and every time she saw Kira she felt her resolve erode a little more. Luckily, Kira seemed to be avoiding her. Abby couldn't help but look for her as they walked around the fairground, and every time she got a glimpse of Kira, she switched directions and disappeared. Abby should feel relieved. Instead of determinedly challenging her boundaries like the mounted team was doing, Kira seemed content to keep distance between them.

Rachel held up a hand and stopped the foursome as a young girl darted out of the crowd and reached to pet Bandit's leg. The same thing happened a few times every night, especially when they were near the kiddie rides, and the horses stood quietly as a few families milled around and visited with them. When they were ready to move forward again, Rachel turned back toward her.

"Are you okay, Lieutenant? If you're too sore…"

Abby gestured toward the pony ride, where several furry animals were attached to a metal pole that spun in a slow circle. "Yeah, Bryce, I'm exhausted. Why don't you tie me and Legs to one of those chains and we'll stay here until you're done for the night."

Rachel raised her eyebrows and Abby realized how irritated her voice had sounded.

"Maybe we should split into pairs tonight," Rachel said after a few seconds of silence. "Don and Billie, I heard there were some gang members hanging out around the main game tent. There will be plenty of officers nearby, but it'd be a good idea to make the horses' presence known. Abby and I can check out the grandstand area since tonight's show will attract a younger audience and I don't want the crowd to get out of hand."

Abby felt the change in Legs as soon as Don and Billie rode away from them. She and Rachel turned toward the central portion of the fairgrounds, and the gray mare shied away from a blue-and-white checked piece of paper blown across their path by a slight breeze. Abby stroked the mare's neck and spoke quietly to her until her muscles relaxed and they were ready to move on again. She had been so caught up in her own problems and her thoughts of Kira that she hadn't stopped to think about how much comfort Legs was deriving from the nearness of her small herd. Abby hoped her pride hadn't jeopardized the safety of her horse or her partner.

"I wouldn't have split us up if I didn't think you could handle it, no matter how much you whined," Rachel said, as if reading Abby's mind.

She *never* whined. Abby was about to protest when she saw Rachel's grin. Was her entire unit bent on joking with her like she was one of the gang instead of their boss? Abby kept quiet and concentrated on keeping a firm but quiet hand on the reins. Bandit walked along calmly, and Legs seemed to relax as she stuck close by his side. Even though Rachel had disguised it as teasing, Abby knew the truth of her statement. As usual, she was well aware of the big picture and wouldn't be swayed from it. Hell, it was the main reason why Abby had come to respect Rachel as a sergeant and a person—she stood by her beliefs and would never put the team at risk just to placate Abby.

"Hey," Rachel said. "Did I ever tell you about the time Cal made us walk across the Narrows Bridge for a training session?"

Abby felt herself disengage even as she laughed along with Rachel's story. She had to keep her focus on the big picture, too. The future of her mounted unit. The good she could do as a member of the police force as long as she maintained a strict adherence to the protocols she'd set in place for herself. She sat comfortably in the saddle for the first time in days, rocking along with the rhythm of Legs's stride as they walked past the carousel. The mare watched with interest as a horde of children ran around the wooden platform, hurrying to claim a favorite mount from the lavishly colored choices. Abby had wanted to experience being part of this team, and she had her chance now on this crisp fall evening, surrounded by the layered scents and sounds of the fair. It was a fleeting moment in time. In two weeks, this would be over—the tempting sight of Kira, the laughter of her temporary teammates, the camaraderie of mounted patrol—and she would be back to normal. Mostly unchanged, but maybe a little stronger both physically from her work on Legs and mentally from her ability to resist both her desire to let down her defenses with Kira and her team. No more bonding during nightly patrols, and definitely no more intimate lunches flavored with tangy barbecue sauce and the sweet taste of Kira's fingers. She exhaled deeply and felt an answering sigh from Legs as they followed Rachel toward the main grandstand.

Chapter Seven

Kira had been confident about her work on the Milford property during the week, but somehow being back at the fair—where he had confronted her only a few days before—made her jumpy. While Julie prepped for and rode in her trail class, Kira spent the day scanning the faces around her, waiting for Tad Milford to show up again. Her career as a wetland biologist regularly required confrontation since developers often disagreed with her environmental impact assessments and her restrictions on building sites. When she had first started in the field, she had never minded a good, heated debate about the ecosystems she studied and fought to protect, but she had changed lately. Before, she had been able to separate herself from the conflicts—arguing with knowledge and data rather than emotions. But now? Even the thought of Tad standing too close to her with a heartless expression on his face made her react physically. A dry mouth and sweaty palms. She felt upside down, and not in a good way. Exposed.

She wandered around the midway, delaying the trip from the busy grounds to the parking lot with all its shadowy hiding spots. She and Julie had parked a few blocks away this morning, to save on the ridiculous parking fees for the main lots, but she had run out there after Julie's class and moved her car to one of the closer, pricey spots. Even so, she dreaded the short walk. She wasn't so much afraid that Tad would follow her or attack her, but she was afraid of—and angered by—her own fear. What had happened to the brave and outspoken woman she'd been after graduate school?

She paused by one of the rides and watched the twirling cars whip through the air. The green and yellow neon lights illuminated the faces of the riders. Wide grins, mouths parted in loud screams. These people had paid to feel fear, to be pushed out of their comfort zones and flung through the air. She'd been like them, once. Kira avoided those feelings as much as possible these days, for her own sake but mostly to create a safer life for Julie. A life of predictability and security—was it even possible? Now danger had approached from an unexpected angle, from her work and not her personal relationships. Julie was part of the reason she reacted so strongly to Tad's threats. She cared about wetlands and would fight to protect the environment, but how much more would she give up to protect her daughter? Her life. Anything and everything she had.

Kira saw Abby and another officer riding toward her, and she ducked behind a stand selling deep-fried candy bars. Yes, another opportunity to be fearful instead of brave. This time, however, Kira was protecting her heart and not her body. Her identity and then her physical security had been subsumed by Dale, and Kira couldn't allow that to happen again. Ever. She was too attracted to Abby to let herself get close. She hadn't been able to find a sufficient reason to keep Julie from attending the mounted police demonstration ride yet again, but she had made an excuse to let her and her friend Angie go alone while she had used the time to move her car. At least that way she had been able to find a safer parking spot without worrying Julie. She wanted to protect her daughter, but at the same time she didn't want Julie to have to face the fear and loss of self she had experienced.

Unfortunately, not watching the police ride hadn't kept her from hearing about the entire thing from an enthusiastic Julie. Officer Hargrove did this…Officer Hargrove did that… Kira shook her head even as she slipped out of her hiding spot and followed the two riders. She was only interested in seeing if Abby really was as amazing as Julie seemed to think. Kira didn't do much riding herself, but she had watched Julie's lessons enough to learn the basics and to recognize a skilled equestrian when she saw one. Abby didn't look as relaxed in the saddle as her dark-haired companion did, but she carried herself with a controlled poise. Her hands were light and soft, and she moved easily with her large gray horse even when the animal shied away from a sudden burst of noise at one of the carnival games. Abby got her horse back under control calmly and without any fuss, and the two officers inched toward the offending sound. Step by step, they moved forward until they were standing right by the wooden counter of the game. Players lobbed basketballs through the air while Abby and her partner watched. A flashing light and shrill whistle announced another winner, but this time Abby's horse didn't react to the sound, and the officers moved on.

Kira walked behind them for another few feet before she realized she was staring a little too intently at Abby's seat on the saddle. Snug pants showed every dip and groove of her muscles as she swayed with the horse's movement. Mesmerizing.

"Oh, excuse me," Kira said when she almost ran into someone. She felt her face heat and looked around to see if anyone had seen her apologizing to a display of T-shirts. She turned around and headed in the opposite direction from Abby's route. She'd be safer facing Tad Milford in the parking lot than following Abby any longer.

Kira went out the gate and hurried to catch up to a large family as they crossed the street and entered the parking lot. The area was brightly lit, but still she circled around her car and checked the backseat before she got in and hurriedly locked the doors. She started the engine but just sat there for a few minutes, letting her heart rate slow down. So strong a reaction to such a simple act. The day had been as full of twists and sudden drops as a roller coaster. Watching Abby had gotten her heart beating faster, but she had to admit that feeling had been exhilarating, like the thrill of being pushed to the limit on an exciting ride. Kira used to crave that kind of reaction to another woman, but now it scared her as much as the walk to the parking lot had. Had she grown more sensible? Or was she too paranoid? She wasn't certain.

She backed out of her spot and drove home. Yes, she was overprotective and overreactive at times, but she had every reason to be. She had learned exactly what happened when she let someone strong get too close. The control happened slowly at first, but then life got too scary too fast. After she had managed to get out, she had been told by family and friends not to worry, that she'd eventually learn to trust again, but she didn't care to. She trusted herself, was slowly learning to trust her own instincts once more, and that was enough. She'd try to teach Julie how to be careful while still being able to love, but for herself? She was better off being alone. Sometimes lonely, but safe at least.

Kira drove slowly through the darkness, leaving the small town of Puyallup and taking the back roads into Tacoma. She bypassed the freeway and only occasionally checked to be sure no one was following her through the quiet residential streets. She was tempted to enter the drive-through of one of the several fast-food restaurants she passed on her way to Tacoma's north end, but she resisted the urge. If Julie had been with her, they'd have stopped, but Julie was spending the night with Angie. Tomorrow night, the two would stay with Kira, and the girls would be sure to want burgers and fries for dinner, so she bypassed the chain restaurants for now. She'd have a sandwich at home tonight and share the more calorie-laden meal with the girls tomorrow night. She smiled at the thought. Competing at the fair seemed to be as much about socializing as it was about winning ribbons. Julie and Angie would probably spend the night strategizing for their upcoming classes and discussing the riders from other counties and clubs. Julie always took her riding seriously and never took for granted the money Kira spent on the activity, so Kira wouldn't begrudge her a few sleepless and gossipy nights. She wanted Julie to have friends and have fun, and Kira herself would be very happy to have chatter and company in the house.

She pulled into the driveway of her small postwar rambler and turned off the car. She had left a light on inside, but the house already seemed lonelier without Julie there to share it. Kira found her house key before she got out of the car. She'd keep the television on all night, preferring to sleep through the low volume rather than feel so alone. She shut and locked her car, and then walked up the path to her front door. She climbed the steps and pushed aside a couple of branches from one of her large rhododendrons. She'd need to trim them back this—

She was on her knees before she registered the pain. Something hard had struck her thighs from behind, making her legs buckle. She put out a hand to balance herself on the concrete steps, but it was wrenched behind her back and a warm hand clamped over her mouth before she could do more than gasp in shock. She felt the sweat from the heavy palm on her lips. She struggled to get enough purchase on the steps to be in a position to fight back, but within seconds her hands were fastened together by something cuttingly sharp, and a piece of duct tape replaced the damp human flesh that had covered her mouth. The tape was tight, blocking all air and pulling the skin of her face into what appropriately felt like a grimace of pain.

She was half dragged, half carried back down her driveway. She fought to kick or elbow the person holding her, but she was unable to do more than look wildly up and down her block, hoping one of her neighbors would come to her aid. The street was deserted, although she could see lights on in a few windows. Flickers of movement, shadows on closed drapes, but no eyes to witness her abduction. A dark cloth was tugged over her head, severing her connection to the world around her with a finality that made tears come to her eyes. With a cry of despair, Kira felt herself lifted off her feet and rolled backward. Her head slammed into something metal, making her wince in pain, before she felt it come to rest on a hard surface. Her legs were bent behind her back and fastened with a tight narrow band of plastic.

The slam of metal on metal. The lid of a trunk…she was *in* someone's trunk. She struggled to breathe rapidly through her nostrils, unable to get enough air. She was going to hyperventilate, but she couldn't resist the need to get more oxygen. More air, please more air…

The roar of the car's engine coming to life reverberated through her body. She was trapped, but felt oddly exposed as the car moved. Cold night air whistled through cracks and chilled her bare arms. Every bump in the road jostled her aching body. Her nostrils flared as she pulled in breath with a growing sense of panic. She'd suffocate in the dark mask and duct tape. She'd die, unable to fill her lungs with air.

Kira kicked at the walls of the trunk. Her attempts were futile. Her own weakness made her sag in despair, but she had to try again. She used all her strength to lift her bound legs and kick at the lid. She had to get out, get free, breathe air that wasn't choked with exhaust. The fumes made bile rise in her throat, but she willed it down. She couldn't vomit, not with her mouth sealed shut. She kicked again, with less strength but with more terror in her movements.

She let her legs drop. She was only a step away from hysteria, from completely losing control in her panic to get out. Get out where? To find whom? The only person who was going to open the trunk was the one who'd put her there. Suddenly the thought of what might happen to her when he *did* open the lid and let her out made the thought of staying inside and suffocating seem the more bearable option. Fear rose again, making her breath shallow and fluttery. She lost touch with every part of her body except the passageway from her lungs to her throat to her nose. She needed more air, dragged it in, but it burned.

You have five more seconds to panic, and then you have to pull it together. For Julie. For yourself. She moaned loudly, felt the material draped over her face dampen with her tears, while she counted slowly. *One, two, three, four. Four and a half. Four and three-quarters.* She gave a choked laugh. She and Julie had played that game many times before. Whenever Julie faced something she didn't want to do, like homework or cleaning her room, Kira would give her to the count of five to complain and whine about it. Then she had to get it done. Julie had become an expert at fractions just to procrastinate more.

Five. No more panic. Awareness and attention. Kira wasn't sure how it would help. Would she find a way to escape? Or would she only gather enough evidence to possibly help the police find who did this to her? She pictured Abby looking for Julie at the fair. Sitting her down and telling her they'd found her mother's body…

And no more following that particular train of thought. Kira tried to focus. On Abby's aura of strength and self-confidence. On the advice Kira imagined she'd give, if she were here, about how to handle this situation. To keep control, to pay attention to her surroundings. Kira couldn't see anything but darkness, couldn't hear anything but the car's engine and the rush of air, couldn't smell anything but the revolting, thick fumes. She still tasted the man's sweat, but once she concentrated there was more. Something bitter and aromatic in her mouth. Aftershave.

Had she been right to be worried about Tad's threats? Kira felt a small glimmer of pride. She had a new piece of information—albeit small and not much help to her yet—but she had controlled her emotions enough to find it. She reached out a little further with her awareness.

She moved her arm and felt the rough carpet chafe her skin. Her right elbow had been scraped, either when she was pushed inside or during her vain attempts to get out again. She remembered the crime shows she'd seen when a victim was transported in a trunk. Detectives looked for fibers, blood, some proof the person had been there. Of course, those shows rarely ended with the victim being found alive, but she quickly pushed that thought away. It didn't help her now, didn't belong in her head. She rubbed her raw elbow on the floor of the trunk and plucked at the hem of her T-shirt until she pulled a few threads loose, letting them drop to the carpet. Yet another act that didn't do her much good at the moment, but it was a tiny victory over her fear. She lay still for a few seconds, her breathing still rough and fast, but not as panic-stricken now.

As she lay there, motionless yet hurtling through the darkness, the aching parts of her body slowly seeped into her awareness. Her heels stung where she'd pounded them on the metal—with more force than she had realized, since the pain was intense. Her core muscles, supposedly strengthened by all the Pilates she did, were weak and tight after a mere few moments of extreme anxiety and the effort of supporting her raised, kicking legs. Useless pain. She had exerted herself but hadn't had any real chance of succeeding in her escape attempts. She couldn't let that happen again, let her panic overwhelm her common sense. Abby's imagined voice rang in her head again: *Don't get exhausted, but save your strength. Don't let images of what might happen in the hours ahead keep your mind from observing and analyzing the present. Don't let a real chance to escape slip by because you were too blinded by fear to see it.*

Good ideas, yes. Easy to follow? Not a chance. The car turned, and Kira helplessly rolled across the trunk until her neck was strained against the cold metal wall. She felt the vehicle slow down and come to a stop. Her breathing increased again, every fiber of her body wanted to scream *No!* The fog of despair was as blinding as the bag over her head—she couldn't see past it to find reason or control. She felt feral. Inhuman. Only the thought of Julie kept her from completely losing her grip.

She was dragged out of the trunk, briefly through the cooling evening, and into a building. She tried to stay lucid enough to pick up clues about where she was, but the short journey left her sore and disoriented. A scraped shin on the pavement, a kick in the ribs, a fisted hand grabbing her hair and shoving her, face first, onto the hard floor. Without her ability to see, the outside world seemed oddly distant. Sounds echoed as if coming to her from the far end of a long tunnel. All she really knew was pain and fear.

Then, as suddenly as it had started, the chaos receded and time slowed to its normal pace. She was hefted off the floor and slammed into a chair.

"Let's get one thing straight." Tad's voice was clear and undisguised. "This never happened. You'll never tell anyone it happened. You won't even let yourself believe it happened."

He's going to kill me. Kira was more certain of that fact than she had ever been about anything. He wasn't even making an effort to hide his identity from her.

"Because if you do, it'll be your daughter next, sitting in this room with me, helpless and trembling while I decide what to do to her."

Worse. Kira would rather die than have Julie experience even one minute of this defenseless terror. She couldn't speak, couldn't move more than an inch without feeling like the plastic ties on her wrists and ankles were about to sever her limbs. But she was able to nod her head.

"Good. We understand each other." Tad's voice was harsh. Cruel. Kira had heard the meanness in it last week and though she had taken a few small steps to protect herself and her daughter, it hadn't been enough. Why hadn't she fully trusted her instincts? Why had she—God, yet again—made such a costly mistake? "Now, let's have a chat about my property. You didn't seem inclined to listen to me last Friday, but maybe you're more in the mood to pay attention tonight. You had a busy week, but you've discovered that my property isn't really as vital a part of Tacoma's wetland corridor as you originally thought, right?"

He'd really put her through this just to build a few damned houses? Kira trembled with rage at her own vulnerability and fury at his violation of her. He grabbed her hair again, pulling the cloth hood tightly against her nose, and roughly shook her head back and forth.

"Answer me when I talk to you," he said. He let go and she sucked in air with spasmodic breaths. "Well?"

She shuddered and shook her head. She was beaten. Defeated. *No*, Abby's imagined voice echoed in her head. She had to cede the battles she couldn't win and wait—and hope—for one she could.

"Nicely done. Let's try another. The buffer restrictions you placed on my site are wrong, and you'll be amending them in my favor Monday morning, won't you?"

Kira nodded. She hated him. Wanted to kill him. Maybe more so because he was right. She'd sacrifice the wetland to keep Julie safe. And, selfishly, to protect herself from his insanity.

"Now we're getting somewhere. I think you and I are going to get along better than—What the hell are you doing here?"

Kira had barely registered the sound of a door closing and someone entering the room. All her focus centered on this new arrival. Friend or foe? Someone who might help her, or someone to make the night even worse? She heard low murmurs of a voice, but the sound was too muffled by the cloth and her pounding heart for her to identify the person's words, let alone their intent or even gender.

Tad didn't bother to lower his voice, and Kira tried to fill in the gaps left in the conversation.

"I told you I'd take care of this…Don't get involved…*I* make the decisions here, not you. Just walk away and count the money we'll make once this little bitch is out of our way."

She heard the hiss of a forceful whisper, and then sensed Tad had returned to her side. His leg brushed against her thigh, and she cringed. He put a hand on the top of her head, not pulling her hair this time but instead almost caressing her with a gesture in between a pat and a too-rough squeeze. She felt the need to vomit again, and now she didn't care that her mouth was sealed shut.

"You can watch if you want to," Tad said with a bark of a laugh. "But you can't stop me."

A crack that made her ears ring. The shudder of Tad's hand before it slipped off her head. The hot splatter of liquid on her arms. Kira pushed her mind to figure out the rapid fire of sensations. Was she hurt? No. Was she safe yet? She had no idea.

The quiet after the gunshot was even more disconcerting. She remained as still as possible, as if she could make herself disappear from sight, while what she assumed was Tad's blood dripped down her arm and off her fingers. The other person—the killer—was still there. Standing close but not touching. Neither hurting her nor letting her go. Kira held her breath, the need for air overridden by the need to know what was coming next.

She heard footsteps, the swish of a door opening, and the click of it shutting again. And Kira was left alone.

CHAPTER EIGHT

Abby sat on her porch and watched the sunrise. She leaned back in the deck chair, stretching her legs out in front of her and breathing in the cool morning air. She felt good. Her muscles had finally adapted to their new work, and her tall leather boots had lost their stiffness as well. She still had blisters and a few bruises, but she had thoroughly enjoyed the week. Legs had been a blast to ride, and Abby had finally let herself...well, just *be*. Not be in charge—she had let Cal lead the demonstration and Rachel lead the mounted team. She also hadn't had to be a Hargrove. Legs had been the focus of everyone's attention. Kids and adults had crowded around the horses, wanting to pet them and ask questions, and they had barely looked at Abby's face, let alone her name tag. She could see why Rachel and the team enjoyed the PR side of their job. There had been an interesting mix of celebrity and anonymity as she had been at once the center of attention, yet merely the one holding the horse's reins.

The deep navy sky was rimmed with color now. Amber and garnet and burnt orange cast Mount Rainier into a silhouette of looming black. Abby took a sip of her coffee and sighed. Two weeks away from her normal life. Away from the department headquarters and away from the private work she did on behalf of those wronged by her family. The former was official leave time and the latter was a gift she was allowing herself. She'd feel guilty about it, of course, but guilt was a constant companion. Any extra would be outweighed by the short-term fun of actually being a part of the team she had envisioned and implemented.

The sky lightened to a soft blue, and the warm tones of the sunrise turned to cooler pinks and peaches. Abby had bought her run-down Victorian for a steep price, even though it had needed a ridiculous amount of repairs. She had walked through the rooms with their water-stained ceilings and windowsills covered with dead flies without really noticing them. She had stepped out on the back porch and had seen the view of Commencement Bay and Old Town Tacoma—the real reason she had come to see the house. The sky had been overcast, but she knew where the mountain would be visible on rare clear days. She had paid the crazy amount of money—expected in this part of the city even for a crappy house—and had gotten the major and priority repairs done to the plumbing and electricity as soon as she was able to afford them. She had always planned to decorate and renovate the rooms, but most of her money went, in various forms, to the people she needed to help. People her family of cops *should* have helped, but hadn't. So she lived one step up from a college student in a dorm room, with mismatched particleboard furniture she'd assembled herself. But she had this view, and the momentary peace it brought her every night and morning.

And now, for a short time, she had the Puyallup Fair, with the mounted police horses and the chance of seeing Kira again. Abby set her University of Puget Sound coffee mug on the table next to her and crossed her arms behind her head. She felt a twinge in her delts as she arched her back and stretched her spine tall. Her feelings for Kira were risky. She was already willing to make allowances on her no dating anyone associated with police work policy. Would it be so bad if she bent her rigid rules just this once? She had made reparations for her brother's misconduct the best way she could, by giving the horse she loved to Kira's daughter. A symbol of acceptance and unconditional love, meant to bring joy to a battered family. Her self-imposed obligation to Kira was fulfilled.

Abby sat up with a jerking motion. Was this how it had started with her grandfather's actions and her dad's complicit acceptance? Was this the direction in which her brother was heading? Make a small allowance—what could it hurt?—and then bigger and bigger ones? No, she was making an unfair comparison. She and Kira weren't involved in any police business, not anymore. She wouldn't be tempted to fix her parking tickets or steal pens for her from the department's supply rooms. Ridiculous. So why should she worry that she'd follow their footsteps in more serious matters?

Because she understood just how easy it would be to fall prey to temptation. And because she wasn't convinced she could overcome heredity by sheer will alone. She had been careful to avoid any hint of misconduct at work. No favoritism, no favors. No friendships formed that would give her even the slightest chance to err. Why was Kira able to tempt her when no one else ever had? Would it be a sin to get to know her a little better, in the context of the fair and the horse show and not in association with the domestic violence call Rick had apparently mishandled?

Her phone vibrated, and Abby checked the caller ID. No name, but the prefix was a departmental one.

"Hargrove," she said. She hoped it wasn't something that would keep her from riding again today.

"Lieutenant, this is Carter from Homicide. Do you know a Kira Lovell?"

Abby knocked over the table next to her as she bolted to her feet. She left the shattered glass on the patio and was heading inside to get dressed even as she answered.

"Yes, I do. What happened? Is she—"

"She's okay. I didn't mean to worry you," Detective Bryan Carter said quickly. "She's a little shaken and bruised, but she'll be fine."

"What happened?" Abby yanked a uniform out of her closet and dropped her robe on the bedroom floor.

"She was abducted from her home last night, presumably by Tad Milford. He's a real-estate developer."

"I'm familiar with the name," Abby said through clenched teeth. Her brother's business partner. Rick had been investing in Milford Corporation's spec building projects for a few years now. Abby was certain there were some shady aspects to her brother's side venture, but she hadn't investigated them fully yet. She had so many other Hargrove wrongs to put right that she'd probably be playing cleanup until long after she retired from her real job. All she knew so far was that Tad had given her a bad feeling the one time she had met him. She had been spot-on, apparently. She was startled by her sudden desire to seriously hurt him for whatever he'd done to Kira.

"He's the victim. Shot dead."

Abby paused as she struggled to fasten the clasp of her bra while holding the phone. "Did Kira…is she a suspect?"

"No. She was tied up next to him. We got a tip this morning to go to his office, and we found them both there. She asked for you." Carter's voice shifted from matter-of-fact cop to human being. "Abby, she was there next to him all night. She couldn't see what was happening, but she might have some clue about who the killer is. I thought, since you're friends, you might be able to help her remember some details."

Abby wasn't sure if his tone or his use of her given name made her most uneasy. She had to get to Kira, help her in any way she could. She hung up and finished getting dressed in seconds. It wasn't until she was in the car and speeding toward Milford's downtown office that she realized she and Kira were now irrevocably and unquestionably connected by Abby's police career. Abby would do her best to support Kira through the long day of questions ahead of her, but any relationship—friendship or otherwise—was now off-limits to her.

❖

Abby stepped under the crime-scene tape strung across the door to the Milford Corporation and was immediately cornered by Detective Carter. He had brown hair and wide-set hazel eyes, a somewhat portly build and quiet demeanor. His nondescript appearance concealed a shrewd and intuitive detective, and Abby usually appreciated his calm and methodical approach. Today, however, she wanted to push him out of the way and get to Kira, who was huddled in a black leather desk chair in the corner of the room, her knees pulled tightly to her chest and a blanket draped over her shoulders. She looked young and exhausted, still wearing the capris and summery top from the night before, and Abby wanted to rush right to her side, especially when Kira looked up and saw her. Abby had seen enough victims of trauma to recognize the shades of pain and haunted memories clouding her expression. She didn't let her impatience show, however, and kept her tone neutral as she talked to Carter.

"What's going on? How did Ms. Lovell get involved?"

"We're still fitting together the pieces of the puzzle, but so far her side of the story checks out." He flipped open his notebook and checked what he had written. "She's a wetland biologist and she was fighting some proposed building he was planning to do because the land is connected to the Snake Lake watershed. She said Milford approached her at the fair last Friday and threatened her if she didn't back off, but she said she wouldn't. She left Puyallup about nine last night, and he must have been waiting at her home. She claims he attacked her from behind, knocking her down and restraining her. Her mouth was covered with duct tape so she couldn't call for help. She was then—"

"Julie," Abby said. She heard the sharp note of concern in her voice, but she didn't care. "Where's Julie?"

"Who? Oh, the daughter? She's fine. She stayed at a friend's house last night, but the parents are bringing her over. She'll be here soon."

Abby felt her shoulders drop as relief made her feel suddenly tired. "Good. That's good. Um, go on, please."

Carter looked at her for a moment before he nodded. "Sure, Lieutenant. So, Ms. Lovell was transported here in the trunk of Milford's car. He put her in that chair over there." Carter pointed at a metal folding chair in the center of the room. Abby had seen it when she first walked in, but the sight made her feel queasy. There was blood spatter on the floor around it. Close, very close, to it. Kira had been right next to Tad when he was shot. And then left there by the killer? That didn't make any sense.

"He roughed her up a little," Carter said. "Threatened to do the same to her daughter if she didn't drop the whole wetland thing. She agreed to his terms, but then someone else came in the room. This is where it gets a little hazy. She can't tell us anything about the killer. All she can say is that Milford was standing next to her, with his hand on the top of her head, when the unknown assailant shot him. The killer left, and several hours later, dispatch got a tip to come here."

"No one reported shots fired? No witnesses to any of this?"

"Nope. All the businesses were closed, and both the victim and the killer seemed to have used the back door from the alley. We're canvassing, but there weren't any 9-1-1 calls. Someone might turn up, but I think our best bet is helping her remember more details about what happened. She's in shock right now, so when she said she knew you I hoped a familiar person might be able to help."

"I'm glad you called me, Bryan." Abby thought for a moment before she formed her next question. "She's not considered a suspect in any way, is she?"

"Not at this time," Carter said. Noncommittal, like any detective would be. Abby had wanted him to say no with more certainty, but this was the best she could have expected from him, this early in the investigation.

"We found her blood on her steps and in the trunk of his car. She was bound with zip ties, and the marks on her wrists and ankles are consistent with the time frame she gave us. Blood spatter indicates she was sitting in the same position when he was shot and when we found her this morning. We're going to check on the wetland story and find out if anyone witnessed their altercation at the fair, but it's clear she wasn't the killer. Was she involved somehow?" Carter shrugged. "We don't know yet. Milford was shot, but she was left alone. Maybe the killer knew her and didn't want her harmed, or maybe the two events are completely separate."

Someone coincidentally came to shoot Tad Milford on the same night he had a kidnapping victim in his office? Abby didn't believe in coincidences, and she had a feeling Carter didn't either. She let the questions raised by the event flit around her mind, diluting the pure rage she felt at the picture of Kira bound and gagged as she sat in the hard metal chair for hours. Covered in Milford's blood. Abby swallowed and took a step back. She had heard enough. She had to get to Kira.

"Thanks for calling me in on this. Keep me informed of your progress, and I'll find out if I can get any more information from her." She took a few steps, and then turned back to face him. "Oh, and come get me when Julie gets here. It might be easier on her if I talk to her before she sees her mom. Give her an idea of what to expect so she isn't scared."

Abby resisted the urge to run across the room, instead slowing her steps as she approached Kira. Kira watched her with a haunted look, seeming to want Abby there and to be afraid of her at the same time. Abby had seen it before, had dealt with victims before. She had often cared about them, hated what had happened to them, but she had never felt such a powerful urge for justice. She wanted to bring Tad back from the dead and shoot him herself. The depth of her involvement in this case—even though she'd only met Kira a week ago—frightened her. She'd been too intrigued after meeting Kira, too captivated by her during their lunch, and had spent far too much time thinking about her and hoping to spot her in the fair crowds. Abby felt connected to Kira, but she really wasn't—at least not by any easily definable relationship.

Since the moment Abby had decided to become a cop, she'd been driven by a fierce need to protect and to right wrongs, but she wasn't prepared for the intensity of her feelings now. She made a decision as she walked across the office. She'd help Kira through this day, as she faced the ordeals to come and as the numbing effect of shock wore off. She'd help Julie cope with the sight of her mother's bruised face and the swollen, crimson divots where the restraints had been. But then she'd back away and let the detectives handle the case. She couldn't get involved.

She hesitated for a moment when she was close to Kira. She was only trying to protect herself, wasn't she? She had spent her career working to undo the shame her grandfather had caused. She had never let her feelings about his misdeeds show, had never discussed the old cases she studied with anyone. What was the point? He was dead and buried. She'd spend her life trying to atone in private for his sins. She bore his guilt and she would fix what she could. Judge, jury, hangman, and hanged. She had taken on all the jobs. Now she was faced with a case involving Tad Milford *and* Kira. Her brother *must* be connected somehow—and he was very much alive and wearing a badge. If she started investigating this case, the trail might lead directly to her family's doorstep. She wasn't prepared for that. She had to stay away.

She knelt by Kira's chair. "Hi," she said. She reached out and took one of Kira's hands, gently massaging her cold fingers and palm. The touch shocked her system as she felt the physical, tangible proof of Kira's horrific night. "I'm so sorry this happened to you."

Kira pulled her hand away and tucked it under the blanket. "I'm cold," she said.

"Can you bring us a couple more blankets?" Abby called to one of the officers standing nearby, who nodded and walked quickly away. Abby looked at Kira again. "Kira, we need your help."

"I already told the detective everything I remember. I'm sorry I can't tell you more, but…"

She stopped talking and squeezed her eyes shut. Abby saw her swallow with a convulsive gulp and she wished more than anything that she could just make the night disappear from Kira's memory, rather than needing to make it more clear in her mind.

"I…I understand. I know it's hard to relive what happened, but if you could just go over it again with me, maybe I can help you uncover something you haven't recalled yet. Sometimes, when you're in the middle of something as traumatic as last night, there are small details that get overshadowed by the more pressing survival needs. You never know what could help us catch a killer."

Kira nodded, her eyes still shut. Abby mouthed a thank-you to the officer who returned with a stack of blankets, and then she draped them over Kira's lap and shoulders, rubbing her upper arms to bring her more warmth. Kira opened her eyes at the touch.

"Tell me everything," Abby said, "starting from the moment he approached you at the fair."

"He…he was standing by Nirvana's stall when we got back to it after talking to you on Friday. I didn't recognize him at first, we had never actually met…but I was nervous around him from the start. Too close…he stood too close. And the smell. Of his aftershave. Why didn't I pay more attention to how I felt? Why did I let this happen?"

Abby cupped her fingers under Kira's chin. "Look at me, Kira. You did not *let* this happen. He hurt you, and it's not your fault at all." Her voice sounded harsh, but she had to make Kira understand what she was saying. Abby had been blaming herself while she listened, asking similar questions to Kira's. Why hadn't she followed Julie and Kira down the aisle that day? She'd have been there when Tad confronted them. Maybe she'd have recognized the real potential for danger and could have kept this from happening. She was trying to convince herself, too, that Tad was the one at fault here. Not her or Kira.

Kira nodded and swallowed again. "Okay. He told me I'd better drop my efforts to stop him from building…"

Abby gave Kira's words half of her attention. The rest of it focused on the red, chafed rectangle over Kira's mouth, where the duct tape had been. She wanted to wipe the residual marks away, clean Kira of any reminders of Tad's brutality, kiss away the pain. Her reaction was uncomfortable, but as Kira continued her story, Abby forgot her own unprofessional urges and listened more intently. She asked a question now and again but mainly let the narrative unfold in its own way. Kira's memories were disjointed and chaotic—no surprise to Abby, given the night she'd been through. The blindfold had separated Kira from her habitual way of experiencing her world and consolidating the input from her other senses, so the night was a series of disconnected sounds and smells and sensations. Abby had known this to happen with other people who were deprived of a sense during a traumatic event. What Abby hadn't expected was Kira's remarkable recall of her experience.

Abby's sense of wonder grew as Kira talked—haltingly, but with full command of her memories. She was braver and stronger than Abby would have guessed. She had thought through her actions, had paid full attention to events that could have rendered her catatonic. Abby's admiration for Kira was the only thing keeping her from losing herself in anger over what had happened. The descriptions Kira gave of her ride in the trunk and of Tad's dominance over her would haunt Abby for a long time.

Abby had been ready to walk away after her talk with Kira. She had promised Carter she'd try to get more information and had told herself she'd offer a short bout of compassion. Then she'd drop her involvement in the case to avoid any conflict of interest given her attraction to Kira and to dissociate herself from any connection if it was discovered that her brother had a hand in this.

Abby was certain Rick was involved somehow. But she couldn't act the coward now, in the face of Kira's bravery. She'd stay on the case long enough to find out the whole story behind Kira's kidnapping, and to be absolutely certain that she and Julie would be safe from now on—even if it meant she was the one to finally expose her family to the public. If Rick had played any part in this, he'd have to pay, like any dirty criminal. Brother or not.

CHAPTER NINE

Kira pulled one of the blankets tighter around her shoulders and winced as the fabric brushed the sensitive, swollen skin of her wrist. She had dozed off occasionally during the seemingly endless night, and every time she dropped to sleep either her wrists or ankles would sag against the cruel zip ties. The only way she had been able to keep pain from them at bay was to stay awake and keep her hands and feet pressed close together. Her body had rebelled against both her physical soreness and her frantically active mind, so she had spent hours in a cycle of drifting to sleep, relaxing enough to put pressure on her restraints, and jerking awake again. Over and over. By the time the police had arrived to release her, she was nearly delirious from lack of sleep. Exhausted, but agitated. She felt like crawling out of her skin.

Abby reached up and adjusted Kira's blanket for her. The small act touched Kira, even as she fought against being protected, against needing anyone to take care of her. The morning had been a gruesome one. The cops had uncovered her head and untaped her chapped mouth, but they had needed to take pictures of the crime scene. They had seemed to be trying to hurry, but the minutes had stretched long for Kira. She wanted to get out of the chair, to stretch, to get the hell away from the stiff body lying next to her. She thought she should feel some compassion for Tad Milford, or even a sense of relief that he was dead. All she had been able to think, though, was that he had bloodstains all over his pressed suit. She had sat there while the detectives snapped photo after photo, just wondering how one would remove so much blood from such expensive fabric.

She couldn't get warm. The blankets had slowed her violent shivering, but she still felt chills running up her spine and sharp frissons exploding in her stomach and chest. Abby took her hand again, holding it between her own and blowing warm breath on Kira's icy skin. It felt nice. It was comforting to have another human being connect with her, but in a gentle way. Kira felt too bruised to be touched with firmness.

Abby was just sitting quietly with her now. Waiting. Kira had told her story to the detective and had repeated it for Abby. She had tried to observe even the tiniest clues, but they needed more. What could she say? Tad had done something criminal, but at least she could understand his reasons. Egomania, greed, a hunger for power. But the unknown person who had shot him and left her there? Kira couldn't grasp the meaning of that. It didn't make sense, and somehow it disturbed her almost as much as the pain Tad had inflicted.

"Lieutenant?" The detective who had first interviewed Kira came over and whispered something to Abby.

She squeezed Kira's hand almost imperceptibly, and then let it go. "I'll be right back," she said. "If you need anything at all, ask one of the officers and they'll come get me. Are you okay if I go?"

Of course, Kira wanted to say. *Don't be ridiculous—I don't need you.* Instead, she gave a quick nod. She hated relying on someone, but she had asked the detective to call Abby. She had said they were friends, but in reality Abby's was the only name she could call to mind. There had been cops everywhere. They were examining every inch of the office space, and every inch of her own person. They had taken pictures and samples of Tad's blood before they had finally allowed her to wash it off as best she could with a handful of paper towels. She hadn't wanted Abby to see her this vulnerable, this weak, but she had to face the truth. She wasn't strong enough to resist the need to see a familiar face: Abby, who was treating her with such gentleness, as if she understood. Who had been able to come to an active crime scene and be treated with deference as she cared for Kira.

Kira winced as she pressed on her wrists and tried to raise herself higher in the desk chair. Her muscles protested and remained flaccid, but she managed to sit a few inches straighter. She saw Abby just outside the office door, kneeling down like she had been when she was next to Kira. Abby shifted a bit, and Kira saw Julie standing next to her. *Julie.* Kira wanted to get up and run to her daughter—no matter how unwilling her muscles—but she stayed where she was. In this one instance, she would let Abby take control. Julie needed someone with Abby's experience to explain what had happened, to prepare her for the wounds she'd see on Kira's face and limbs.

She watched Abby put her arm around Julie's shoulders while she talked. Kira had no idea what she was saying, but she appreciated the kindness she saw in Abby. She had noticed it Friday, too, when Abby had held Nirvana's head in her arms and stroked her neck, and again last night when she had calmed her gray police horse. A sense of calmness, straightforwardness. She might not personally like Abby's assertive nature, or want to have someone like that in her life again, but during this crisis Abby was exactly what she and Julie needed.

The two finally walked over to where Kira was sitting, still wrapped in her thick blankets. She wanted to hide her wrists, but she couldn't resist holding her arms out to Julie.

"Mama," Julie whispered, using the age-old name for her mother in a barely audible whisper. She burrowed close, but gently. Kira figured Abby had warned her about the bruises and sores. "Are you okay?"

"I'm going to be fine, honey," Kira said, stroking Julie's hair.

Julie pulled back and looked at her mother. She carefully touched the raw skin around Kira's mouth and the furrow on her wrist. "Abby told me what happened. No one else would, but she did. It was scary not to know."

Kira nodded at Abby, who was standing a few feet away and watching the interchange. Again, she was seeing Abby's apparent penchant for honesty. She didn't understand how one Hargrove could have a full dose of integrity while the other had very little. Was the Abby she was witnessing the real person? Or was she putting on a show of openness to hide her true nature? Kira had been exposed to the confusion of duplicity in her past relationship. Moments of brutal honesty mingled with blatant lies until she hadn't known what to believe. The intention then had been to keep her off guard, uncertain and insecure. What were Abby's motives? "She was right to tell you. I know Angie's parents were trying to protect you, but it's worse not to know what's going on."

"I should have been with you last night instead of staying at Angie's. I can't believe we were playing computer games while you were being—"

"No," Kira said.

"Don't," Abby said at the same time. She crossed the distance between them in two long steps and turned Julie to face her. "A few minutes ago, your mom was saying it was her fault because she walked onto your front porch and was assaulted. Do you think she's to blame for this?"

Julie shook her head. "No, of course not."

"Then don't blame yourself, either. Please."

Kira was silent, thankful that Abby was helping Julie see that she shouldn't feel guilty about not being with her. Kira needed a few moments before she was able to talk again. All she could think about was what might have happened if Julie *had* been with her last night. The images in her imagination made her cringe inside.

"I hate that he did this to you," Julie said. She stood close to Kira's chair.

"So do I," Kira admitted. He had paid for it, but even though he was dead, the memories of her abduction would never go away. She'd learn to live with them, but they were part of her now.

"Angie's going to take care of Nirvana for me today, so I can take care of you. Abby said she'd drive us home."

Kira looked from Julie to Abby. They were willing to let her rest, to take care of her. The thought was tempting, but she didn't want Tad to have destroyed her. "Abby, can you take us to the fair instead? We can still make it for Julie's hunt seat equitation class. Or do I have to stay here any longer?"

Abby watched her in silence for a moment. Kira had a feeling she wanted to argue, to urge Kira to go home and sleep. But she must have understood what Kira was going through. Being at home, quiet, with too much time to think? Not helpful. Going to the fair and letting the busy atmosphere and Julie's competition fill her mind for a few hours would give her more rest from her anxiety than she'd find in bed.

"I'll check with Detective Carter, but I'm sure it'll be okay for you to go back to Puyallup. He'll be able to contact you through me if they have more questions. We can stop by your house for you to shower and change first."

"Are you saying you don't like my shirt?" Kira asked. She looked down at her blood-spattered and torn T-shirt. Abby and Julie laughed.

"You look great, but perhaps it's too formal for the casual atmosphere of the fair." Abby held out her arm and Kira used it to pull herself out of the chair. She hadn't walked for a couple of hours and was still stiff from the long night. She worried her legs might give way and she'd collapse in front of Julie and everyone else, but Abby casually kept her arm as they walked to the office door.

"I have a sequined tuxedo at home," Kira said, happy to hear Julie's tentative laugh at their teasing. "It'll be more suitable."

❖

Kira sat on an upturned bucket and watched Julie warm up for her class. She wasn't as comfortable riding English style as she was Western, but she had managed to qualify for state in both seats. One of the things Kira liked most about Julie's 4-H experience was her exposure to different styles of riding. Abby stood on the sidelines, and Julie paused near her every few laps while the two talked and gestured. Then Julie would ride off again.

Kira watched in amazement as Julie and Nirvana seemed to improve after each stop. Whatever advice Abby was giving her must be helping, because Nirvana's stride seemed to stretch longer and Julie sat taller and more relaxed on her back. Kira smiled. She still wasn't convinced it was safe for her equanimity to get too attached to Abby, but she was starting to believe Abby was a good influence on Julie. Not only was she helping with her riding, but she'd been invaluable today as both Kira and Julie coped with what had happened last night. Kira wanted to resist Abby's assistance because it might turn into control, and Kira wasn't going down that road again. But she'd allow Abby to hover close by for a while longer. Julie needed her. Kira didn't.

Abby had driven them to Kira's house, where she had taken a hot shower and changed into non-bloody clothes. She'd stood under the spraying cocoon of water and hadn't wanted to get out again. Her muscles were still tight, but the warmth of the water helped loosen them up again. Even better were the heated seats in Abby's car. Kira had nestled into the warmth, finally feeling the deep chill leave her bones. Quite an improvement over her ride in Tad's trunk. After a quick stop at Abby's while she ran into her house and picked up her riding clothes for the day, they had come to the fair. Abby and Julie had talked horse all the way, leaving Kira to just rest in the heat and comfort, and by the time they reached the fairgrounds she was feeling human again. Now, Kira angled her face to the sun and thought about Abby's home. She'd expected sleek and modern, not the ancient Victorian with its faded and peeling yellow paint with white trim and the tidy but simple front lawn. Abby wasn't what Kira had expected at all, based on her first impressions.

She took out her cell phone and dialed one of the volunteers who was working with her on the Milford project. She needed to distract her mind from thoughts of Abby and from any attempt to understand the woman beneath the uptight cop exterior. She'd get back to work, back to her pre-fair reality. She listened to the voice mail message and waited for the beep.

"Keith, hi. It's Kira. Tad Milford, um, passed away last night. We need to find out who's going to inherit the land—whether it will go to an heir or to the investors. I'll stop by the courthouse Monday and check the deed, and then we can pull together a meeting to plan our next steps. I want to get this development stopped. Talk to you Monday. Bye."

"Jeez, what happened to you?"

Kira stood up, nearly knocking the bucket over in her haste. "Dale," she said, her voice as icy as her bones had been this morning. "What are you doing here?"

"Last I heard this area wasn't closed to the public." Dale stepped closer and took Kira's hand. She closed her fingers around Kira's slender wrist where the zip tie had been. Her touch was gentle, but Kira felt as if a manacle had been locked on. "What happened?" she repeated.

Kira tugged her hand away. The movement bruised her swollen skin, but the sharp bite of pain was preferable to Dale's soft touch. "Get your hands off me," she said. Dale smiled at her, seemingly unperturbed by Kira's demand.

"Okay, okay. Calm down and lower your voice, please." Dale put up her hands in a sign of surrender. She wore a button-down chambray shirt and dark jeans, in her usual business-casual style of dress. Kira smelled the sea-breeze scent of her familiar cologne when Dale pushed her bangs out of her eyes. Dale's hair was short, but she always had worn the front about an inch too long—Kira remembered how she had used to feel the itch to reach out and push those damned bangs aside, revealing Dale's shockingly blue eyes. Dale was pretty in a powerful, androgynous way. Charismatic. Kira had been drawn to the very qualities that had eventually been turned up in volume and turned on her.

"I just wanted to find out why you're sitting over here looking like you've been worked over." Dale moved closer again, into Kira's space without touching her. Kira wanted to back away, but she stood her ground. She wouldn't let Dale intimidate her until she was pushed back against the barn wall. "Well, I guess you always did like it a little rough."

The rage Kira had felt churning inside her since last night seemed to coil in her stomach like a serpent. First Tad had humiliated and threatened her, and now Dale was up to her old tricks. She had never asked, always *told* Kira who she was and what she wanted and had never really paid attention to Kira's own truths. The police had failed Kira when Dale had finally pushed past her limits, but Kira hadn't failed herself. She'd gotten away on her own, without any assistance, and she was damned sure she wasn't going to be dragged back into Dale's self-serving fictions.

"You need to—"

"Everything okay here?" Abby's voice was professional and cold. Her casual stance was belied by her hand resting on the hilt of her Taser, and Kira felt Abby's authority like a tangible thing.

"You must be the one who made those marks on Kira." Dale gestured at Abby's duty belt. "Did you handcuff her to the bed for a game of cops and robbers?"

"Why don't you stop talking and move along," Abby said, seemingly unfazed by Dale's insinuations. "This is a place for kids and families."

"Why do I need to go? Am I breaking any laws, Officer?" Dale asked. She didn't move from Kira's side.

"Lieutenant," Abby corrected her.

Kira wanted to punch both of them. She had pent-up frustration from being so helpless the night before, and she had already proven to herself that she was strong enough not only to resist Dale, but to stand up to her. She could feel how much she had needed to take control after being out of control last night, but Abby had taken the chance away from her. She might be trying to protect her, but she had pushed her down and silenced her instead.

"Abby, I can handle this on my own. Dale, you need to—"

"Lieutenant? Hmm, too bad they don't pay you public servants enough, so you're forced to work as riding teachers to make ends meet."

Abby smiled in a predatory way. "We're just enjoying the fair and minding our own business. If you can't do the same, I'll be happy to escort you out."

"Maybe I'd rather hang around and talk to my good friend Kira. How about you escort yourself straight to—"

"Stop, both of you," Kira hissed with enough power to make them stop their pissing contest and look at her. She saw Julie riding toward them with a concerned look on her face, and she wanted this over before she got to them. "Dale, I've told you this before. Get the hell out of my life and stay away. I am *not* in the mood for your games, and I never will be again. Go."

Dale grinned and shrugged one shoulder. "Whatever you want, my darling. Your wish is my command. See you later. Lieutenant."

Dale walked past Julie and patted her on the leg. "You look good out there, kiddo. I'll be cheering you on from the stands."

"Mom, why's Dale here? Is everything all right?"

"Yes, of course. Nirvana has a mud stain on her back leg. You should clean it off before you go in your class."

Julie leaned to the right and looked at Nirvana's dirty white sock. "Oh, cripes. I didn't notice that before."

She hopped off her horse and led her down the aisle. Kira tried to count to ten before she exploded at Abby. She had been supportive today, for Kira and Julie, but now she was overstepping her bounds.

"Nice friend you've got there," Abby said. "Maybe you and Julie should stay at my house tonight, just to be sure—"

"Thank you, but no," Kira said, her voice and words unyielding.

Abby looked at her and frowned. "Are you sure everything is okay? Do you hurt anywhere?"

"Look, Abby, I appreciate what you've done today. For me, for Julie. Even for her riding. But what happened with Dale is none of your business. I was handling it, and you had no right to push me aside and take over."

"Hey, Kira, I wasn't trying to—"

"Of course you weren't. But you did." Kira shook her head. "I'm not helpless. I'm not a damsel in need of rescuing or a child in need of parenting. Don't ever treat me that way again."

She walked away before Abby could answer. She had known better than to get involved with someone like her from the start. Abby was the type who would always be in control, would always assert herself in any situation. Kira didn't need her. She was strong enough to stand on her own.

CHAPTER TEN

A bby watched Kira walk away from her, disappearing down the aisle after Julie and Nirvana. Talk about overreacting. Abby had only been trying to assess the situation. Kira had been visibly upset by her friend Dale's appearance, and Abby…well, she hadn't liked the woman from first sight. Something seemed off about her. She'd been standing too close to Kira and she'd been outright rude and disrespectful to Abby. Kira hadn't needed to jump down her throat just because she had done what any cop in the same situation would have done. Still, Kira had been through a traumatic experience, and mood swings and emotional outbursts were to be expected.

She should walk away and leave Kira in peace, but she had promised Julie she'd watch her class. She went into the arena and leaned against one of the metal railings. When she'd competed in 4-H, classes had been held in the old wooden barn-style arena. This newer one was huge, with good dirt footing and plenty of room for the horses, as well as the other events held there throughout the year. Abby felt it was too harsh, though. The halide lights, shining down from the metal-beamed ceiling, were overly bright, and the aluminum bleachers clanged and squeaked every time someone climbed up to a seat. The ring itself was surrounded by a high concrete barrier, and the concrete extended to the seating area. The open ends let in a little natural sunlight, but the atmosphere was chilly.

Inside the ring, though, the horses circling with barely audible footfalls gave the place a softer feel. There were hundreds of kids competing during the fair, and each division was separated into sections of ten or more riders. Abby watched the class—the one before Julie's—and hoped the rhythmic trots and canters would seep into her and restore her equilibrium. She was confused by Kira. She had been determined to avoid her, and then she'd given herself permission to get to know her if their paths crossed during the fair. She'd been prepared to walk away this morning after Kira became police business because of the kidnapping. She had relented yet again, though, and had crossed one of the strict boundaries she had set for herself when she decided she'd stick around for the investigation. She should have left Kira with Detective Carter and—as she had just been told to do—minded her own damned business.

The group in the ring lined up while the judge took one last look at them and made her final decisions. Each class was judged separately, and the championship riders from each section would return to compete against each other. Abby could see Julie and Nirvana waiting outside for their turn to ride. She wanted to go out and talk to them, but she knew the rules. 4-H kids were supposed to handle most of the event by themselves, on their own for everything from cleaning to prep work to time management.

Abby judged the class in her own mind, not surprised that she picked the same top horse-and-rider combinations as the judge. The group filed out of the ring, and Julie entered with her section. Abby looked for Kira among the other spectators and finally saw her sitting next to some other parents. Abby returned her attention to the ring and smiled at Julie when she trotted by. Nirvana looked good, but Julie held her inside rein too tightly and was restricting the mare's movement slightly. Abby sighed in frustration. She was getting too involved with Kira and Julie and she didn't understand why she'd broken her own clear rules for the two of them. *If it's personal, stay out of it. Work is work, it's never personal.* Kira had blown all her strong resolutions out the window, and she had the gall to say Abby was the one in control?

"Loosen your right rein," she hissed when Julie rode by again. She watched in relief as Julie did what she asked and let the mare move more freely. They weren't the top pair in the group and probably wouldn't be champion, but they ought to get a high ribbon. Because she'd stepped in instead of letting Julie figure out how to fix her riding on her own.

God, maybe Kira was right. Maybe she *was* too bossy. Earlier, Abby had had a suspicion that the woman she saw approach Kira—causing her to startle so violently—was the ex from the police report her brother had written, when he claimed there was no sign of domestic abuse, and then she'd recognized Dale Burke's name once she heard it. She had felt compelled to get her away from Kira. She had been through too much—she didn't need to deal with an abusive ex-girlfriend right after her kidnapping.

She thought about exactly what Kira had suffered last night. Indignity, loss of control, and abuse of power and control. Abby had been trying to rescue her from more of the same when she intervened with Dale. But had she really done the same thing as Tad and Dale? Had she taken away Kira's right to control her own life?

Damn. Abby gripped the metal rail. She'd used her strength, her position, in the wrong way. She'd abused them, just like she had promised herself she'd never, ever do. She watched Julie pick up her ribbon, and then she hurried out the door. She'd congratulate her quickly, even though she wanted to avoid Kira. She was in too deep to stop now, but as soon as she knew who had shot Tad Milford and why, she'd get the hell away from Kira and Julie. She had to make certain her brother wasn't involved and that Kira was truly safe. The killer had let her go without harming her—although mystifyingly without helping her either—but as the investigation went on and the detectives got closer to finding the shooter, he or she might get spooked. Worry that Kira had heard something, had some clue to the killer's identity. Then she'd be in danger yet again. A cold-blooded murderer wouldn't hesitate to get her out of the way.

"Well done," she said when she met Julie near the arena's exit. Kira hovered in the background, obviously waiting for Abby to leave before she congratulated her daughter. Abby kept a smile on her face while Julie gushed about Nirvana's performance and Abby's help, but Abby barely heard a word she said. Everything receded, leaving only the mental echo of the phrase *cold-blooded murderer* juxtaposed with the actual presence of Julie and Kira. Abby was fooling herself when she pretended she could walk away anytime.

"I shouldn't have reminded you about your rein," Abby said when Julie paused to take a breath. "Next time I watch you ride I can give you some ways to evaluate yourself while you're riding. So you won't have to rely on me or anyone else when you're in the ring."

Julie nodded. "I felt something was off, but I didn't know what until you told me what to do." She leaned forward on Nirvana's neck and lowered her voice. "Was it cheating? Should I give my ribbon back?"

Abby had to laugh at Julie's serious, yet weirdly pleased expression, as if she was imagining a dramatic and valiant entreaty for the judge's forgiveness. She patted Julie's knee. "You can keep your ribbon with a clear conscience. You didn't break any rules—I was the one who should have kept my mouth shut. Now go talk to your mom. She's bursting with pride over there."

Abby stepped back and watched Kira and Julie. She had two duties toward them, whether Kira liked it or not. First, she had to keep them alive. Find the killer and make sure they were out of danger. Second, she was determined to help Kira get past the fear and helplessness Tad had driven into her. If it meant standing by while Kira did her own yelling at her ex, so be it. She'd sacrifice her own vanity and protective instincts and not rise to Dale's bait if they met again.

Abby had another source of support for Kira in mind, but asking for it required Abby to tear down another of her barriers. She entered the police aisle and looked in the stalls until she found Billie in Ranger's stall. She was crouched down with her back to the aisle, painting the gelding's hooves with an oil-based conditioner, but she stood and faced Abby before she had made a sound.

"Hey, Lieutenant. How's your friend?"

So, news of not only Kira's abduction, but also her relationship with Abby had already spread through the ranks. Abby wasn't surprised. News moved quickly through the small department, and transference was nearly instantaneous in a tight-knit unit like her mounted team.

"She's doing all right. She came out here to watch her daughter ride and she's been keeping busy." Abby rubbed her wrists, picturing Kira's wounds.

Billie twisted the cap back on the jar of hoof oil and came out of Ranger's stall. She was only a few inches over five feet and had delicately beautiful features to match, but the entire department knew better than to underestimate her because of her size. The few who had, never did so twice. Abby had read Billie's file, but it was merely an outline of her time in the military and on the department. Her actual experiences were locked away behind those intense dark brown eyes.

"You're worried about what will happen to her once she slows down," Billie said. She tucked black hair behind one ear. "When she's alone and has time to think."

"And remember," Abby said with a nod. She'd figured Billie would understand.

"Hang on," Billie said. She went into the team's tack room and came right back out with a pen and a piece of paper. She wrote her information and handed it to Abby. "This is my personal number. Tell her to give me a call anytime, if she ever needs someone to talk to while she's coping with the memories."

Coming from anyone besides a team member, Abby would have suspected a hidden motive behind the offer. A motive based directly on Kira's beauty. But Abby knew the gesture was made because of Billie's connection to her, to Abby. She had come to Billie for this same reason—because she was beginning to feel connected, too. Able to ask for help, for something personal. She was getting too close to too many people, but this time she'd allow herself to accept an overture of friendship from someone at work. For Kira.

"Thank you, Billie. I appreciate this." She put the folded piece of paper in her breast pocket and pulled out her phone when it began to buzz almost simultaneously. She checked the name of the caller and quickly answered. "Detective Carter. Any leads?"

"We have a possible ID on a car in the alley. It's a long shot, possibly from well before the murder, but I called Ms. Lovell in to listen to some audio samples. She'll be here tomorrow afternoon. I thought you'd want to know."

"Thanks for keeping me in the loop," Abby said. She ended the call and tapped the phone against her chin.

"A break in the case?" Billie asked.

"It doesn't sound too promising, but at least it's something. He's having Kira come in tomorrow afternoon to check it out."

Billie nodded with a shrewd expression. "Tomorrow. This meeting wouldn't happen to interfere with our demo ride, would it?"

Abby frowned. Was she so transparent? Or was Billie actually a mind reader? "The two might be at roughly the same time."

"Of course you'll want to be there for her. Don't worry about skipping the ride. Don has organized a routine for tomorrow, and the rest of us will only need to do a short ride. We'll be fine without you for one day."

Abby was caught on the first sentence, realizing she couldn't let Kira think she was being chaperoned. She'd have to find an excuse to be at the station at the same time. A coincidence, not control.

"Thank you, Billie. I want to be…Wait, *Don* is planning a routine? On Fancy?"

"Yes. He's been working on it for days. Don't worry, it'll be fun for the audience."

Fun. The demonstration was supposed to be professional. She didn't want Don turning it into a circus act with his beloved, but scraggly pinto. She frowned at Billie. Since joining the unit, Billie and Don had become—oddly enough—good friends despite their differences in age, temperament, background…basically every trait. Of course she'd stick up for him, no matter what bizarre show he was planning. "What exactly is he going to do?"

"Sorry, Lieutenant. I'm sworn to secrecy," Billie said. She made a motion of locking her lips shut, and then retreated into Ranger's stall. "All I can say is that he won't embarrass you or the team."

Abby was still doubtful, but she gave up on her interrogation and left the barn. Billie would never crack, anyway. She hesitated by the door to the 4-H barn and peeked around the corner. Kira was sitting on her bucket again, leaning back against the barn wall with her eyes closed. Nirvana's stall door was open, but Abby couldn't see either her or Julie from this angle. She stared at Kira for a few more minutes, noticing the signs of fatigue in her posture and lowered head. Let Don and Fancy perform the Macarena in the ring tomorrow if they wanted to—she didn't care. She'd be at the station with Kira.

CHAPTER ELEVEN

Kira parked in the public lot in front of the police department headquarters and pushed through the large glass door. She felt a perplexing cascade of emotions when she saw Abby standing at the desk chatting with another officer. She wanted to attribute her feelings to surprise, but why should she be startled to see Abby here, where she worked? She was happy to see her, even after Abby had tried to bulldoze her the day before, but there was something deeper than that. Desire, yes. Vulnerability? Definitely. Too much to process.

"Hi, Abby," she said briefly before addressing the officer on duty. "I'm Kira Lovell. Detective Carter is expecting me."

"I'll show you the way," Abby said once she had her visitor's pass. When the door buzzed, Abby held it open for Kira and followed her through. "That is, unless you think I'm being too bossy?"

"Ha-ha," Kira said. She tried to look stern, but she couldn't help but answer the hint of a smile on Abby's face. "I'm not going to apologize for what I said yesterday. You should have backed off and let me handle the situation with Dale, and I was right to point it out to you. So don't sulk."

"I do not sulk," Abby said in an indignant tone. "I merely hold grudges for an extended period of time."

Kira laughed and jabbed Abby with her elbow. "It's a very attractive trait."

"I know. I'm irresistible to the ladies."

I'll bet you are. Abby's voice was self-deprecating and

humorous, but Kira knew—based on her own reaction to Abby— that the words were all too true.

"Thank you for giving Julie some pointers before her class yesterday," Kira said, changing the subject and hoping to get the image of Abby with other women out of her head. "She looked great out there, and hunt seat usually isn't her strong point. She doesn't always have the patience for it."

"I had fun coaching her, but she did all the work. As she gets older, she'll be able to focus better. Riding in these equitation classes takes discipline."

"I'll bet you had more than your share of self-discipline even as a preteen," Kira said. Abby laughed and shrugged but didn't refute her statement. Kira had watched Julie struggle to maintain her concentration and work on her riding position when she often just wanted to go on trail rides and have fun. Kira tried to help her find a balance so she was progressing, but still enjoying her favorite pastime. "She's improved over the past year—not just in her lessons but in school and at home. She wants to do well and she understands the effort required."

Kira paused. She had been proud of Julie this last year, and of herself as well. She'd been strong enough to get away from Dale when she had nowhere else to turn. She'd rebuilt the life Dale had taken away from her and was in the process of rebuilding herself. Both she and Julie had flourished as they met and conquered challenges head-on. "You were part of it, in a way," she said. "I spent the past year wishing I had the chance to thank Nirvana's anonymous donor. Now I have the opportunity, but I'm having trouble finding the right words."

Abby stopped and faced her. "No need. The look on Julie's face when she's with her is thanks enough."

"Yes, she loves Nirvana, but it's deeper than that," Kira said. Over the past week with Abby, Kira had been forced to dredge up past memories. She had expected pain, but instead she was feeling a sense of healing—the distance of time, perhaps? And Abby's understanding, nonjudgmental attitude when she listened—they hadn't known each other long, but Abby seemed to be on Kira's side. "We were both lost when I finally made the choice to get away from Dale. I had tried a few times before, but she'd managed to coerce and convince and cajole until I came back. She was never abusive to Julie, instead they practically ignored each other, but Julie changed while we were living with her. I didn't realize how much until we were out of the house."

Abby reached over and squeezed her hand briefly. "I have no doubt that you'd have left sooner if Julie had been in danger."

Kira agreed, but she still harbored secret guilt for letting the situation go on as long as it had. Two years of their lives, wasted. Dale had provided well for Julie, compensating for Kira's meager income from her unglamorous career saving wetlands, and she had thought the financial benefits outweighed the emotional upheaval Kira was experiencing. She had also thought Julie was doing well and was happy with her private school and her nice clothes. When they left, Julie had given all of it up without a murmur of complaint.

"You're right. She wasn't thriving, but she wasn't in danger. As soon as I thought she might be, we were out of there. But back to Nirvana. She rescued us. I still don't know why you gave her to Julie, or how you knew about us at all, but I'm grateful you did." Kira hesitated again and searched for the right phrasing. "Julie is devoted to that mare. She gave her direction and purpose when we were going through so many changes. She brought the two of us closer together since I got involved in the 4-H group. She was good for me, too. I don't think Julie realizes this, but just being around animals and spending time outside was very…restorative."

"She understands," Abby said. "She wrote about it in her essay."

Kira stared at Abby in surprise. "She did? She wouldn't let me read it. What did she say?"

"She talked about how hard you work to protect the environment and how you've been an influence on the way she sees her world. She wrote about how much it meant for the two of you to spend time together close to nature, and that having a horse of her own would be a way of connecting with you and the earth."

Kira blinked away tears at Julie's perceptive statements. She hadn't realized Julie was aware of the broader meaning of their time together, but her daughter never failed to surprise. "She can be a little melodramatic at times, but she's spot-on. You did something very special when you gave her to us, so thank you."

"You're welcome." Abby brushed her thumb over Kira's cheek. Her touch was as soothing as Tad's had been unwelcome on the same part of her face. One cutting her open, the other sealing her shut. "Your skin is already less red. In a few days, you won't be able to see any of the reminders of that night."

Kira couldn't meet Abby's eyes after the tender way she touched her. Abby was talking about her chafed mouth after her ordeal with Tad, but Kira felt the old, remembered wound start to close as well. She held her hands in front of her and looked at the divots from the zip ties. "The memories won't fade as fast, but they'll go away, too, eventually."

"If they don't, tell me," Abby said. She hesitated for a long moment before continuing. "I have a…friend who knows firsthand about dealing with bad memories. I'm sure she'd be willing to talk to you. Come on, let's see what Carter wants."

Abby started walking again, toward the conference room where she'd seen Carter this morning. She had been fighting the growing attachment between herself and her team, but she knew without a doubt that Billie would be someone Kira could talk to about healing after a trauma. She would understand what Kira might experience in the days and weeks to come.

"Cozy place you've got here," Kira said as she looked around the sparse station. "Very warm and inviting."

"We don't encourage visitors," Abby said with a laugh. She liked the new industrial-style building, with its open floor plan and gleaming metal accents. Everything was bright and light, from the white tile floors to the high, fluorescent-lit ceilings. It encouraged distance and muted voices. "It's a green building, though, so it should appeal to you."

"I like that aspect, but function without form isn't always the way to go."

"I happen to like the aesthetics of the place," Abby said. She was in the minority with her opinion, but she stood by it. "We're here to work. The old station downtown had too many private rooms and empty corridors. Here, everyone can see what's going on. Who's visiting whose office."

"So, no more secrets and subterfuge?"

"Oh, they're still everywhere around here," Abby said. She opened the door to a room furnished with a black Formica table and a half dozen gray plastic chairs. "But now we have to work harder to keep them hidden."

Kira laughed and followed her into the room. Carter got out of his chair and came to greet them.

"Lieutenant. Good to see you again, Ms. Lovell. Thank you for coming back so quickly."

"Any more information on the case, Bryan?" Abby asked.

He motioned toward the table where he had placed a small recorder and a file folder. "We found a couple of witnesses to the gunshot last night. Neither reported it, but they heard it and were accurate enough with their times. One of them lives in an apartment overlooking the alley, and he looked outside a few minutes after and saw a car driving away. Ms. Lovell, I have some recordings of car engines. If you'll listen to them, one might jog your memory. You might have heard the car without registering that you did."

"Sure. I'll try."

"I need to finish some work in my office," Abby said. "Why don't you come say good-bye when you're done here?"

Kira nodded and Abby left the room. She looked back from the doorway, but Kira seemed relaxed enough as she sat in one of the uncomfortable chairs. Abby figured she wouldn't want her to hover, so she climbed the clear staircase and unlocked her office door. The second- and third-floor rooms ringed the large open space in the center, and she could open her door and see most of the activity in the building if she wanted to. Usually, she didn't. She left her office door open today, though, so Kira could find her.

Abby sat at her desk and turned on her computer. She was glad Bryan had called her to keep her updated on the case and to let her know Kira would be coming in to see him. She wanted to be here in case Kira's talk with the detective stirred up too many memories. Just a courtesy to her, and nothing more.

One week. Abby toyed with the hole-punch on her desk until it was neatly lined up between her computer and the phone. She'd only known Kira in person for a little over a week, but their interchanges had run the gamut from a frivolous conversation over barbecue to a rehashing of Kira's night of abduction and homicide. Extremes. Abby had recognized the potential intensity of a relationship with Kira from the start. She was attracted to her in a way she'd never before experienced. She was connected to Kira through her family, from the shame engendered by her brother's actions and by her own attempts to rectify them. She understood the complexity from Kira's side, too. Her past. Dale and Rick. Her need to protect her daughter from the physical and emotional forces she'd encountered far too often.

Only one week, but Kira had burrowed deep into Abby's life. Right now, on a single afternoon, she was choosing Kira over her team and her brother. Abby slid the hole-punch to the other side of her computer. It flipped over the lip of her desk pad and tiny white circles dropped out. After Kira's terrifying night, she deserved whatever considerations and allowances Abby could give, and she couldn't ignore the way Rick's fingerprints seemed to be all over this crime, but she couldn't get in the habit of putting Kira before everything important to her.

One week, and Kira would be out of her life. The fairgrounds would be empty except for windblown burger wrappers and ride tickets. Not even an echo of steel horseshoes on the bare concrete barn aisles. Kira, Nirvana, and Julie would be home again. Abby would be back at work here in her office, keeping tabs on the mounted unit through Rachel's emails, and poring over her grandfather's indiscretions whenever she had a spare moment.

She scooped up the spilled paper circles and tossed them in the empty garbage can next to her desk. She'd miss Kira, but she'd be better off when her life regained the equilibrium she'd come to rely on. She'd miss her team, but she'd have the memories of riding with them and the pride she felt in their accomplishments.

Unless, of course, Don's demonstration was such a fiasco the entire unit was disbanded. Always a possibility. Abby turned to her computer and tried to erase the images of Fancy wearing a frilly pink skirt and jumping through a hoop. Don knew she'd kill him if he did anything to make the unit look foolish, didn't he? Maybe she should send him a text...

But Billie wouldn't lie to her, and Rachel could handle the demo rides without her input. Kira was right—she had a hard time letting go of control. She would let her team do its job and she'd let Kira run her own life, as soon as this case was over. For now, though, if her brother was involved in the shooting or had played a part in the kidnapping, she sure as hell was going to be right in the middle of things. She'd give her brother the benefit of the doubt— even a Hargrove was innocent until proven guilty, after all, but she had to make sure Rick wouldn't be a danger to Kira. *Then* she'd back her bossy self out of the picture and let everyone do as they damned well pleased.

She searched records for Tad Milford and found only one reference to him, in a report about a suspected DUI from a few years earlier. He had destroyed some property, a neighbor's parked motorcycle, but he had never been charged with drunk driving. His breathalyzer test had been inconclusive and no witnesses had come forward at his court hearing. The primary officer—surprise, surprise—had been Richard Hargrove. Abby could fill in the gaps missing from the inexplicably vague report. Tad had probably paid his neighbor handsomely for his bike and his promise not to testify. Rick had somehow managed to recalibrate the breathalyzer so the results couldn't be used in court. In exchange for what? Abby couldn't remember when her mom had first mentioned Rick's real-estate development investments, but Abby had a feeling they had started about four years ago, soon after this DUI.

Interesting stuff, but not much use to her. It established a possible timeline for the origin of her brother's relationship with Tad Milford, but they could have been working together before the accident happened. Either way, Rick had done Tad a favor and gotten him off the hook for a DUI. She wondered if her brother would have done the same thing if Tad had hit a person instead of the parked motorcycle. She hoped not, but she wouldn't bet money on it. She was about to close the report when she noticed a link to a secondary one that had been filed by the other officer on the scene. She opened it and skimmed the information. There were a couple of witness statements that had conveniently been left out of Rick's official report. Neither witness had shown up for court. One was a teenaged boy who had been playing basketball near the entrance to the community when Tad came in at high speed.

The other was Dale Burke. Accused's stepsister and passenger in his vehicle.

She said he hadn't been drinking at all. He had swerved to avoid hitting a squirrel, and his car had skidded on a wet spot on the pavement caused by the motorcycle owner's sprinkler system. A bullshit story.

Abby was about to search for more records involving Dale when Kira tapped on her office door. She hastily closed the window on her computer, as if she'd been caught reading porn.

"Kira, hi, come in. You're done already?"

Kira came in and sat in the metal chair on the other side of Abby's desk. She looked around with a curious expression while she talked. "Yes. I don't think Detective Carter is happy with me."

"Because you couldn't identify the car engine?" Abby shut off her computer and set it to one side.

"I don't think he really had much hope I'd be able to do that. He said it was a long shot, but they wanted to give it a try. What are you doing with that?"

Abby followed Kira's gaze and looked down at her hand. She was flipping a small stapler end over end with her fingers. "Habit," she said. She set the stapler down on the edge of her desk calendar.

"You're a fidgeter. I should have expected it from someone who keeps everything bottled up inside."

"I don't…" Abby realized a little too late that Kira was baiting her with a teasing smile. "Is fidgeter a word?"

"You knew what I meant, so it works as a word. Anyway, Detective Carter played the tape of the car engine six or seven times—which I thought was overdoing it—and then he asked me if anything sounded familiar. I said I didn't remember hearing that engine and he said, *Which one?* Turns out, he had played seven different car sounds, and I was supposed to identify the right one. I said they all sounded the same to me…"

"Uh-oh," Abby said. Her mind had been spinning as she tried to figure out what the new connection between Tad and Dale meant, but Kira's story made her laugh. Carter was a car guy and would talk about spark plugs and engine blocks for hours if anyone let him. "Which lecture did you get? The one about how computer chips are destroying the bond between owner and car, or the one about the endless variety of cylinder configurations and how they differ?"

"Neither of those. This was about how you can identify problems with your engine just by listening. It was a good lecture. It had sound effects."

Abby laughed. She liked seeing Kira look so at ease. The taut and wary expression she'd worn when Abby first saw her this morning was fading away. It reappeared for seconds now and again, as if Kira was remembering some detail from two nights before. "His nickname around here is The Car Whisperer. I think he's the one who started using it first."

"I'll remember that the next time I talk to him." Kira stood up. "I need to get back to the fairgrounds to pick up Julie and her friend Angie. Do you still have work to do here?"

Abby stood up as well. "No. I can come back and finish another time, but I'm heading the same way as you."

She'd be back later to do more research, but now that she was assured Kira was okay, she wanted to get to the fair in time for the second demo ride. She wouldn't have time to warm up and ride Legs in it, but she could at least watch Don parade Fancy around like a trained seal before she got ready for a night patrolling the midway. The trip here had been fruitful, though. She'd seen Kira laughing and looking normal even after her talk with Bryan Carter, and she'd also learned some valuable information. She wasn't sure what to make of it yet, but it helped to explain why Rick hadn't done anything to help Kira when he answered the domestic call.

Abby locked her office behind them. She had never understood why he hadn't made an arrest that night. She'd assumed it was because Kira and Dale were a lesbian couple, but the explanation hadn't been convincing to her. Her brother hadn't displayed any pattern of homophobia in the calls she'd researched. He seemed motivated by money alone and made his decisions based on what he'd get out of the victims he blackmailed or the accused he let go without charges. Knowing Dale was his business partner's stepsister suddenly made his actions that night more consistent with his other behavior. She had to ask Kira eventually if she'd known about the connection between Tad and Dale, although she had said she hadn't met him before yesterday.

"What did you think?" she asked instead, as they went down the stairs and back to the open main floor.

"About what?"

"About my office. You were checking it out."

"I was not!" Kira said. "Well, okay, I was. Your office looks exactly like I thought it would. Spartan and clean and colorless. I expected your house to be the same, but you surprised me with the big old Victorian."

Abby wasn't sure how to respond. Home was…well, where she could be herself. The steel and metal of her office furniture and supplies were part of the armor she wore here at work. She was about to change the subject when someone did it for her. Rick was coming through the front door and directly toward them.

She was ready to whisk Kira away from him, but he was looking right at them.

"Hey, Goody-Goody," he said, using his nickname for her. Goody-Goody Hargrove. The name made her nostalgic for Hard-Ass. "This your girlfriend?" He gave Kira a slow once-over. "Nice, little sis. I didn't think you had it in you."

He seemed awfully cheerful for someone who'd just lost a friend and business partner, but Abby realized he might not know yet. He was coming back to swing shift after his weekend off, and his usual routine—she felt disgusted that she knew his routine—included a trip to a bar after work and then a couple days holed up with whatever woman he picked up, or whoever needed to screw her way out of a speeding ticket. Then he'd sleep in, work out, and come to the station. He was a creature of habit. She had that in common with him and the rest of her family, but she hoped her habits were more productive and positive than theirs. Unless he'd been involved, he probably hadn't heard about Tad's shooting. She wanted to get Kira out of there before he got the news.

"You look familiar. Have we met?" he asked Kira. She was staring at him with her mouth open, and Abby guessed she was about to start screaming at him.

"C'mon, we need to get going." She tugged on Kira's arm. "He's not worth it."

She got Kira to move, and they walked away with the sound of Rick's laughter following them.

"He didn't even remember me." The words exploded from Kira when they got to the parking lot. "He made my night hell, abandoned me in a clearly dangerous situation, and he has no clue who I am. Why'd he do it? Abby, why?"

Abby was still heading toward the car, but Kira had planted herself on the pavement and didn't seem ready to move until she had some answers. Abby went back to her.

"I didn't understand myself, until today," she said. "He didn't arrest Dale because she was his business partner's stepsister."

"Dale has a stepbrother?" Kira repeated. The shocked look on her face convinced Abby this was the first she'd heard of it. "I didn't know. I never met any of her family. Do you know who he is?"

"You've met him already," Abby said. "It was Tad Milford."

CHAPTER TWELVE

Abby was in the audience just in time for the second police demo. Since she had been called in last minute to fill in for Clark Jensen when he had to fly back to Connecticut for a funeral, she hadn't had a chance to prepare with the other riders, but she'd had fun riding with the group. Rachel and Cal had organized several different rides so audience members who came more than once wouldn't be seeing the same set show over and over, and they used Abby and Legs to demonstrate the easier versions of each exercise. They never told the audience that she and Legs were inexperienced, which might have diminished their authority and put them in danger when they were on patrol. Instead, they showed the stages of training and desensitization for the horses, and Legs and Abby usually performed step one. As she had grown comfortable over the past few days, however, she and Legs had participated in more of the advanced phases of the exercises. Abby was pleased with the way the rides had gone—not just from a personal standpoint, but also as the team's supervisor.

Cal, playing the part of emcee, was funny and charmed her audience. Rachel competently led the riders through a series of exercises with large, bright props. The entire team captured the essence she had hoped for when she first started drafting her proposal for a mounted unit. Although the team had originally been expected to fail, the end result was a success. The horse-and-rider pairs were polished and calm during the maneuvers and friendly and approachable with the kids and adults who crowded around to visit them after they were finished.

Abby felt a pang of regret because she wasn't riding right now, since she had so few days to play at being a real member of the group. The afternoon had been worth missing the ride, though. She had learned about Dale and her connection to Tad. She had also discovered more about her brother's offenses and the reasons behind them. Most important, she had been there to support Kira. She'd even managed to make Kira smile even though she was at a police station reliving her traumatic experience with the detective.

After she had gotten a stunned Kira into her car and on her way, Abby had raced home and into her private office where she had copies of reports related to her family stored in locked file cabinets. They were the ones she'd considered suspicious from her grandfather's career and now her brother's as well. She had taken out Kira's file again today, after so many months. She had reread Julie's essay, now able to put a face and personality to the words. She had also gone through the report from the night Kira had called the police in an attempt to get help. According to Rick's words, Dale had been cooperative and Kira had recanted her allegations of assault. A lover's spat, with no visible marks on either person. No arrest warranted.

Abby hadn't discovered anything new in her rereading, but she'd felt a deeper pull toward Julie and Kira. They were her responsibility. They had been since the moment she had made an unauthorized copy of the report and taken it into her home. She had thought giving them Nirvana was enough, but it wasn't. They were real people now, not abstract symbols representing her family's sins. She had to be sure she didn't get too involved, didn't follow the path of familiarity that led to ethical compromises, but she had to see this through.

Now, in the arena, she paid attention with half her mind as the team worked through some warm-up exercises from Cal's polo repertoire. Once Don and Fancy took center stage, however, she forgot about her obligations to Kira and leaned forward to see what would happen next. There were huge piles of debris scattered around the arena, and Abby had been eyeing them with concern while the rest of the unit performed their exercises around them. What was Don planning to do? A trash obstacle course? She watched with a mix of trepidation and curiosity as Don came forward with a clip-on microphone and introduced himself to the crowd. She had to put aside her skepticism and trust her team, but she rubbed sweaty palms on her uniform pants.

"I'm Officer Don, and this is my horse and partner Fancy. She might not be the prettiest horse in the world, but she's pretty special to me."

Abby groaned. Hopefully he was going to do more than a lame stand-up comedy routine. She might have to fire him if he kept this up.

"Hey. Scoot over."

Abby started when Kira spoke from the bleacher behind her. She put her hand on Abby's shoulder while she climbed over the back of the seat and sat down. Julie and Angie followed, squeezing in next to them. Kira's thigh was pressed flush against hers. Abby tried to concentrate on Don's words, but the scent of gardenias threatened to transport her to a tropical island. Where Kira was wearing a bikini and frolicking in the warm surf…

"And Fancy's trot is so bumpy, I sometimes think we're having an earthquake when she and I are jogging back to the barn for our lunch break."

Leave it to Don to cool off her passion. Abby wanted to get out a hook and pull him off the stage, but she heard Julie and Angie laugh when he tried to sing a song while he trotted Fancy around the ring. The other kids in the audience were laughing as well. Even she had to smile at the vibrato Fancy forced out of him.

He halted again and made a show of being out of breath and stiff after his short workout. Once he recovered, he spoke more seriously.

"We know earthquakes can occur anytime in our state. How many of you have felt one happen before?"

Most of the people in the audience raised their hands. Abby didn't at first, but Kira jabbed her in the side and cleared her throat.

Abby rolled her eyes and put her hand in the air. She wasn't an audience-participation kind of person, but she wasn't about to ignore Kira's insistence.

"After a bad quake, some buildings are destroyed and people might be trapped inside. There are dogs trained to search for survivors, and I've been training Fancy to do the same thing. If there's a natural disaster in Tacoma, she'll be ready to rescue some citizens."

Okay, this was getting interesting. Abby heard Julie and Angie whispering together about training their horses as search-and-rescue animals and she felt Kira's sigh echo through her where their arms were resting next to each other. She had a feeling Kira would be hearing about this new plan for a long time. Abby listened to Don explain the difference between the way a dog sniffed the ground for a scent while a horse sniffed the air, and she was intrigued with his initiative. Yet another way for the mounted unit to be useful to the city of Tacoma—they needed anything they could use as leverage when officials inevitably started looking for ways to cut back on expenses.

After his talk, he left the ring and Cal took over as announcer again. She picked a young audience member and had him point to one of the debris piles. Billie wedged herself under the plywood and brush the kid had chosen, and Don rode Fancy into the ring again. He wove around the piles until she stopped at Billie's pile. Abby hoped Billie wouldn't be injured by Fancy's enthusiastic pawing, but she climbed out unscathed while Don gave Fancy a sugar cube as her reward.

Abby and Kira led the girls out of the arena while the riders walked around and answered questions from the audience. They were talking and gesturing as they planned a training regimen to turn their horses into bloodhounds.

"She seems like a smart horse," Kira said.

"Well, she's exceptionally food motivated," Abby said. "She'd do almost anything except move fast for a lump of sugar."

Kira laughed. She gestured toward the girls who were standing a few feet away, deep in conversation. "We're going to walk around and see some of the other 4-H exhibits. Do you have time to join us?"

Abby glanced at her watch. She knew what time it was, but she wanted a moment to consider the offer. Innocent as it was, she had already gotten too involved with Kira. But she had some questions for her about the night of her domestic, and the casual atmosphere of the fair might make it easier for Kira to talk about such personal topics.

"I have an hour or so before I need to get out on the midway. I wouldn't mind seeing more of the fair than the horse barns."

"Great. So, girls, where are we going first?"

"Scones," both said at the same time.

"Are scones an exhibit now?" Abby asked. "I thought they were something to buy."

"We need sustenance for all the walking we're about to do," Kira said. "Besides, have you ever come to the Puyallup Fair without getting a scone?"

"Never," Abby said without hesitation. She remembered her mother bringing bags of them home when she was little. She and most of the kids in her school had them in their lunch boxes for a couple of weeks every September.

Abby got in line and bought them each a scone, plus waters for the girls and coffee for her and Kira. The prices were ridiculous, but the first bite into the soft biscuit with its butter and raspberry jam filling made it worthwhile. It was a taste of the past.

She and Kira trailed behind the girls as they walked toward the opposite corner of the fairgrounds from the horse barns. A carousel turned lazily here, far from the flashier midway rides, and people used the splashing fountain as a meeting place. In the evenings, music and cheers from the grandstand shows would filter into this space. They entered the Pavilion and took the escalator upstairs.

"I haven't been in here for years," Abby said, looking around the large second floor. This was where handmade products and photographs were judged and displayed. Quilts and articles of clothing hung from the ceilings, and glass cases were filled with plates of food and canned goods. In a fair teeming with commercialism and displays of cheap souvenirs, these simple objects took on more meaning than they would have in a less incongruous setting. They stood for home and community and sustenance.

"I entered a carrot cake here once," she admitted to Kira when they paused by some jars of jellies, their contents glistening like jewels under the bright fluorescent lights. The confession was hard for her to make because of the memory it triggered. Standing in the kitchen with her mother as they followed her grandmother's recipe. Her mom hadn't been a cop, but she'd known exactly what her husband and father-in-law were doing. She—like Abby and her father—had benefitted from her grandfather's actions.

"I can't imagine you baking," Kira said, looking at her with her head cocked to one side.

"Well, my mom helped. On my first attempt, I forgot the baking powder, so the cake could have been used as a discus in a track meet. The second try was more successful. It got a blue ribbon."

"Now *that* I can believe. You seem to have a competitive streak, whether it's with horses or carrot cakes. I'll bet you'd even enter a police officer competition if there was one."

"*Pfft.*" Abby dismissed Kira's ridiculous notion with a derisive sound, but she secretly reveled in the way Kira had come to really know her in such a short time. She wasn't about to admit she had been considering taking her team to compete in a national mounted police competition at the Kentucky Horse Park.

Kira had stopped under a colorful patchwork quilt hanging from the ceiling. Her head was tilted as she tried to read the information card, and she pushed a wave of hair behind her ear. Abby took a step back as the sudden urge to kiss Kira's exposed neck caught her off guard. She'd been lost in the past for a few moments, and the sight of Kira's skin yanked her back to the present.

"What about you?" she asked, sticking to a more neutral topic. "Do you like to compete?"

"This quilt has pieces of clothing from five generations of one family," Kira said. She looked down again and moved on to the next case of food. "I played soccer when I was younger, but I never had a strong drive to win. Except in grades, though. I always wanted to be the top of my class."

"Why?" Abby asked. She stood next to Kira and pretended she was more interested in the plate of petrified chocolate chip cookies than in nuzzling the nape of Kira's neck. "I mean, I understand wanting to do well in school, but what made you need to be the best?"

"It made my grandparents happy. They were so proud of me when I'd bring home a report card full of As." She paused. "I lost my parents when I was four, and my grandparents raised me. I liked making them smile."

Kira left it at that and turned to a display of handcrafted toys and stuffed animals. Abby filled in the rest herself. Survivor guilt. Kira had been raised by a mom and dad who had lost their child but were pushing through their grief to raise their grandchild. She'd probably sought all sorts of ways to give them moments of joy and to rarely give them a moment of trouble. She knew Kira's life wasn't as simple as Abby's pop psychology made it sound, but she had a feeling it was close. Kira was a peacemaker. She was strong and independent and capable, but she craved peace. Her world had been shaken by Dale and Rick and Tad, and Abby wanted to be there until Kira found secure footing again.

"I do have something entered here at the fair," Kira said in a conspiratorial whisper when they were standing side by side near some knitted sweaters.

"This year? What is it?"

"Guess."

Abby smiled at the dare she saw in Kira's eyes. "What do I get if I'm right?"

"What do you want?"

"Um…" Abby ran through a tempting variety of possibilities in her mind. *A kiss. Take off your top.* She shook the visions out of her head and gave a somewhat more sensible answer. "You have to go on the roller coaster with me."

"Deal," Kira said with a smile. "Although maybe someday

you'll tell me what your other ideas were before you picked that one. You're blushing."

"I am not," Abby said indignantly. She turned away and scanned the room.

"It might not be on display here," Kira warned.

Abby thought about the other exhibit halls. "Let's see," she said, listing the possibilities while she mulled over her choice. "You might have grown a prize-winning tomato or one of those enormous pumpkins. Or maybe you have a collection of Disney memorabilia in the hobby hall. Perhaps a vase of geraniums in the floral section?"

Kira watched her with a smug smile, apparently certain Abby wouldn't guess.

Abby snapped her fingers. She pretended she'd been going over options, but she went with her initial idea. "A photograph. Probably of one of your wetland projects."

Kira's jaw dropped open, confirming Abby was right. She seemed as taken aback as Abby had been to find out Kira already knew her well. "How'd you know?"

"Superior deductive reasoning," Abby said. She was weirdly pleased with herself for getting it right and surprising Kira. She hadn't spent much time with Kira, but she felt she understood her in some ways. "I'll bet you can make great chocolate-chip cookies, and I saw your garden when I took you home, so I can guarantee you'd win a prize with your flowers. But you wouldn't bother to compete just for the sake of getting a ribbon. You'd have to have a reason for wanting to share whatever you'd created. Now, you have to show me the picture."

"Don't look so proud of yourself. It isn't becoming," Kira said, but with a teasing smile. She led Abby through the maze of photos and stopped in front of the nature and landscape section.

Abby picked out Kira's photo before she read her name on the placard. The shot was taken from the ground, looking up through a stand of cattails. Treetops in the distance added asymmetrical layers to the picture. Clouds of different shapes crisscrossed the sky, in waves and puffs and wispy curls. A red second-place ribbon was attached to the frame.

"It's beautiful," Abby said. "I love how you gave texture and depth to a two-dimensional medium. It's…It shows how you feel about these city wetlands you work so hard to save. They might be surrounded by houses or businesses, but they are pieces of nature. You connect to the earth and up to the sky. Self-contained, but connected."

Kira watched Abby as she examined the photo. Her words captured what Kira had been trying to portray in the picture, but Abby's appreciative scrutiny of it meant even more than her intuitive interpretation. Abby understood her, she'd proven it when she had figured out what Kira entered in the fair. Kira might be a private person, keeping things to herself, but she wasn't able to do the same thing when it came to her work with the environment. She had to shout to the world about the value she saw when she studied the plants and wildlife coexisting in the endangered ecosystems. She had to fight like a mother wildcat to protect them from development and pollution—whether by people who were too wealthy or too little informed to care about the harm they did.

Kira had been lying on the muddy edge of the water that day, tracking the sound of a red-legged frog and hoping to get a picture, when her supporting hand slipped and she toppled into the muck. She had saved her camera by rolling onto her back as she fell, and she had found herself staring up at the waving cattails with clouds wafting behind them. The sound of nearby traffic receded, as did the anxiety she'd been feeling because the whole area was slated to become yet another strip mall if she wasn't able to save it. Her world narrowed to a single frame, and she captured it on film. As Abby had guessed, Kira had needed to share her vision with the public, somehow, even if no one besides her understood it. But Abby had.

"Come on, Mom." Julie appeared from behind the display stands. "We need to get back to the barn because the chicken judging is going to start soon." She paused. "It's an awesome photo, isn't it, Abby? You should have seen Mom the day she took it. Head-to-toe mud. It was disgusting."

"Chicken judging?" Abby repeated with disbelief in her voice.

"When you asked me to see the fair with you, I don't think I realized what you actually meant."

"You were expecting the Extreme Scream and a funnel cake, I suppose?" Kira took Abby's hand and hurried them to the escalator. She had done it automatically, because the girls were already far ahead, and Abby seemed inclined to stay put in the Pavilion, but the rightness of it scared her. Having Abby's hand in hers felt as natural as if it had been created for just that purpose. The feeling was deceptive. She might enjoy Abby's company, and Abby might be connected to her life right now in some very confusing ways, but the whole situation was too complex for Kira. If she were stupid enough to repeat a dangerous pattern with another dominant woman, then all her self-pride would rightly disappear. She and Julie deserved better than a life spent under someone else's control. Seeing Abby and Dale facing off with each other had made her realize how dominant Abby was. Would the trait ever be used against her? She didn't believe so—after all, Abby had been defending her, not attacking her.

Kira tried to act casual when she dropped Abby's hand. "Julie and Angie have a friend who raises chickens for her 4-H project. They actually bathe them in the sink." She couldn't keep the note of horror out of her voice. She loved birds in the wild, but the thought of chicken poop in her kitchen made her skin crawl. She'd have to eat out for months after.

"That sounds…unhygienic," Abby said as they rushed across the fairground, dodging around groups of people. "And it must be disturbing for the chickens to be so close to the stove. You'd have to be sure to keep the lemons and capers hidden."

Kira stopped speed-walking and pointed her finger at Abby. "You cannot make me laugh when we're in there. Promise?"

"I wasn't telling a joke," Abby said in her deadpan way that made Kira want to crack up. "I really think they'd be traumatized if they happened to see the ingredients for a nice piccata sauce on the counter next to them. They'd need counseling afterward."

"Maybe the therapist could put a silver platter on his couch for them to sit in. He could close the dome lid if they got too emotional."

"I changed my mind about chicken judging," Abby said with a

grin. She started walking again and called to Kira over her shoulder. "I think this is going to be fun. Let's go."

"You have to behave," Kira pleaded when she caught up to Abby and they joined the crowd around the judging area. Her entreaty lost some of its effectiveness because she'd joined in with Abby's joke, but she hoped it would work. She was feeling punchy from lack of sleep, but at least she was inclined to laugh and not sob. A small but significant victory for the day. She stood in front of Abby, and the large number of spectators in the small room meant she had to stand close enough so the full length of her back was against Abby's front.

Kira leaned back. She'd been aware of her body's reaction to Abby since the first moment they'd touched. Electric and arousing. Abby stirred desire with the flick of her tongue against fingertips or the press of a thigh against hers. But when Abby put her hands on Kira's hips and anchored them together, Kira felt an entirely new response seeping through her. She felt calm and protected. She sighed and felt her body shudder as the tension she'd been carrying broke free and floated away.

The feeling of belonging was more frightening than her original, undeniable sexual response to Abby had been.

Kira looked around the room, searching for some way to distract herself from the bewitching pressure from Abby's body. Long tables were placed around the room, with dividers between the contestants. Kira supposed it was because they might peck at each other if they weren't separated. The judges walked to each station and examined the birds, prodding them and looking at beaks and feet.

"What do you think she's saying?" Abby leaned down and whispered in her ear.

The warmth of her breath bombarded Kira's ear and radiated outward. She felt it everywhere, as if she was made of dry kindling and the mere tickle of air ignited her. She blinked, trying to concentrate on Abby's words and the judge in front of her who was poking at a large hen's breast.

"Maybe *Hmm, I could make at least* twenty *McNuggets out of this one*," she said. She covered her mouth in an attempt to conceal her snort of laughter that echoed Abby's, but the judge gave them an angry glare. Abby grabbed her arm and pulled her outside where they collapsed in giggles against the side of the barn.

"I can't believe you said that," Abby said, wiping her eyes.

"Me? You started it, you and your piccata sauce. I'll probably be banned from all future chicken judging."

"How can I ever make it up to you?" Abby asked. She skimmed her fingers through Kira's hair and down the side of her neck.

"Do you want a list? Because I can make a long one right now." Kira was too worn out, too depleted to be able to filter her thoughts and keep from saying them out loud. Her body felt energized by Abby's touch, even as her mind seemed to slow down, and all she wanted was for Abby to lean a little closer and kiss her, no matter how bad a decision it might prove to be.

A burst of commotion from a passing group of teenagers caught their attention for a moment. Abby looked at them, and then back at Kira. She sighed and stroked Kira's hair once more, but this time Kira felt her letting go, not reaching closer.

"You must be exhausted," Abby said. "You should get home and sleep, and I need to get to work."

She walked a few steps away before turning back toward Kira, where she was still leaning against the wooden building. "Maybe I'll ask you about that list of yours another time."

Kira watched her until she was swallowed up by the crowd. Abby was right. She needed to get to bed, but she sure as hell wouldn't be going to sleep anytime soon.

CHAPTER THIRTEEN

The next afternoon, Abby slid off Legs and pulled the reins over her head. She was stopped several times before she got back to the barn by people who wanted to take a picture with her and the pretty gray mare. She smiled for the cameras and chatted with the bystanders while they patted her horse, but she felt out of sync with the whole process. Today, she had put on a friendly expression the same way she put on her uniform. It was something she was supposed to wear, not something that felt natural. She was relieved when she got back to the more private aisle where Legs and the other police mounts were stabled, but even there they were on display. They were separated from the public by a mere piece of yellow tape, as if they were in a crime scene, and people stood just beyond the fragile barrier and watched the riders work as they untacked and groomed the horses.

Abby was carrying her saddle back to the makeshift tack room when a man with a little girl on his shoulders called out a question about it. She carried the bulky saddle over to him and explained the various parts of it while he asked question after question until she wanted to conk him on the head with one of the heavy stirrups. She would have publicly berated any of her officers if they were rude to a citizen when they were supposed to be goodwill ambassadors for the city, so she had to maintain the same pleasant and friendly attitude she'd expect from them. She eventually disengaged from the conversation, and she took the saddle into the stall Rachel had filled with saddle racks and grooming equipment. She sat on a small trunk and rested her hands on her knees while she inhaled and exhaled slowly. She could use more time and privacy to decompress before they went on duty tonight, but she didn't have the luxury of either.

"You did well today," Rachel said as she entered the stall with Bandit's bridle in her hand. "You and Legs looked like old pros out there. You looked settled, I suppose."

"Thank you," Abby said. She had felt more natural on horseback, finally, as if she hadn't had so much time off. She wasn't sure how much of it was because she was adapting to the work and the routines and how much was because her mind was occupied and so her body had been able to perform without constant overthinking. She had been dwelling on Kira, replaying their interactions over the past days. The events had been crazy—from her recognition of Kira to their playful lunch to Kira's kidnapping to their near-miss moment of passion. Time had been compressed because so much had taken place, and she had gotten too close too fast. She couldn't believe they'd only met last Friday, but she'd been ready to kiss her yesterday. No wonder she had strict rules about not dating anyone connected to her work. She couldn't handle the mix of personal and professional very well at all. She hoped Rachel's words were prophetic in more ways than one and that Abby's feelings toward Kira would settle. Disappear.

Rachel hung the bridle on a hook and picked up a tote full of horse brushes. "Are you all right, Lieutenant? You look a little tired. You took part in the demos more than usual today, so if you need to—"

Abby held up her hand. "Don't tell me to take the night off, Sergeant. I'll be fine." She would be. As long as she reminded herself where her boundaries were and why they should be maintained.

"Okay." Rachel turned to go, but paused in the doorway. "Cal and I are going to grab some dinner before we go on patrol. Why don't you join us?"

Abby was tempted—a regular experience for her these days—but she shook her head. Boundaries didn't just apply to romantic involvement with Kira. Abby had waded in the shallow end of friendship with her team, joking on their patrol rides and even asking Billie for help in case Kira needed it. But she wouldn't allow her ethics to drown because she was lonely and wanted friends.

"Thanks, Rachel, but go on without me. I'll meet you back here in an hour."

Abby stood up and braced herself for the walk back to Legs's stall. Luckily, there were fewer people clustered around the barn door than before.

"Hey, Lieutenant," Don called out to her as she walked by Fancy's stall. "Are you hungry? We're going over to the International Village during our break, if you wanna come."

"Um, no. But thank you, Don." Abby wasn't accustomed to her team—or anyone from work, for that matter—making so many overtures of friendship toward her. She met Billie coming out of Ranger's stall and raised her eyebrows, waiting for her chance to refuse yet another meal invitation.

"Don't worry, Lieutenant, I already heard you say no twice, so I'm not going to ask." Billie grinned at her and walked on a few steps before turning around. "But if you change your mind, you know where to find us."

Abby shook her head and ducked into the stall with Legs, irritated that she felt as transparent as she did. Abby had been hesitant about bringing Billie on as a mounted officer after their first interview, but she was damned glad she had listened to the recommendation of Billie's sergeant at the time and had gone against her first instincts. She didn't admit to having wrong gut feelings often, but in this case she'd been way off the mark. She'd been concerned about Billie's lack of prior riding experience. In fact, her only time with horses had come when she had returned from the Middle East and had taken part in a therapeutic equestrian program for soldiers suffering from PTSD. The records were in Billie's file, but she'd been very close-lipped about both the PTSD and her time with the program. Well, she'd been reserved about everything during her interview. Abby had eventually hired her but had kept a close watch on her progress and had carefully read Rachel's evaluations. Billie might not have been taught long, but she'd been taught well. Abby had never regretted making her part of the team, but she had always considered herself to be as much an enigma to the rest of the department as Billie was to her. Now, she felt exposed. Maybe it had been a bad idea to join the team this week and be seen as one of them, instead of as their aloof lieutenant. She had liked being here with the horses, but she hadn't chosen her career to have fun.

Once the other riders had gone to dinner, she left the stall and walked quickly through the barn. She hadn't seen Kira today, not that she'd been looking, and she didn't want to run into her now. She was confused by the time they'd spent together yesterday. They'd looked at some canned goods and joked about chicken judging. Hardly a romantic afternoon. So why had the pull toward Kira strengthened yet again? Sure, Abby had found her attractive at first. Breathtaking. And yes, she'd seen more facets of her every day since. Her admirable strength and bravery. Her wacky sense of humor. Her artistic and passionate side.

Abby stopped her train of thought. She was supposed to be talking herself out of a relationship, but making a list of Kira's good qualities wasn't the best way to do so. She concentrated instead on finding a place to eat. Maybe some food would give her the energy to resist Kira's charms. After their near kiss, she'd been distracted while on patrol and restless once she got home. Kira had been too present in her bed, and Abby woke after a fitful sleep certain the scent of gardenias had just wafted through her room.

The smell of the open wood pit at BBQ Pete's made her mouth water—due more to her memories of eating there with Kira than to the tempting scent of food—but she saw Rachel and Cal eating there. They were sitting close together, tucked on the same side of one of the picnic tables. While she watched, Rachel laughed at something Cal said and gave her a playful shove on the arm. Abby walked on. They were good-humored but steadfast. They made it look easy. She hesitated for a moment, but the momentum of the people around her jolted her back into motion. She had experienced the same ease and natural closeness with Kira yesterday afternoon and at their lunch together. For brief moments, they fit together. She didn't have faith it would last longer than the hour they'd spent in each other's company, but it had been intoxicating in its simplicity. Dangerous in its potency.

Abby moved to the edge of the sidewalk when she noticed Billie and Don coming toward her. Don was eating pieces off what looked like a huge brick of curly fries while they walked, and Billie was carrying a salad in one hand and gesturing with the other as she talked. Abby had never seen Billie eat anything remotely unhealthy, and she wondered if her animated discussion was a lecture on good dietary habits. If so, she was wasting her breath on Don.

All team members accounted for. All she had to do was hope she didn't run into Kira and Julie, and she'd be fine. She went to one of the burger stands housed together in a large warehouse-type building and got the cheeseburger with extra grilled onions she'd been craving since Friday. She ate quickly, sitting in a relatively quiet corner of the building and wondering why she was feeling so irritable with herself and acting so testy with her teammates. She had been growing closer to them and to Kira, despite her better instincts, but now she was determined to maintain distance. She had come full circle, back to the person she'd been on the first day of the fair. Why? Because it was nearly the last day of the fair. She scooped up the last bite of onions and crumpled her wrapper into a tight ball. She tossed it in a garbage can and headed back to the barn.

Legs was waiting for her when she got back with her nose pressed against the bars on the upper half of her stall. She seemed restless, but Abby wondered if she was communicating her own agitation to the sensitive horse. She did a hasty grooming job since she had already made sure Legs was spotless before their demonstration this afternoon when Cal had decided it would be fun to have a mock uniform-judging class. This was one of the categories they'd compete in if she took the team to the national competition, so Abby had been interested in the trial run. Cal had judged them on the condition of their clothing, tack, and horses, and she'd involved the audience in selecting winners in the different categories. Rachel had won all of them, as expected. Not because she had an in with the judge, but because she had some magical ability to polish a saddle and horse to a brilliant shine.

Abby was relieved she'd already done most of her grooming, because Legs was growing more impatient as she worked. She finally put the brushes away and got her saddle. Legs probably needed to get out and move around, and Abby's whirling thoughts weren't helping her be the calming influence the horse needed.

She led the fully tacked mare out of the barn and put her foot in the stirrup to mount. Legs swung around and bumped into her, almost knocking her down while she was off balance, but Cal was there in a second, taking the reins and soothing the horse so Abby could get on.

"She seems nervous," Cal said. "The horses are used to more exercise than they're getting here, and they might be going a little stir-crazy since they're in their stalls so much. But if she doesn't settle soon, bring her back here."

"She's been great out there on the midway," Abby said, reassuring herself as much as Cal. "I doubt we'll have any trouble."

"Probably not," Cal said, giving the mare another pat. "But there will be a lot of people around you. Safety first, for them and for you."

"Yes, ma'am," Abby said, with a mock salute. She smiled and walked Legs around the area behind the barn. By the time Rachel came out with Bandit, Legs had calmed down and was moving in a brisk stride but with a long, easy rein.

"Ready to go?" Rachel asked.

"We sure are," Abby said.

Rachel nodded. "Good. But if she acts up at all, we'll take her to the warm-up ring where she can move a little faster. She might need a good trot around to settle her nerves."

Abby frowned. Rachel and Cal didn't seem to take a breath without the other knowing. "Did Cal actually speak to you about Legs, or did she communicate with you telepathically?"

Rachel only laughed at her sarcastic tone. "The safety of this team—your team—is our top priority. We don't ignore or hide anything from each other that might be a danger."

"We promise we'll jog right back to the barn at the first sign of trouble," Abby said. She adjusted her reins and gave a light squeeze with her legs. She and Rachel merged into the human traffic at the far end of the barn and headed toward the midway.

They started their rounds in the kiddie area where the sedate rides went slowly around their tracks. Every few yards, they had to stop for a photo op or to answer a question. They'd gone through the same ritual every night, but Legs had apparently decided she'd done enough PR work. She danced in place, swinging her rump dangerously close to a group of people standing in line to buy ride tickets. Abby kept chatting with people even as she struggled to hold her horse in place without letting Rachel or the fairgoers see any tension on her face or in her body. She was explaining to a young girl why she shouldn't feed Legs a piece of pizza when a man walked by with a huge stuffed dragon on his shoulders. Legs had seen hundreds of toys like this, hanging enticingly on the walls of game booths and draped over the people who'd won them. Tonight, though, she gave a snort of fear and leaped in the air, coming down with her legs spread wide, ready to bolt. Abby stroked her neck, feeling her own pulse race to match the thumping beat of Legs's heart between her calves. She was debating whether to admit defeat and return to the barn when Rachel's walkie-talkie crackled.

"Sarge, we have a fight over by the Matterhorn."

"On our way," Rachel said. She clucked to Bandit and moved toward the increasingly loud yells coming from Don's location. "Coming through," she called to the people in front of her. "Police! Stand aside."

Legs followed in Bandit's wake, her nose nearly pressed against his tail as she tried to outpace him. Abby pulled back on the reins, now slick with sweat from the mare's neck, but Legs didn't seem to notice. Rachel trotted the steady Bandit into the midst of the brawl, helping Don and Billie separate the combatants, while Abby kept to the sidelines. She dropped her feet out of the stirrups and was about to dismount and regain control of her horse when a roller coaster car clattered by and Legs reared suddenly and plunged to the right. Abby pulled desperately on her left rein to keep Legs from crashing into the throngs of people who had gathered to watch the fight.

Legs spun in a tight circle, to the left, and Abby braced her arm against the mare's neck so she didn't fall off during the quick direction change. She choked up on the curb rein, and Legs backed up so fast she was almost trotting. Abby swung her to the left again, toward a booth with a small pool of rubber ducks in it. Pay a quarter, pick a duck, get a prize. Abby's thoughts were as chaotic as her ride, and all her focus was on getting the mare under control before she killed anyone. The mare skidded to a stop inside the small tent and spooked at the floating ducks, jumping sideways a few feet and crashing into the wooden pole supporting the flapping canvas. Abby heard a crack—her wrist, or the wooden beam?—and she jammed her now useless right hand against Legs's neck where it was foamy with sweat. She yanked hard on the other rein and leaned back in the saddle, shouting, "Whoa!" with all the authority she could muster.

The emergency stop, a maneuver she had learned early in her 4-H days, worked long enough for her to get her feet back in the stirrups and her reins looped around her left hand. Before Legs could explode again, Rachel was by her side, side-passing Bandit until he was inches away from Legs.

"Hey, Lieutenant." Don moved Fancy to her other side, hemming Legs in between the two calm and stocky horses. "Looks like you and Legs were doing an imitation of the Tilt-A-Whirl."

"Felt like it, too," Abby said. She grimaced when Legs threw her head in the air and bumped her right hand. The pain spread all the way to her toes like an electric shock traveling through her veins.

"Let's get you back to the barn, Abby," Rachel said. "We don't want people to panic about the horses, so we'll just walk nice and slow."

Abby felt Legs trembling underneath her, but the mare seemed to have given up. She walked between the steadying horses without a fuss.

"What about the fight?" Abby looked back and saw Billie and Ranger boxing her in from behind.

"Fancy and I got it under control," Don said, giving his mare a pat. Abby heard Billie's snort of derision from behind. "Oh, yeah, and Billie helped a little. She stood by and cheered us on."

"They stopped the fight, and foot patrol came and took the two guys into custody," Rachel said in a low voice. She looked as pale as Abby felt.

Halfway to the barn, they found Cal sprinting toward them. "I heard you on the radio," she said to Rachel. "Are you okay, Abby? Can you get back to the barn?"

"Of course. And you can all stop treating me like a little old grandmother who's broken her hip." She was relieved, though, when Cal surreptitiously took hold of her reins and led Legs, making it look like she was scratching her under the chin. As soon as they were behind the barns, more private than before now that night had fallen, Don moved to the side and gave her room to slide off her horse.

Abby felt dazed from the pain in her wrist. She'd had broken bones before, but this was something else. Still, she hated leaving Legs behind when the horse was obviously upset.

"I'll take her," Cal said. She grabbed the reins from Abby. "Don't worry. Rachel's going to take you to the hospital."

Abby watched her lead Legs down the aisle, followed by Billie with Bandit and Ranger.

"Don't worry, Lieutenant," Don repeated Cal's words. "We got this."

Rachel put her hand on Abby's shoulder and drew her away. She wanted to protest that she only needed an aspirin and a ride home, but she felt close to passing out from the pain. She silently went with Rachel through the back exit and to her car.

Chapter Fourteen

Rachel drove through the deserted early morning streets from Puyallup's Good Samaritan Hospital to Cal's family home. She wound past the barn and down the private lane leading to her and Cal's bungalow. As soon as she shut off her engine, she heard Tar and Feathers, Cal's two border collies, barking to announce her arrival. Even if Cal had already gone to bed, she'd be wide awake now, but Rachel knew Cal would be waiting up for her.

Cal opened the door before Rachel could get her key in the lock, and she took Rachel into her arms. Rachel stood silently for a few moments, relaxing into the heated softness of her. Cal was wearing an old pair of sweats and a tank top, and Rachel bunched the thin fabric in her fists as she pulled them closer together.

"How is she?" Cal asked, turning her head toward Rachel's neck so she felt the words breathed on her skin even as she heard them spoken.

"She came out of surgery without any problem. The doctor had to put a metal plate on her radius, but he thinks she'll regain full use of her wrist eventually. She'll be in a brace for a few months, though."

Rachel bent down to pet the dogs as they whined and twisted around her legs. Feathers always greeted her the same way no matter if she'd only been gone a few minutes, but tonight even the usually reserved Tar welcomed her more effusively than usual. Cal must have been worried and transmitted her emotions to her perceptive dogs.

"Come. Sit with me," Cal said. She led the way into the brightly lit kitchen. A liquor bottle and two glasses were waiting on the table. Between Rachel's work with the mounted police and Cal's grueling training schedule, they ate more takeout there than home-cooked food, but the kitchen had been the first room they had decorated together. They spent most of their time when both were home either sitting at the table and talking or in bed. Not talking.

Cal had some canned soup simmering on the stove, and she ladled out a bowl and set it in front of Rachel before sitting across from her and pouring each of them a glass of bourbon. Rachel hadn't had anything to eat since their barbecue dinner, and she was sure the hospital coffee had burned a hole in her stomach lining. She had refused to leave until she knew her lieutenant was going to be okay, so she had waited through the MRI and the surgery that followed. Only when she had grilled the doctor and said good night to a groggy and half-drugged Abby did she feel comfortable leaving the hospital.

She had been texting Cal with news all night while she sat at the hospital and Cal took care of the horses. Unstable fracture of the radius with a trapped tendon. Floating bone fragments from the scaphoid. Rachel crumbled a handful of crackers into her tomato soup and stirred them around. She had been a confused mix of guilt and relief and anxiety over what could have happened when Legs went berserk. She concentrated on her soup and tried not to cry. She had been wrong to let Abby ride with the team without having practiced with them. To be fair, she hadn't been given the option to say no when Abby stepped up to take Clark's place, but she should have found a way to deny her. And the choice to give her Legs as a mount? Rachel wasn't sure how she'd forgive herself for that one. She had thought the quiet horse would be good for Abby. Abby knew the mare was inexperienced, so she'd be inclined to stay out of any real action. At least, that's what Rachel had hoped would happen. She'd been wrong. Nearly dead wrong.

Cal was watching her closely, with a look of concern on her face as if she could read Rachel's thoughts. "Strychnine," Cal said. She took a sip of her bourbon.

Rachel swallowed a mouthful of her soup. "In here?" she asked, pointing to her bowl.

"In Legs."

Rachel put down her spoon and stared at Cal. She knew Cal had called their vet, Dr. Westmore, to have him check the gray mare, but she'd assumed it was only a routine visit to make sure she hadn't been injured or gotten sick after her escapades.

"She was poisoned? Will she be okay?"

"Technically, yes, and yes. She should be fine once it wears out of her system. Westmore took her to the clinic with him. Keep eating, please. You must be starving, although you seem to have more crackers than soup in your bowl."

"I like it that way," Rachel said. She took another bite without really tasting it. "What do you mean *technically*? Did you know this before you called Westmore?"

"Technically, because I don't think the dose was meant to be a poison, but a stimulant. I suspected something like this when I saw her and heard how she had acted. I stayed with her until he came, and he tested her blood and urine. He'll send some to the lab tomorrow for a full workup, but he tested what he could when he got back to the clinic. He called just a few minutes ago."

Rachel gave up the pretense of eating her meal and pushed her bowl aside. She swallowed the bourbon in one quick gulp. She wanted to wash away the tide of despair she felt threatening at the edges of her mind. "I thought we'd put the days of sabotage behind us. I can't believe someone is still out there who wants to hurt our horses. Why strychnine?"

"It's been used for ages to jazz up a tired or sore horse." Cal poured another shot in Rachel's glass. "Too much is a poison, but a small IV dose gives a horse more energy. It increases agitation and the startle reflex. Any one of our horses would have likely been as unmanageable as Legs was if they were given the same dose."

Rachel's mind struggled to comprehend the full meaning of Cal's statement. Her first thought was relief. Abby's accident hadn't been the result of her poor judgment. Her second thought, however, was much more disturbing. "Was Legs chosen on purpose? So Abby would get hurt? Or was she randomly picked, and the whole unit was the target?"

Cal shrugged. "That's the question, isn't it?"

Rachel took another drink. "She hasn't been in patrol for years, but we should find out if any of her arrests have been released recently. And I'll check with dispatch to see if there've been any threats against the mounted unit, although I'm sure we'd have been informed, especially before the fair. Oh, and I'll stop by the fair office tomorrow and talk to the head of security. This might possibly be aimed at the fair itself, not us in particular. And I should—"

Cal stood up, took the drink out of Rachel's hand, and set it on the counter. She rested her hand on the top of Rachel's head and massaged her scalp with gentle fingers. "Yes, we'll have a lot to do starting tomorrow. But right now you're safe and Abby's safe and Legs is safe. The rest can wait until you've had some sleep."

Rachel took both of Cal's hands in her own and laid her cheek against them. "I can't bear the thought of going through this again. Worrying about the team. Wondering why someone is out to get us."

"I know, sweetheart. But it's different this time." Cal tugged on Rachel's hands and got her to stand. She kissed her lips until Rachel sighed and relaxed. "This time, we're in it together from the start. There's nothing we can't do."

Rachel wanted to share her optimism, but she had too great a responsibility. Everyone counted on her to lead and protect the team. Even tonight, when Abby was injured and Legs was acting up, Rachel had made the call to get out of the situation with as little fuss and attention as possible. With all the chaos around them, she didn't think most people had noticed Legs and Abby because they were so busy watching the fight. She could have had Abby dismount right there while she called the medics and had someone lead Legs back to the barn. She had evaluated the situation and decided Abby would be better off riding back to the privacy of their deserted aisleway. Legs was less likely to get free if someone was riding her and not leading her. The other horses had surrounded Legs and kept her calm and quiet. But how much of Rachel's choice had been based on Legs and Abby, and how much on the fragile reputation of the mounted team? She wasn't sure.

She wrestled with the questions in her mind while Cal led her into their bathroom. She wasn't sure which thread to follow first, but she knew her top priority without a doubt. Cal. She had to do her best to convince Cal of it, too.

"I need to ask a favor of you, love."

Cal was fiddling with the temperamental faucet in their shower. She didn't turn around when she spoke. "No, I will not stay away from the fairgrounds until this is over. If you're there, I'm there, too."

"But I can focus on solving this better if I'm not worried about you."

"We'll have two brains working on the puzzle, yours and mine, so it won't matter if you're using only half of yours. Abby and your teammates can take up the rest of the slack." Cal took off her tank top and sweatpants. Rachel swallowed hard when she saw Cal standing in front of her naked. She'd seen her without clothes plenty of times since they'd started their relationship, but the sight never failed to turn her on. Rational thought was draining away, soon to be replaced by pure lust, but Rachel tried one more tactic.

"What if it's like last time, when Eugene's goons tried to shoot you? It paralyzes me to think of you being hurt."

"Well, you're going to need to get over it," Cal said. She unbuttoned Rachel's uniform top, managing to hit all her most sensitive spots as she worked her way down.

"Get over it?" Rachel repeated. She was trying to make her voice sound stern, but it came out breathy and with a definite catch as Cal brushed against her nipple.

"Yes. We're a team now, you and I. So get used to me being around, even if it isn't convenient for you. Now get in the shower and we'll wash those hospital germs off you."

It wasn't a matter of convenience, but one of pure fear. Rachel couldn't bear the thought of Cal being hurt, but her involvement with the mounted unit had taken a dangerous turn yet again.

Rachel stood still in the shower stall for a few minutes, while Cal soaped her from hair to toes. Her touch was exciting, turning the things Rachel did every day, like shampooing her hair, into erotic acts. Rachel was so tired. Tired of being a target. Tired of watching her team go through constant trials. But Cal brought her back to life. Made her realize she was strong enough to lead her mounted unit, even when they were at risk. Cal supported her when she felt weak and made her strong again.

Cal was rubbing her scalp as she rinsed shampoo out of her short, curly hair. Rachel grabbed her hands and spun Cal around so she was facing the shower wall. She kept them both under the spray of hot water.

"You're right," she whispered in Cal's ear. She flicked her tongue inside and smiled as Cal gasped. Cal's whole body seemed to quiver at her touch, no matter how brief. She held nothing back when she gave of herself, and she deserved the same from Rachel.

"I usually am," Cal said. She ground her hips against Rachel and almost made her come right then, from the sheer, beautiful friction she created between them. "But what was I right about this time?"

"Modest, aren't you?" Rachel laughed and held Cal's wrists captive over her head with one of her hands. She slid her other down Cal's wet stomach and stopped when she felt her damp hair. She moved her hand back and forth until Cal moaned. "You're right when you say your place is with me. I worry about you, but I need you there."

She dipped her hand lower, until she slid her fingers between Cal's lips. She was dripping wet, and Rachel groaned and bit Cal's neck. Cal needed her, too. Rachel felt it here, in Cal's responses. She felt it in Cal's touch, whether sexual or tender. She felt it every time Cal looked at her.

"We'll get through this together," Rachel promised. She increased the pressure of her hand until Cal's breath came in hard, shuddering gasps. She had fought against needing anyone for too long. Cal made her weak in the knees, but strong where it counted. "Together," she whispered again as Cal climaxed under her touch.

Chapter Fifteen

The next day, Abby parked next to the nature center at the Snake Lake nature preserve. She reached across her body to put her car in park with her left hand and climbed out. She wasn't supposed to be driving yet, but she decided the doctor would have arranged for a chauffeur if he'd really been serious about that. He hadn't, so she was driving. Everything was awkward without the use of her right hand, but at least the pain had eased to a dull ache since the doctor had released her tendon from its pinched position between two ragged edges of bone. Her wrist was still tender and swollen, but she'd get by.

She paused by the Discovery Pond play area and watched a couple of preschoolers splash in the shallow water while their mothers chatted on a nearby bench. The little pond, with its strategically placed rocks and bridges, was a human-made depiction of nature, condensed into a small space with a view of a gas station and a huge grocery store. The entire preserve was ringed by civilization. A Highway 16 overpass roared over the southern edge of the lake, and there were stores, a high school, and apartment buildings on the other sides. Kira might feel this was a success story, but Abby couldn't help but see it in a more cynical way. It was a token piece of nature, barely able to keep out city growth and noise. Of course, the only times she'd been on the trails leading around the lake, she'd been there as a patrol officer chasing out illegal squatters. Perhaps she hadn't fully appreciated the area's beauty and importance because it had been the middle of the night and she'd been up to her ankles in slimy mud.

Abby stopped by a large wooden map and checked out the trail system. The various options were labeled with different colored paint. One mile, a half mile. None of them were very long, but she hoped Kira had gone on one of the shorter walks with her group. Abby had barely slept the night before, and as soon as morning had come, she'd made an effort to be wide awake every time a nurse stopped by her room so they'd believe she was well enough to go home. She hated hospitals.

The doctor had finally discharged her, and Cal had come to pick her up and take her to the fairgrounds, where her car was parked. The news there had made her want to go back to the hospital and pull the covers over her head. Strychnine? Another case of sabotage against her mounted unit? Rachel and the team were organizing guard duty yet again, and one of them would be with the horses every minute until either the fair was over or they figured out who had drugged Legs. Abby was thankful the mare was recovering well. She also felt a selfish pang of relief because she'd been worried that the horse's behavior was a response to her own rusty riding skills.

Abby started down the main path that circled in a loop around the lake. Kira had been leaving messages on her phone since last night, but Abby hadn't had a chance to answer yet. She hadn't been sure how to explain the accident, especially to someone outside the team, but something in Kira's voice made her realize she couldn't put off their conversation for long. In her last message she'd said she'd call again after she led a tour here at the nature center, so Abby had decided to stop by on her way home.

A few yards along the path, the sounds of the city started to fade. The decaying greenery and lush mossy undergrowth coated the air with a thick woodsy smell. Abby took a deep breath, and then another. She'd been carrying the tension of her wild ride on Legs deep in her shoulders and spine, but the packed-dirt path and protective towering trees loosened something inside her. Small birds flitted by her head, and the occasional squirrel came to watch her progress. She guessed that plenty of people ignored the signs asking visitors not to feed the wildlife because they seemed eagerly expectant of a handout.

Abby was almost sorry when she heard a group of people chattering up ahead. She wouldn't have minded walking alone for a while longer. She heard Kira's voice rise above the muddled voices of the group, and she felt her body grow tense again. No, not tense. She stopped and paid close attention to the unfamiliar feeling. Anticipation? Yes. Eagerness, even. She was overly exhausted and susceptible to every little emotion running through her. All she needed was a good night's sleep—helped by some of the painkillers her doctor had prescribed—and she'd be able to control those responses again. Kira couldn't keep this hold on her when she was in full control of her faculties. Well, maybe she could, but Abby had plenty of experience resisting personal urges. She'd be fine.

Or maybe she wouldn't. She came around a corner of the path and saw Kira standing on a wooden footbridge while she addressed a group of a dozen or so seniors. She was brightly dressed in a sunny yellow T-shirt, khakis, and those red sneakers, but she somehow fit in her environment without needing to resort to the props of earth tones and naturally dyed fibers. She wore her hair in a short braid and had a pair of binoculars around her neck.

She noticed Abby as soon as she rounded the corner, and Abby heard the falter in her voice before she picked up the thread of her lecture again. She gave a brief wave, and Abby returned it with her left hand. She edged closer to the group and listened to Kira speak.

"You're going to see many different species of flora and fauna on our short tour, and you might wonder why it'd be important if we lost any one of them. For instance, think about these willow trees you can see rimming the lake. There are plenty of other varieties of trees here, so why should this one type matter to conservationists? Willows often grow along the water in lentic or riparian—lake or river—ecosystems. When they're destroyed by development, overgrazing, or some other destruction of their habitat, the cascade effect can be significant. The willows provide shade for fish, cooling the water and offering places to spawn and feed. If those areas are removed because the willows are gone, there will be a reduction in the number of fish in the stream or lake. Predators that eat fish will have a decreased food supply, and if the fish had been feeding on plankton, their numbers will increase. A similar process will happen with songbirds that nest in the trees, and beaver that use tree limbs for food and dams. The system is no longer in balance if it loses a single part. Sadly, we often don't realize or recognize the value of each particular species until it's gone. And then it might be too late to restore the balance we've destroyed."

Kira paused and studied the lake around her. Although she had hesitated when she saw Abby, the passion she had for her wetlands had seeped back into her voice as she spoke. She had a true calling to do her job. Abby had as deep a connection to her own career, but it wasn't based on passion. Still, she was as tied to what she did as Kira was.

"If you look to your right, you'll see several types of waterfowl. There are hooded mergansers and wood ducks, and about five others I recognize. Why don't you use your guidebooks and see how many you can identify?"

She squeezed through the group as they filed onto the narrow bridge. Her smile faded when she saw Abby's bandaged arm.

"What happened to you? Please tell me there were no zip ties involved."

"Just a little accident while I was on patrol last night. Legs and I had an altercation with a tent pole. I lost." She tried to joke her way out of the full explanation, but Kira's face showed too much concern for her to ignore.

"I'm fine, really." She held up her hand and wiggled her fingers even though the movement made her grit her teeth.

Kira gently grasped her fingers and stopped their motion. "Please stop proving how little you hurt, or you're going to pass out. I'll just pretend I believe you, okay?"

"Thanks," Abby said. She disengaged from Kira's touch and cradled her arm against her stomach. "You, on the other hand, are looking much better. I barely noticed the marks on your wrists."

Kira held out her hands. "It looks like I'm wearing bracelets now, unless you're close. My face itches still, but at least the tape mark is fading. I hated getting such blatant stares whenever I was out in public."

She looked over her shoulder at her tour group. Some of them were still watching the ducks, but most were getting restless. "I need to talk to you, but I have to finish this tour first. I'll only be fifteen minutes or so if you want to follow along."

Abby was tempted. She loved hearing Kira talk with so much conviction and verve, but she gestured toward a bench carved out of a tree trunk instead. "I wouldn't mind just sitting for a few minutes. Can you come back here when you're done?"

"Of course."

Kira walked back to her group and asked them about their duck-identifying experience. They walked farther along the bridge and Kira stopped to point out some more native plants. Abby listened as long as they were within earshot, and then she leaned back and closed her eyes. She hadn't been lying when she said she'd rather sit alone than join the group. She enjoyed the sound of Kira's voice too much for comfort. More than self-protection, though, she wanted to try to recapture the sense of peace she'd felt before she'd met up with the tour. She let the sound of chirping birds and rustling leaves lull her past the frantic thoughts on the surface of her mind and deeper to a place of quiet. She sighed and slipped closer to sleep.

❖

Kira quietly sat down on the bench next to Abby. She looked terrible. Her skin was too pale, and her cheekbones stood out too prominently, as if she'd lost significant weight since Kira had last seen her, only two days ago. Abby had tried to brush off Kira's concern about her wrist, but her little finger-wiggling stunt had about done her in. Kira had watched pain move across Abby's face like a tangible wave.

She wanted to smooth Abby's frown lines with her fingers. To kiss the side of her jaw where her skin pulsed, most likely in reaction to tension and clenched teeth. But she figured Abby wouldn't appreciate the compassion. She had seemed touchy around Kira after their brush with physical contact, and then she'd practically disappeared. Admittedly, Kira was feeling just as hesitant to spend time alone with Abby. Touching her had seemed more innocent, less significant and dangerous, when they'd been eating barbecue together. Now Kira knew Abby better and she craved her in a deeper way. Maybe Abby was feeling the same way toward her. Just now, she'd have preferred if Abby had kept with the group so they could have talked when they got back to the nature center, instead of meeting alone on the isolated path. The preserve was always quiet on weekday mornings and would be the ideal place for a romantic tryst. Kira knew a few private places where they could slip off the public path and conceal themselves behind a lattice of branches and shrubs. The needle-covered dirt would be cool and scratchy on her back, and pliant under her clawing fingers...

She had to rouse Abby. Get her the hell out of here. She wanted to let her sleep since Abby seemed to need it, but she couldn't stay here and watch or she'd be waking Abby with a kiss instead of a shake of her shoulder.

"Abby, time to wake up," she said, shaking her firmly.

"I'm not sleeping," Abby said. She sat up and looked around her, tucking a loose strand of auburn hair into her French twist. "Well, maybe I was. Just a little."

Kira smiled at Abby's confession. She felt more comfortable with Abby when she was able to show an occasional weakness. Kira had more than enough experience with someone who would never admit to being at fault or out of control.

"Are you going to tell me what really happened last night?" Kira asked. She didn't believe the nonchalant version Abby had given earlier. "I watched you on Legs, and I can't believe you accidentally ran into a booth. She seemed like such a quiet horse, and you're too good a rider."

"Thank you," Abby said with a weary-looking smile. "We're still trying to figure out what happened, so I can't give all the details, but...well, Legs was drugged. She was given a stimulant and she became...hard to manage. I didn't fall off, but I hit my wrist hard enough to need very minor surgery. It'll be fine soon, though. The doctor says I'll probably regain full use of it, and Legs is going to be okay. So it worked out fine."

Abby's attempts to keep the story light and worry-free failed miserably. Kira had a hundred questions, but she didn't know how to ask. She guessed Abby would gloss over most of the real facts, anyway. She tried to reconcile the beautiful, delicate Abby who had been sleeping on the bench next to her with the hard-edged and imperturbable police officer. Her world was one of violence, where people hurt horses and put the lives of cops and bystanders in danger. She knew how easily the situation could have turned deadly, with a drugged horse and so many pedestrians in the way...

Before Kira had time to wrap her mind around the half-told story and its implications, Abby was changing the subject. "What did you need to tell me? You left six messages on my phone."

Kira frowned. She had been anxious to talk to Abby about her discovery, but now that they were face-to-face, she wasn't sure how to broach the subject or what Abby's reaction would be. Still, if she had uncovered the information, the police detectives would soon know it as well. Better if Abby heard it now, from her.

"I had one of the people in my wetland coalition check into Milford's properties. It's important to me—to the *city*—that we keep fighting to preserve the land he owned." Kira didn't want to admit her personal vendetta against Milford. He had nearly succeeded in getting her to derail the efforts to protect the wetland, and she felt ashamed at her weakness. She'd have done what he asked because Julie was in danger, but now she wanted to increase her efforts and reclaim some of the power he had wrenched from her. "Anyway, we needed to know who would inherit the deed to the land if he died, so we'd know what our next steps should be."

Abby nodded. "I get it," she said.

Kira had a feeling Abby really did get it, that she understood Kira's deep need to protect this land because she hadn't been able to protect herself during his assault. Abby understood violence, in all its forms.

"Do you need me to do some checking for you? I might be able to find out—"

"Abby, I know who'll get this tract of land as well as quite a few others. They'll all go to Tad Milford's investment group. It's small, only three people, but they're all very influential in the city."

"And you had to tell me this because…?"

"Because one of them is Richard Hargrove."

She watched Abby as she processed the information. Her expression wasn't as unreadable as before, and now Kira could see a heavy weariness on Abby's face. Was Abby too tired to conceal it well, or was Kira learning how to look at her? She stayed silent while Abby examined whatever thoughts were in her head.

"Damn," Abby said. Kira agreed. She had seen the list of properties to which Abby's brother would have claim after Tad's death. He'd have made good money as an investor, but his profit margin had increased significantly over the weekend. Before, as an investor, he'd have made one-third of half the profits Milford made. Now he'd jumped to a full third of all profits. He'd doubled his take with, what, one easy bullet?

"I knew he'd invested with Milford, but I didn't realize how heavily. Still, is it enough to kill for?"

Abby shook her head, but Kira didn't know if she was answering her own question in the negative, or if she was unwilling to picture her brother as the killer.

"It's a lot of money," Kira said. "Milford seemed to have a sixth sense of when people were about to sell. My friend at the tax assessor's office said he'd buy properties for a low price from people who wanted to build commercially but couldn't because of one or two residential holdouts. Soon after, the holdouts would sell to him, too, and he'd make a huge profit."

"You have spies in the county offices," Abby said with a smile.

Kira grinned back, happy to see the worry lines on Abby's face relax for even a brief moment. "I'm usually fighting a losing battle by trying to protect instead of destroy. I need all the information I can get about what's going on behind the scenes. We have ears all over," she added in a conspiratorial whisper.

"So, Sage of Pierce County, what are some of these moneymaking ventures my brother and Tad had going?"

"The new medical building on Twelfth and Union is one," Kira said. "There's also a strip mall on Proctor, a proposed apartment building near the university, yet another strip mall on—"

Abby held up her left hand to stop Kira. "Twelfth and Union, near the church?"

"Yes, it was—"

Abby was on her feet and walking down the path before Kira could finish her sentence.

"Where are you going?" Kira got up and jogged after her. "What is it?"

"The address is familiar, but I need to check something at home." Abby had seemed agitated by their entire discussion, but now she had the calm manner of someone who was on the cusp of answers. If they had anything to do with the person who had stood in the room with her and splattered her with Milford's blood, then Kira had a right to know, too.

"I'm coming with you," Kira said. Abby looked about to protest, but Kira wouldn't be swayed. Abby could be as bossy as she wanted, but Kira was going.

Abby nodded, as if Kira had spoken her defiance out loud. She handed Kira her keys. "Okay. You can drive."

CHAPTER SIXTEEN

Kira gave Abby her phone while she drove, and Abby skimmed through the long list of addresses Kira's source had sent her. When she had first started her conservation work in Tacoma, she went to the courthouse on an almost daily basis to research records and zoning maps, and Keith—just out of high school at the time and working as an intern—had helped her untangle the messy county system. She'd shared some of the work she was doing, answering his eager questions and explaining her reasons for wanting to protect the vulnerable wetland areas, and he had eventually become one of her most loyal volunteers. He had helped her streamline the process of filing zoning permits with the county, and his technical knowledge made him a successful grant writer as well. Some of the people who joined forces with her only stayed until their own neighborhood issues were resolved, but some remained involved in a citywide capacity. She appreciated all of them, whether their motive was to keep a fast-food restaurant off the corner lot on their own street or whether they truly believed in the need to save these precious and endangered environments. Keith was one who saw the big picture, and Kira didn't know how she'd managed before him.

Abby whistled. "What's the name of the kid who got you all this information? He seems like a handy person to know."

"Hey, keep your paws off him. He's my...what do you call it?"

"Your CI? Confidential informant?"

"Yes, and I found him first. Besides, he's the type who needs a cause, not just a paycheck or a get-out-of-jail-free card."

Abby didn't answer. Kira glanced at her and saw she was no longer scrolling through the list. "Did I say something wrong? I didn't mean to imply that what I do is noble, and your work isn't."

"I know. So, no, there's nothing wrong. I'm just tired."

"Ah. Code for *I'm not going to talk about it*." Kira wasn't sure what had happened to make Abby shut down, but she let it go. Abby had been through a hell of a night, and Kira herself was barely recovered from Saturday. She had slept enough to enable her to get through her daily routines as if nothing was wrong, but she still felt the effects of her time in Milford's office. The fact was, they were both tired. Kira was prepared to leave it at that, but Abby seemed to want to explain.

"It's just…some of my family members have used bribes as a way to get information. I never would, but people hear the name Hargrove and…" She shrugged.

And they judged Abby by the low standards her relatives had set. Kira had done something similar when they'd first met, but she thought she knew Abby better now. "I can't imagine you ever crossing a line that way, but I can see why you'd be sensitive about the subject. The get-out-of-jail card thing was just a joke."

"I know," Abby repeated. "I guess that's why I told you it hurt. Come inside. I need to tell you more about my family."

Kira got out of the car and walked up the path to the faded but graceful Victorian. She was interested to see the inside of Abby's house. Would it be like her office, all black-and-white and pointy? Or would it match the exterior of the house in a shabby-chic style?

Or would it be nearly empty? Kira stood in the doorway and looked around the grand living room. She could easily see the original features like the intricate crown molding and the dark-grained hardwood floors because the room was completely bare.

"I don't spend much time in this room," Abby said.

"Obviously. So why bother furnishing it?" Kira said. She followed Abby through the narrow hallway to the eat-in kitchen. At least there was furniture in this room. A card table had been set up near a huge bay window. There was a coffee mug on the table, and a newspaper, but Kira forgot about the monastic feel of the house when she saw the back patio. "Wow, I expected you to have a decent view in this neighborhood, but this is gorgeous."

She went through the back door and took a deep breath. She caught a whiff of the industrial Tideflats, and just the merest hint of fishy odor. Wonderful. "I love the smell of the sea," she said. The mountain was partially covered with a high, thick layer of clouds, but the view was phenomenal. Abby had a set of plastic deck furniture and a fancy grill that looked like it could fit an entire kalua pig. Who cared if she didn't have anything in the rest of the house. Kira would spend all her time out here if she…

She couldn't stop herself in time. As soon as she had pictured herself living here, she had a vision of being in Abby's bed—did she even have a bed?—with Abby's hands on her. She turned to find Abby watching her with a curious expression. She must not entertain much, unless she had people over for a barbecue, so maybe she was uncomfortable having someone in her space.

Kira sighed. She doubted it. She figured plenty of women would be happy to spend time here with Abby, couch or no couch. She followed her back into the house.

"Do you want something to drink?" Abby went over to the fridge and pulled it open with her good hand.

"Do you have a couple of rib eyes in there?" Kira asked. "Kidding. Just wishful thinking after seeing your grill. A beer would be good."

"I'll have you over for a steak dinner sometime," Abby said. She got two beers out and set them on the counter. "I don't cook much in here, but I can grill the hell out of anything out there."

"I'll bet you can. Here, let me open those for you," Kira offered quickly. She ignored Abby's polite mention of an invitation, but she wouldn't hold her breath waiting for a real one to come. Abby pulled away from her every time she got a step closer. Kira couldn't fault her for it since she was guilty of doing the same thing. She twisted off the tops of the Alaskan Ambers and handed one to Abby.

She followed Abby up the wooden staircase. The house would be stunning if Abby only took the time to fill in some cracks and repaint the walls. Maybe sand the floors and replace the worn carpet in the hallway. Add a chair or two and some photos—Kira stopped. No wonder Abby hadn't done much with the house. The list was daunting, and she wasn't the one who'd have to do the work.

Abby opened the door to a room at the top of the steps, and Kira stared inside in amazement.

"Holy Bat Cave, Batman," she muttered as she slowly walked around the perimeter of the room and studied the charts and pictures pinned to the walls. Abby had furniture here. A desk, a chair, a large table. Three tall file cabinets. An office-sized copier, a fax machine. "What is this place? Do you control an army of spies from this command center?"

Abby set her beer on the desk and opened one of the file drawers. "I do a little extracurricular work here," she said.

"Hmm. Family history?"

One of the walls was completely covered with corkboard tiles. There were two names listed, Richard Hargrove and Albert Hargrove, and each one had a string reaching across the wall with different colored pins spaced at intervals. Small pieces of paper with dates written on them were pinned along the timelines. Albert's line spanned long-past decades, but Richard's was much shorter and more recent.

Abby came and stood beside her. "I come from a long line of cops," she said. "They haven't been very good people, so I'm trying to make things right."

Kira opened and closed her mouth several times. She wanted to respond somehow, but she didn't know what to say. Abby's voice was casual, but the set of her jaw and the whiteness of her knuckles where she gripped a file folder were anything but. It clearly hurt her to make that judgment against her relatives.

"Can you…can you walk me through exactly what you do here?"

"It's simple," Abby said with a shrug. "I go over my grandfather's old case files whenever I get a chance at work. And Rick's now, too. If I see something fishy, I look into it more closely here at home. If someone was harmed in some way by one of them, I try to make it right."

Kira wasn't sure what part of this stunned her more. The sheer volume of cases Abby was reviewing—if the pushpins and notecards were any indication—or the way she'd devoted her whole world to this project. Hundreds of cases spanning a cop's entire career. And now Rick's, to add fresh pain to Abby's solitary labor. Kira understood why Abby had been so touchy about her little joke, and why the rest of the house was bare. This room was Abby's home. She lived here with her guilt. No, not *her* guilt. Her family's. "Do you wear a cape and tight underwear while you do it?"

Abby laughed at her comment. "Yes. I have a big *H* on the front of my chest, and a little mask so no one recognizes my alter ego."

Kira took a drink of her beer. "Abby, this is not normal. Do you get that?"

"Of course I do. But it's my life, so it's my normal. Here's the file I was looking for. Come over here and read this."

She set the folder on a large bare table and opened it. Kira wasn't ready to return to business as usual, so she stayed where she was.

"Abby, is my file in there somewhere?"

Abby had expected the question. She'd never brought anyone here before, had never even hinted about what she did in this place, but she was glad Kira had seen it. Abby could have said no when Kira insisted on accompanying her from Snake Lake. She could have left her downstairs while she came up here alone and got the file. But she wanted Kira to know everything. Why Julie had been given Nirvana, and what Abby had done to make things right for them. Kira deserved to know the truth about their relationship. While Abby was in it, she had to be in it all the way. Like she did with everything else in her life—everything that mattered.

"Yes. I have a copy of the report Rick wrote that night in your folder. I also have notes I took about you and Julie, as well as the essay she sent. Do you want to see it?"

Kira shook her head slowly. "No. Julie wanted the essay to be private, and you gave me a hint of what she wrote in it. The rest... well, I'd rather not read it."

"The contest was a front for giving her Nirvana, I admit that, but she'd have won hands down even if my decision hadn't already been made. I read all the essays, and there were some touching ones, but Julie's was special."

Abby didn't know if she'd have parted with Nirvana in the end if she hadn't been moved by what Julie had written. She'd felt the threads binding them together even then. She'd needed to do more than her normal fix for Kira, and she'd needed to share her beloved horse with Julie. She didn't know why they had stood out from the seemingly endless files in these cabinets, but they had.

"How do you decide what will make things right, in your mind? How do you put a value on the lives that have been ruined?"

"I don't have a magic formula," Abby said. She'd struggled with her inability to truly make amends every day of her professional life. "I do what I can. What feels appropriate for the situation."

Kira turned toward her with an angry expression. "Help me understand here," she said. "You *know* your grandfather and Rick have done bad things. You have charts listing the dates and times. So why don't you go to the authorities with this? Make them really pay for what they've done instead of making yourself suffer?"

Abby watched the fury seethe in Kira's eyes. Was she angry because of her own brush with the Hargrove family, or because of the principle of the matter? Or was she actually concerned with the weight Abby made herself bear?

She took her time before answering, wanting Kira to truly understand. "By the time I joined the department, my grandfather had died. Even if I gave my notes to the chief, nothing would change for most of the people who'd been hurt. Don't you see? Nothing would happen except what I make happen. And Rick? I'm still trying to sort through his cases. I might be wrong about him. And if I'm right, there's still a chance he can be stopped. He could change."

Abby rubbed her temple. She didn't like to bring Kira's personal case into this, but she had to make her point. "You know what happened the night you called the police because of Dale. You were there, you have the facts. Can you, right this moment, prove beyond a doubt that my brother's report was wrong?"

"I know it was—"

"Yes, and I know it, too. That's why I have your file here. But can you *prove* it?"

Kira was silent, but she gave a jerky shake of her head.

"Right. And neither can I. So I do what I can to fix things. But this"—she tapped the folder lying on the table—"this connection to Tad Milford is something I can prove. If Rick killed him, it'll have to be made public. I promise you, if he had any part in your abduction, if he's truly crossed the line into corruption, I will take everything about him to IA."

"But you don't want that. You want to protect him."

"Not him. My name. It's different."

"I don't know if it is."

They watched each other in silence. Abby pulled the desk chair over to the table and gestured for Kira to sit. "No matter what you think of the way I handle these other cases, this one is something we can solve together. We can find out who killed Milford, and whether you're involved beyond the kidnapping or not. I'll do it on my own if I have to, because I'm used to it, but it'd be easier if you help me. You know the work you've been doing on his property and you are more familiar with his business than I am. You might notice clues in these files that I wouldn't. Your safety might be in jeopardy here, so put aside your negative opinion about my life and let's get to work."

Abby didn't add that Julie might still be in danger if Kira was, but she had no doubt Kira knew it. She wasn't trying to threaten her, but to get her to look beyond her distaste for Abby and her family. Abby felt defeated. She'd let Kira have a glimpse into her private world, and she'd been judged and condemned along with the rest of the Hargroves. It was a familiar feeling, but this time it reached beyond her surface and cut deep.

Kira seemed to battle her desire to run out of the room and away from Abby, but she slowly walked to the chair and sat down. She started looking through the pages in the folder while Abby got another armload of them from the cabinet. She carried them awkwardly under her left arm, and when she put them on the table, the pile skittered across the polished surface. She started to gather them again, but Kira put her hand on Abby's arm and squeezed.

"Let me," she said. She gathered the files into a neat stack. "Abby, I'm not thinking you're the bad person here. I'm disgusted by the way your relatives have handled their positions of power in the community, but what they've done is no reflection on you. *You* are the one who's chosen to involve yourself in their crimes. And you're the only one who can step away from them and start living your own life. You've known me a few days and you've been doing all this"—she gestured vaguely around the room—"for God knows how long. What I say won't make a difference, but I hope you'll at least consider letting them go."

Abby didn't tell Kira how much she'd wanted to just walk away from her endless work here, and she certainly wasn't going to tell her that even though they had just met, Kira was somehow the only person who had made Abby believe she actually could. Right now, she needed to stay focused. She had to keep open the channels she'd formed between herself and these cases because they possibly held the clues that would lead to Kira's safety.

"I appreciate your concern, but I've made my choice." Abby cleared her throat and stood behind Kira's chair. She rested her injured hand lightly on Kira's shoulder while she pointed at the report with her left one.

"See here, Rick claimed that he got a tip this guy Sal Hendrick was selling drugs. They found some coke at his house, but not enough for an intent to sell. When I first saw this report, I thought it seemed odd, so I brought a copy home. This guy didn't have any priors, and he wasn't living in a high-drug-traffic area. It just didn't sit right. Meanwhile, I remember seeing this lone house in the middle of cleared land on Union, and then one day it was gone and they were building the medical center. I hadn't connected it with this case until now, but it's the same address, and this alleged drug bust took place about the same time as the demolition."

"So he had a house Milford needed, and he didn't choose to sell until your brother happened to find drugs on his property. Yeah, there's nothing suspicious here." Kira pulled the rest of the files toward her. "What do you need me to do?"

"Let's just go through these cases and see if anything jumps out. I've been through them dozens of times, but now we need to look at the addresses and the dates. Rick might have been coercing people to sell somehow, if he and Milford would benefit from it."

"If we find enough evidence, your detectives will have to investigate further, won't they? Then you can actually make him stop instead of just following behind and cleaning up after him."

Abby didn't share Kira's enthusiasm for that part of the plan. She got a folding chair from her bedroom and sat at the table with a pile of folders in front of her. She'd spent too much of her life cleaning up—as Kira put it—the Hargrove mess, and she didn't relish the thought of being associated by name with a public scandal. But somehow, as they worked side by side, Abby felt the burden she'd carried alone so long ease just a little.

CHAPTER SEVENTEEN

"Here's one," Kira said. "An older couple thought they heard someone in their yard. The cops found footprints around the back window and a pry bar and splintered wood beneath it. The house was on a large corner lot on Ninth Avenue and it's a Wendy's restaurant now. Thanks to our friend Milford."

She added the file to the three other suspicious ones they'd found. "He could have been working this in a couple of ways," Kira said. She mentally pictured herself in the couple's situation. She knew how she had felt the past few days when she walked onto her porch, even in broad daylight. Her pulse quickened, her breath was strangled, and her fingers shook as she fumbled to get the key in the lock as quickly as she could. A normal reaction to what had happened to her, but a disheartening one. She wouldn't be any safer on a different doorstep if someone was after her, but the thought of moving was tempting at times.

"What do you mean?" Abby asked. She looked up from the report she was scanning and rubbed her right palm. The gesture seemed unconscious, since Kira didn't believe Abby would admit to being in pain, and it pulled at Kira's heart. Abby was staying strong for her, not just to gather evidence against her brother but to keep Kira safe.

"Well, the drug charge from the first file was probably made up to get the last holdout to sell his property, like we thought, but maybe your brother also looked for unexpected opportunities. He takes a report from a couple who are frightened in their own home. The lot is in a prime location, so maybe he mentions how many break-ins there've been in the neighborhood lately—"

"And a few days later, in swoops Tad Milford with a low but adequate offer on their house," Abby finished the thought. "Chicken or egg. But either way, it's an abuse of power. The first instance is criminal—planting evidence and blackmail—but the second is a hazier moral gray area. I hate those."

"You mean you avoid those, because the rest of your family seems comfortable living smack in the middle of them." Kira was reading the reports and paying attention to the pertinent details, but her attention kept straying to Abby and the cocoon she'd built in this room. At first, Kira had been appalled by the degree of corruption in the Hargrove family and by the apparent lack of repercussions they'd faced. More and more now, her concern was for Abby. What she'd given up, and the terrible burden she'd nobly chosen to bear. Kira had made jokes about her being a superhero, but they weren't far from the truth. Frustratingly, Abby seemed instead to identify with the shame her family had caused.

"Whatever," Abby said with a wave of her left hand. She read a little more before tossing the folder she was holding into the pile of those unassociated with Milford. Instead of picking up another one, she finished off her beer and watched Kira.

"Tell me about Dale," she said.

Kira frowned. She rarely talked about Dale anymore. She had confessed everything about their relationship to Rick Hargrove, and her painful honesty had been disregarded. Since then, she hadn't told anyone else. But she didn't need to convince Abby of anything. Abby had believed her side of the story from the very first, even after reading the falsified report.

"I get embarrassed when I even think about it, let alone talk about it," she admitted. "I should have—"

"No should-haves," Abby said. "Who hasn't been fooled into thinking the mask they see is the real person? I'm not asking you to justify your life, but I'd like to know more about it."

Kira wondered what masks had fooled Abby. She was sure

there had been a time before Abby knew about the extent of this corruption. Somewhere along the line she'd gone from being a blissfully ignorant, adoring granddaughter, to being holed up in this room atoning for the world's sins. Abby would understand Kira's desire to believe the best, even when the worst was proven over and over again.

"We met at an Earth Day celebration at Wright Park, about five years ago, after I'd moved back to Tacoma." Kira remembered the sadness accompanying her that day. The skies had been blue and the music loud, but she'd been locked inside her own world until a woman with crazily blue eyes had bumped into her, and then gallantly apologized by buying her lunch. "My grandparents moved to Oregon to help me take care of Julie while I got my degree, and they passed away within two years of each other. We needed to make a change and had just come back here, and I was lonely. Julie was making friends in school, but I didn't know many people and I was grieving."

Abby reached across the table and laced just the tips of her fingers with Kira's. The touch was tentative and noncommittal, but comforting in a cautious way.

"Dale was great at first. Funny and charming. Always interested in my work and asking about my day. She made me the center of attention whenever I was in the room with her."

"But, then…?" Abby prompted when Kira got silent.

"But then, as soon as we moved in together, she changed. Not all the time—there were days when she was the same woman I'd fallen in love with. Just part of the time, enough to make me feel insecure. She'd go from hot to cold in an instant. Loving and attentive one minute, but distant and angry the next. She was never wrong. Even if I had a legitimate complaint, she'd twist it around until I was the guilty one. I never knew what to expect, so I always felt unsettled and nervous about what I'd face when I got home from work."

Work that had been distracting and full of confrontation given its subject matter, but it had also been a source of friendships and pride. The more Kira had accomplished in her field, the more resentful

Dale grew. Kira had only wanted peace in her home life—both for herself and for Julie. She'd always believed that if she could just say the right thing, do the right thing, she could restore the harmony that had defined the first days of their relationship. Control had been taken from her in increments. She didn't like looking backward, because the past was hard to face.

"She was good to Julie, like I've said. Financially, but not emotionally. She was distant and cold, but I didn't realize it at first because she was so charming. I don't know if it was an act or not, but even when she stopped being that way with me, she was charismatic and friendly to anyone we met outside the home. There were a couple of shoves along the way when we were alone—always followed by apologies and explanations and excuses—but nothing clearly abusive until that night."

Kira paused. She wanted to stop, but Abby had already read the report. Kira had already talked a little about her brush with the police. The hard part was over and she could talk to Abby.

"I was out a little later than usual working on the final details for a proposal I was presenting to the city council the next day. She had been drinking while she waited for me to get home, and we got in a fight. She hit me, hard enough to cut my cheek with her ring. I called the cops, and you know what happened then. They separated us to get our stories, and then they left me with her. She was still angry and drunk, but I managed to keep things calm until she passed out. Then I left. Julie was staying at a friend's house, so I went and got her and we never went back."

Abby gripped her hand more tightly. "I'm proud of you. I know how difficult it must have been to let go of hope and make the changes you needed to make. You're very strong."

"Someone strong would have left right away," Kira argued, but without much conviction. She loved hearing Abby's words because they echoed the ones she'd whispered to herself at night. Outsiders might judge her differently, but she'd been the one in the situation. She alone knew what she'd faced, and she knew what it had taken to get out.

"No," Abby said with a firm shake of her head. "Someone strong leaves when it's necessary. You did."

"Thank you," Kira said. "Abby, what your brother did was wrong, but in an odd way it helped me. It forced me to make the decision to go on my own, without assistance or approval from anyone else. I was lucky I was safe until I was able to get out. In the end, I found my own strength."

"You can't be making allowances for what he did to you—"

"I'm not," Kira said. She wasn't even thinking about her own situation anymore. She was trying to find a way to use what had happened to her to help Abby. "I think I'm just saying things are more complex than they appear. Yes, your brother did a bad thing, but it also was a catalyst for me to take charge. And yes, Nirvana helped me and Julie through a time of change, but we would have survived on our own. I'll always be grateful for her, and for what you did, but the retribution you're seeking won't ever balance everything back to zero. You're caught in a never-ending battle between good and evil, and you don't always know how far the scales have been tipped to either side. You'll never find complete resolution so you can rest."

Rest. The word made Abby's head hurt. She longed for the feeling, and she had experienced it a few times with Kira over the past week and a half. Playing with her at the fair, sleeping beside her next to the lake, and sharing this secret world with her. She'd even found some rest when she was riding with her team, even though her time on active duty as a mounted officer had been a record-breakingly short one.

Still, Kira's words wormed their way into her mind, and she'd need to give them more consideration after this case was settled. She'd read Kira's file and had made assumptions about the truth behind Rick's words, but she hadn't known the full, human picture until now. She saw each situation, each case, as clearly right or wrong, but there were variations of which she wasn't aware. How much of what she saw was factual and how much was colored by her perception? She knew her brother felt as much contempt for her as she felt for him. Goody-Goody Hargrove. Was she really the one who saw the clearest? She was too exhausted to get out of the shade and into the truth.

She needed to get out of this room and away from these files. She went over to her desk and opened the laptop.

"What are you doing?" Kira asked. She'd been silent while Abby mulled over her words, and now she twisted in her chair to watch Abby as she typed.

"Looking up Sal Hendrick's new address," she said. "Ah, here he is. Living in an apartment on Jackson. Not exactly an upgrade from his old house."

"I'm sure Milford bought his old one for practically nothing, if the alternative was going to jail for selling drugs."

"I believe you're right," Abby said. She held out her hand and pulled Kira to her feet. "But I'm tired of reading and forming hypotheses. I want to hear his version of what actually happened."

"How are we going to find out?" Kira asked as she followed Abby down the stairs.

Abby shrugged. "I'm going to ask him."

She locked the front door behind them. "I'll take you back to your car at the nature center and—"

"No way," Kira said. She grabbed the keys from Abby's hand. "I'll drive us to his apartment, and then we'll take me back to my car."

Abby wanted to protest, but Kira had as much at stake in this situation as she did. Maybe more. There was nothing official about this interview, so Kira might as well tag along. "If there's any sign of danger, you have to listen to me and get the hell out of there, okay? I don't care if you think I'm overbearing and protective. Unless you promise to trust my instincts in this situation, we're not going."

Kira seemed to struggle with Abby's words, but she eventually nodded. "Okay, but only because you're the one with experience."

"Exactly," Abby said. She got in the passenger seat and buckled her seat belt awkwardly with her left hand.

"So, how do you shake the information out of him?" Kira asked. "Do you get out the thumb screws if he doesn't want to talk?"

She sounded like she was joking, but Abby saw a hint of concern on Kira's face. She'd be sensitive to any use of coercion or manipulation, especially given her own experience with Dale and the cops. Abby wouldn't have gotten physical with the guy anyway, but she'd need to be especially careful how she approached him with Kira along.

"I'm not planning to toss him around the room until he confesses," she said, matching Kira's light tone. "We just need to get some confirmation of our suspicions before we go further along this avenue of investigation. I'll ask him what happened, and we'll decide if we think his answer is truthful or not, whatever it is. Most likely, if he really was set up like we think, he'll be eager to tell his side of the story to someone who is willing to listen."

Kira drove the short distance from her house to Hendrick's, and she and Abby walked from the visitor's parking area to the back unit of the apartment complex. The surrounding fence was painted a tan color, but there were multiple white patches where graffiti had been covered up. The landscaping was plain and unkempt, and the garbage bin overflowed into the parking lot. Some of the units had balconies, but they were mostly filled with toys and plastic storage containers so they looked like outdoor junk closets. Abby and Kira walked up a rickety staircase to the second floor.

Abby knocked on the door, positioning herself so she'd be able to protect Kira if Sal was inclined to barge through it and into them, and she was surprised by the short, middle-aged man who answered the door. He resembled Mr. Rogers, complete with cardigan, more than some drug-selling kingpin.

"Mr. Hendrick?" she asked.

"Yes. Who are you?"

"I'm Lynn," she said, using her middle name instead of the more recognizable Abby in case he contacted the department after she left. "I'd like to ask a few questions about the drug charges you faced before you sold your house."

"I don't buy or sell drugs."

"I know," Abby said. Her quiet words seemed to startle him

out of his defiance. He had been prepared for disbelief or for an argument, and she'd deflated his belligerence with her immediate acceptance of his statement.

"You're a cop?"

She shrugged. "I'm familiar with the officer who found coke on your property," she said vaguely. "What would have happened if you hadn't agreed to sell your house?"

He looked past her to Kira. "Who are you?"

Kira met his gaze with her direct one. "I'm someone who was screwed over by the same cop."

Abby gave her a quick smile and turned back to Sal. Kira's honesty seemed to have won him over.

"I don't want trouble. I was warned not to talk to anyone about what happened, and to be thankful I was only arrested for possession, not intent, so if anyone else comes asking about this, I'll deny it. But he had two bags of coke in his hands. One was small, the other was big. He said I had the choice about which one he'd happen to find in my pocket. If I agreed to take an offer for my house in the next week, he'd find the little one. If not, I'd be going away for a long time."

"I'm sorry about what happened to you, Mr. Hendrick. I won't tell anyone what you said here today."

"I don't want trouble," he repeated.

"I know." Abby motioned for Kira to go down the stairs ahead of her. She was shaking inside, imagining her brother hefting the two bags of coke in his hands while Sal stood by helpless to do anything but agree to his terms. "Thank you for talking to us."

"What are you thinking?" Kira asked her when they got in the car. "Are you going to buy him a house to make up for this?"

"I don't know," Abby said. She felt overwhelmed by the information he'd given her. She'd expected it after their research, but it had been abstract then. Now there was a face attached to the report in her mind. She'd been suspicious of her brother's dealings with Hendrick from the start, but she hadn't realized the extent of the damage. "I don't know how to make this right."

Kira took her hand as she drove, and Abby appreciated the

gesture. She was caught up in the relief of having someone else with her to share the frustration and helplessness she often faced when she dug into the cases her family had botched, and she was almost too distracted to see the Tacoma police car several places behind them when they stopped at a light. She told herself not to be so paranoid. She was in Tacoma, so a patrol car was hardly a sight worthy of concern. But still, she watched it turn to the right when Kira turned left into the nature center's lot.

"What now?" Kira asked.

"I'm not sure. I'll need to think this through and decide what the next step should be."

"Come home with me," Kira said. She blushed and stammered as she rushed through an explanation of her words. "To dinner. With me and Julie. She'll be home from school soon. She'd be glad to see you, and besides, you can't cook like that."

She gestured at Abby's wrapped arm. Abby's thoughts were as much on the possible interpretations of Kira's first statement as on the patrol car that might have been following them. Either way, she was going to make yet another concession to her carefully formulated set of personal rules.

"I'd love to."

CHAPTER EIGHTEEN

Abby parked along the curb behind Kira's car and followed her to the porch. She was watching both ends of the street in case a patrol car drove by, and she almost didn't notice how vigilant Kira was as well. She wasn't looking down the block like Abby was, but she was scanning the yard near her front steps, where a recently trimmed rhododendron grew. Abby encouraged people to be aware of their surroundings, but she knew the reason for Kira's nervous-looking glances. She was angry that Kira had to feel afraid at her own home, but she hoped her presence for one evening would help a little. She was certain Kira would balk at any sign of protectiveness from Abby, so she didn't mention the possibility of a car following them, and she definitely wasn't going to tell Kira that the reason she had accepted the dinner invitation was because she worried about her.

Abby wasn't just worried about Kira's safety, but also about her own. She had been semi-teasing when she had offered to grill steaks for Kira, but the thought of having her over for an intimate dinner was very appealing. Then she had barely considered the wisdom behind accepting Kira's invitation. She was being pulled closer, and she was losing the ability to resist. Or the desire to resist...

Abby went into the living room and stared around her. The space was as full of warmth as her own was barren. The furniture was nice, but plain. A green sofa and a plaid recliner, a few end tables and lamps, a TV. Standard and unremarkable. The objects scattered around the room gave it life. Julie's coat, thrown over the back of the couch. Horse figurines and an open math book with a sheet of penciled calculations next to it. A towering pile of field guides and a dozen different leaves and branches on the coffee table. A backgammon board, set and ready for a game. Abby had a vision of Kira and Julie working and playing here together in the evenings. She'd love to be part of something like this, but where would she fit in? Would she be stretched out in the recliner, with a stack of old crime reports next to her? Would she share details about her grandfather's sketchy relationship with a prostitute while Julie and Kira told her about their days?

She didn't belong in this type of normal.

"Why don't you sit in here while I cook," Kira said. She gestured toward the stools placed near the kitchen's island. "I'll get these out of your way..."

Abby perched on one of the stools while Kira gathered the papers that had been strewn across the granite countertop. She picked up a form when it slipped from Kira's grasp and read the address at the top of the page. It was a soil analysis from Milford's wetland. She handed it back to Kira.

"Why wetlands?" she asked. She needed to focus on the murder, not on the floral scent of Kira when she stood so close. The fragrance permeated Abby's car now, and she had barely been able to focus on driving as she had followed Kira here. She had to get her mind back on track. Once she found out who had killed Tad Milford, she would know whether Kira was safe or not and how she was connected. The wetland property seemed to be at the heart of the crime, and Abby needed to learn as much as she could about it. "What drew you to this field?"

Kira looked thoughtful as she got a bottle of wine and a corkscrew out of a cupboard. "I was a sophomore in college, but I hadn't picked a major yet. I was torn between chemistry and biology. Do you like chianti?" Abby nodded and Kira opened the bottle with one smooth twist of the corkscrew. She poured them each a glass and took a sip before she continued. "I didn't date much in high school since I was more concerned about grades than anything else, but I had a more active social life once I got to college. A few boyfriends, girlfriends. A little pregnant..."

She laughed and took another drink of wine. "I can't imagine my life without Julie now, but at the time I was frightened about what my grandparents would say, and what would happen with school. I came back here from Eugene to tell them the news in person, but I was dreading the conversation so I stopped at a yogurt shop in a strip mall near home. It had been built while I was at college, and I was sitting there eating a bowl of strawberry frozen yogurt with mini chocolate chips when I remembered how I used to play on the property when I was in grade school. There had been a small pond and lots of plants and birds and trees. I'd even seen raccoons and salamanders."

Abby toyed with the stem of her glass while she watched Kira lose herself in a far-off memory. She could picture the little girl Kira had been, running along a mossy path and exploring the banks of the pond while birds sang in the trees. She took a drink of the dry red wine and let the hints of cherry and violets linger on her tongue. Better than any painkillers her doctor could give her.

"I was stunned by the loss," Kira continued. She went to the fridge and pulled out an onion and several packaged items. "Hundreds of types of birds and plants had been wiped out, replaced by a cement lot and an ugly building. All so I could eat a bowl of artificially colored frozen yogurt. I went to my grandparents' house with a new mission. I wanted to save these areas, keep them from all going the same way as the one I had played in as a child. I had been worried I might need to leave school, but after making the decision about what I wanted to do with my life, I knew I couldn't. How could I raise a child in this world without fighting to preserve what was valuable and beautiful in it for her to enjoy? Anyway, my grandparents didn't just support me emotionally, but they went back to Eugene with me and we raised Julie together."

Abby watched Kira chop some pancetta and toss it into a hot frying pan. She spun the wineglass in a circle on the countertop. Sitting here and listening to Kira's soft alto as she spoke made memories resurface in Abby's mind, too. She had sat on the peninsula in her mom's kitchen. Doing her homework, talking about friends and school. But Kira's story ended with a tale of generations coming together to make an individual family stronger, and to make the world a better place. Abby's ended just the opposite.

"I didn't go the traditional route with Julie. Marriage, or even being a single mom. But I wouldn't change a thing. She has wonderful memories of living with the three of us, and I'm grateful for that. I might have been looking too hard for a replacement for our extended family when I met Dale, but still—even my experience with her made us stronger."

Kira diced an onion and added it to the pan. She watched Abby twirl the wineglass and wondered what was on her mind. She had noticed Abby's tendency to fidget with increasing intensity as her mind worked through some agitation or another, but she kept silent. A broken glass could be replaced, and Abby seemed to need a kinesthetic outlet when her thoughts were troubling. Kira had a few ideas about other outlets she might provide for Abby's fidgeting needs, but she was definitely keeping those to herself.

She dumped a container of Manzanilla and Kalamata olives onto her cutting board and gave them a rough chop. She wanted to ask about Abby's career choice, too, but she had a feeling the answer was tied in with the secret lair in Abby's house. "What would you have done?" she asked instead. "If you hadn't joined the police force?"

"Something with horses. I was planning to apply to WSU's vet school when I…changed my mind."

"Hey, Mom. Hi, Abby! I was wondering whose car was in front of the house." Julie burst through the door, dropping coat and backpack and shoes as she traveled through the living room. Her arrival kept Kira from saying she was sorry that Abby had given up her dream. All for the best, since she knew Abby wouldn't want her pity.

"Hi, Jules. How was school?"

Kira winked at Abby as Julie chattered on about her upcoming field trip, her friend's new outfit, and the pop quiz in her English class—totally unfair since Ms. Campbell knew she was showing at the fair this week—while she busied herself getting a snack from the fridge. Kira was accustomed to the way Julie filled the empty space in the house until it felt ready to burst with her enthusiasm and energy, but Abby seemed startled by the crackling change in the atmosphere. Julie handed each adult a brownie before she plopped on the stool next to Abby with one for herself and a glass of milk.

"What's for dinner? Is Abby staying?"

"Flatbread pizzas, and yes, she is." Kira took a bite of her brownie and saw Abby look at her with raised eyebrows before she did the same. "Don't worry about eating dessert first. These are made with pureed prunes and wheat germ, so they're healthy enough to eat as a meal."

"Hmm. I can barely tell," Abby said as she chewed the brownie. "They taste almost like the real thing."

Julie laughed and finished her milk in a quick gulp. "Hey, what happened to your arm? Did you fall off Legs while you were chasing a felon?"

Abby looked at her as if asking how much she wanted Julie to know about the accident. Part of Kira wanted to hide the truth from Julie, to protect her innocence, but she chose honesty instead. "Someone gave Legs an illegal substance, Julie. It made her act a little crazy, and Abby got hurt."

"How's poor Legs?"

"She'll be fine," Abby said. Kira watched her rub her palm again, just above the edge of the bandage. "She's staying with our vet for a while."

Kira sprinkled some pine nuts on a baking sheet and put them in the oven to brown. Julie was less reticent than Kira, and she was peppering Abby with questions about the accident. Abby managed, without much difficulty, to turn the conversation back to Julie and her upcoming championship classes with Nirvana. Kira sliced a lump of fresh mozzarella and wondered how the evening had spun away from her original goal for it. She had been concerned about Abby's pale cheeks and weary eyes, and she had guessed that without her invitation, Abby would have had a beer and some aspirin for dinner.

She also hadn't been able to bear the thought of Abby sitting alone in her house, probably working on more files until she fell asleep in her desk chair. Kira had wanted to take care of her, partly in repayment for Abby's kindness on Saturday, but mostly because Kira wanted to be with her. To soothe her weariness and to learn more about her and the person she'd been before she took up her crusade. But watching Abby and Julie talk, listening to their laughter, gave Kira something she hadn't expected. A sense of family, of home.

Kira nearly took a slice off her index finger as she was cutting. She shouldn't feel that way about Abby. About a woman devoted not only to her dangerous career as a police officer, but even more to her secret battle to save the world from her family. Kira admired Abby for what she was doing, but she didn't want Abby's cause to infiltrate her life. Because where Abby went, her family's past was sure to follow. Kira interrupted Julie and Abby's discussion about the best way to slow down Nirvana's trot during the showmanship class.

"Come over here, you two, and make your pizzas." Keep focused on the mundane. Food and wine, Julie's homework, the protection of her own heart. Daily life. She topped her flatbread with an orderly arrangement of olives and pancetta bits and pine nuts, covered with a thin layer of mozzarella. Julie used her condiments to make flowers and smiley faces, and Abby topped her cheese with an intricate picture of a galloping horse.

Even the everyday was more fun with Abby there. Except for Julie's friends and an occasional volunteer who stayed for a meal, Kira didn't invite people into her house often. She was social enough and enjoyed her friendships, but home had become a sanctuary for her. A private world she shared with Julie and hadn't expected to share with another woman ever again. Yet here was Abby—so different and so unsuitable, with her family ties that kept her in bondage and her take-charge attitude—and she somehow *fit*.

While the pizzas heated in the oven, Kira made a quick salad using some purslane and cress she'd found in one of her wetlands. They ate dinner off trays in the living room while they watched an episode of *Jeopardy*, competing to see who could come up with the correct questions the quickest, and then Julie did her homework while Abby and Kira played a game of backgammon. Kira would have figured that having Abby over for dinner would have been like having a guest, someone to entertain. Instead, Abby slid right into their normal evening routine as if she'd been there for years.

"Thank you for this," Abby said when they were out on Kira's back porch, sitting on a wrought-iron bench and wrapped in blankets to ward off the evening chill. Julie had disappeared into her bedroom with the phone as soon as her homework was finished, and Kira had poured the last of the wine into their glasses.

"For beating your ass in backgammon?" Kira asked. "You're quite welcome."

"I still think you have weighted dice. How many double sixes did you roll in those three games?"

Kira shrugged, feeling the warmth and pressure of Abby's arm against hers as she moved. "I didn't cheat, I just have incredible skills. It's all in the wrist." She mimed tossing the dice with a flourish, and then gestured toward Abby's wounded arm with an exaggerated gasp. "Oh, sorry. No wonder you lost."

She felt the vibrations of their shared laughter as Abby slid her arm along the bench behind her shoulders. Abby stroked a stray strand of Kira's hair, tracing the edge of her earlobe, and Kira leaned into her hand. Abby's fingers only skimmed her surface, but the sensation traveled all the way into Kira's bones, into her heart. Abby's touch, like everything else about the evening, felt too right. Kira knew she was supposed to fight her urge to want Abby—her company, her touch, her kisses—but she couldn't remember why. Abby was bossy and domineering, yes, but she had also shown her vulnerable side. Her strength was real and steadfast, not just for show or to mask insecurity, like Dale's had been. Kira had been thinking earlier about how Abby would bring her fight for justice into any relationship she had, but Kira brought along a few battles of her own. To conserve as many wetland areas as she could. To remain strong and independent. She'd expect those to be part of the life she built with a partner, just like Abby would expect to have her needs respected. Kira sighed and felt her defenses weakening as Abby tugged her hair loose from its braid and wrapped her fingers in it.

"Seriously, Kira, thank you for inviting me here tonight. I don't remember the last time I spent time with a normal family."

Kira heard the catch in Abby's voice and she wondered if Abby really did remember that last time. The final moment of innocent family life before she was thrown into her quest. "I'm glad you came," she whispered. The words were too simple to express how happy she was to have Abby here with her instead of alone in her empty house.

Kira sat close against Abby's side and she saw Abby's head move toward hers. She was expecting Abby's kiss, she was waiting for it, but she wasn't prepared for her reaction when their lips finally touched. The contact was brief and tentative, but Kira inhaled sharply and involuntarily. She heard and felt Abby do the same. Kira paused for several breaths, only millimeters from Abby's mouth, and then she closed the distance between them and kissed Abby again.

After the first shock of connection, Kira felt herself melt into the heat of Abby. Kira had thought Abby would be more assertive, taking the lead in romance the same way she would on the job, but instead there was a quiet exchange of roles. Kira was the one to deepen the kiss, angling her head to get better access to Abby's lips. Abby's tongue was the first to brush along Kira's mouth, seeking access. Instead of an onslaught, Kira felt a subtle give-and-take, asking and answering, as their kisses grew more insistent.

When Abby tugged on her hip, Kira willingly shifted onto Abby's lap, straddling her thighs. She felt the pull of still-tender muscles when she knelt on the bench, and the raw chafe of her damaged wrists against the fabric of Abby's shirt. Reminders of hours spent tied in a chair. A moment of claustrophobia hit her when Abby wrapped one arm around her back, holding her close. Kira's muscles tensed, ready to propel her away from Abby and from the confinement of her arm.

"Shh," Abby whispered in her ear. Her hand caressed Kira's

back, and the barely perceivable touch broke through her rising panic and soothed her racing mind.

Kira's body relaxed against Abby and her awareness returned slowly to the present. To her breasts pressed against Abby's. To the heat where her crotch rested on Abby's. As Kira felt Abby's touch heal and calm her, her desire grew proportionately. The more her flight instinct eased, the harder she kissed Abby until she was moaning with obvious pleasure against Kira's mouth. Kira moved her hips in rhythm with her kiss. She wanted more, wanted all Abby could offer.

Kira pulled back. She didn't want to stop, but she wasn't ready to continue, either. Her relationship with Abby had been like riding a whirlwind, erratic and unpredictable, and she needed a moment to catch her breath. She had been prepared to bolt off Abby's lap out of fear. Once she'd allowed Abby's touch to heal her instead, she'd sought more of the balm Abby offered for her wounds. Both were related to her abduction, and Kira needed time to figure out her confusing reactions to a wonderful and much-desired kiss. She wanted Abby—she'd been acutely aware of her attraction since their first meeting. But having Abby here in her home and picturing her settling into this life was more than Kira could handle. A fling to release pent-up energy was one thing. Letting anyone, even Abby, too close to her shielded home life was too significant a decision to be made based on her arousal alone.

"Um, that was…" Kira searched for the right words to describe Abby's spellbinding kisses.

"A wonderful end to a very nice evening?" Abby said with a question in her voice.

Kira nodded, appreciating Abby's willingness not to push. She ran her hands through her mussed hair and quickly braided it again. "I should say good night to Julie."

"And I should go home." Abby stood up and wobbled slightly, reaching for the back of the bench with her left hand.

Kira put her palm against Abby's cheek and felt the flush of warmth that wasn't just from their kisses. She shouldn't be on her feet after her accident and surgery, let alone out on the roads. "You'll stay here," she said. "Take my bed and I'll sleep on the couch. I'll drive us to the fair tomorrow so we can watch Julie's championship classes and you can check on your team."

"I…okay," Abby said. The fact that she didn't fight Kira's orders worried her more than Abby's ashy complexion and her drooping shoulders. Kira helped her back into the house and showed her to the bedroom. She was tempted to stay—just to hold Abby—but she shut the door between them instead. Abby was functioning on willpower alone now, and she needed rest. Kira checked on Julie and then wrapped herself in a pile of blankets on the couch. She thought of Abby only a few steps away. In her bed. Maybe naked? Kira turned out the lights and sighed. It was going to be a long and sleepless night.

CHAPTER NINETEEN

Kira woke up groggy after a fitful night of sleep, but Abby emerged from her bedroom looking refreshed and as flawless as a painting. Her cheeks had color again, and she strategized with Julie about the day's classes while she ate a big bowl of cereal with her left hand. The only proof of her mishap with Legs was revealed when she let Kira change the bandage on her wrist. Abby seemed unfazed by the sight of her wound, but Kira stared at the neat row of stitches and could only see what might have happened—how much worse Abby could have been hurt.

Abby proclaimed herself fit to drive, and Julie elected to go with her, of course, so Kira followed them with her own car. Too much time alone, to think. Last night had been great. Comforting and stimulating at the same time. Abby had seemed to belong in the family atmosphere, but Kira had to acknowledge that it wasn't her reality. It had been a nice fantasy, fueled by her attraction to Abby, but dreams had to end when the sun rose. And what dreams they'd been, starting with the kisses she and Abby had shared, but moving far beyond them.

After a quick stop to feed Nirvana her breakfast, Kira went with Abby and Julie to the police barn. Don took Julie on a short tour to meet Fancy and the other horses, and Kira hoped he wouldn't encourage Julie's new ardor for search-and-rescue work. She was proud of her daughter for wanting to help people but had been a parent long enough to know that this week's passion would be replaced by something new soon enough.

Abby took Kira into the tack stall and introduced her to the officers. "Kira, this is Rachel, Cal, and Billie. Everyone, this is Kira Lovell."

Kira shook hands with them. "Nice to meet you."

"You, too, Kira," Rachel said. She kept hold of her hand for a moment after shaking it and looked at the still-visible slash of red on her wrists. "Zip ties, huh? Nasty. You might have a little scarring, but it'll be barely noticeable." She let go of Kira's hand. "How about you, Lieutenant? Are you taking it easy with your wrist, like the doctor told you?"

"Of course. I'm obeying his every command. For the most part."

"Right," Cal said. "I'm sure Kira could tell us otherwise."

Kira laughed with the others, but she wasn't sure how she felt about their assumptions. Did they think of her and Abby as a couple? Sure, she and Abby seemed to have a strong physical attraction. Kira had felt it from the start and she'd seen the look in Abby's eyes when they had kissed last night. Even more, she'd felt the connection when they talked or laughed together. But Abby's reality was here, where intrigue and danger were met with confidence and even an eagerness to attack any threats.

Kira sat on a trunk that had the police logo on it while Abby and the other riders talked about their strategy for the night's patrol. They were acting as if the incident with Legs had been meant to harm the group as a whole, but Kira—and Abby, too, she believed—thought differently. The act was personal. The intent had been to hurt Abby specifically, Kira was sure of it. But even if Abby hadn't been the sole target, her job put her in a dangerous position. Worse, in her self-appointed role of vigilante, she was putting herself at risk without the department to back her up. At least her mounted unit seemed determined to keep her safe.

Kira left the tack stall while they discussed security for the day's demonstration rides. Julie was still talking to Don, no doubt grilling him about Nirvana's future as a search-and-rescue horse. Kira walked past them and ducked under the tape at the end of the barn. She leaned against the wall and watched the quiet activity as the fair came to life. It was still early, but a few spectators wandered around with the 4-H kids and their horses. Sounds of splashing water and the occasional neigh accompanied the pre-competition routines of feeding and bathing the horses. Kira loved getting up early with Julie on horse-show days. She'd sip her coffee and watch while the competitors prepared. They were busy mornings, but quiet, since most of the kids were still half-asleep.

Kira liked watching Abby at work, too. When she talked to her mounted team and when she had questioned Sal, she changed subtly. Her voice took on more authority, but in a natural way, not like she was injecting more force for show. Her posture shifted so she gave the impression of strength and immovability. She was damned sexy when she was in her element and in uniform. But her element was a violent one. A world of criminals, danger, and corruption. Things Kira avoided at all costs in her own life. Abby plunged in head-on. Kira couldn't reconcile her conflicted feelings. When Abby had been home with her last night, playing games and eating dinner as if she was part of the family, Kira had been afraid to give in to her desire. But here, where Abby was overpoweringly strong and clearly moving in a different world from Kira's, she was ready to find the nearest empty stall and rip Abby's clothes off. This place was more neutral than Kira's home sanctuary. The fair belonged to both of them, and Kira felt safer allowing her fantasies freedom here than she had been able to do last night.

"Sorry I was in there so long, but I needed to catch up with the unit." Abby leaned her shoulder against the wall beside Kira. Even in her civilian clothes, she had the aura of authority that even some cops in full uniform weren't able to project.

"It's all right. I just needed some fresh air. Should we rescue Don from Julie?"

"She went out the other end of the aisle. She's going to the arena to check her pattern for the showmanship class and meet us back at Nirvana's stall. Are you sure you're okay?"

"Coffee would help," Kira said. And a bucket of ice water dumped over her head. Kira had trouble thinking when Abby was so close. Abby must have used Kira's shampoo, because Kira's head was filled with the scent of gardenias every time she inhaled. Abby's hair was held off her face with one of Kira's gold clips, but it had a softer look where it framed her cheekbones than it did when she had it slicked back in her usual twist. The intense look on Abby's face made something inside Kira melt into warm liquid, and the intimacy of having Abby in her bathroom and using her personal items was more erotic than Kira could have anticipated.

Abby leaned a little closer, and Kira stopped breathing for a few thudding heartbeats. Was Abby a good match for her, for the life she wanted? Her body seemed more determined than ever to betray her common sense and keep her mind from taking the time to make a sensible decision. Maybe she was better off listening to the nerve endings clamoring for Abby's touch.

"I know what will wake you up," Abby said. Her shoulder brushed against Kira's where it rested on the wall.

Kira cleared her throat before she spoke. "Better than coffee?"

"Oh yes. Come on. We're going to ride the roller coaster."

Abby led her down the aisle to Nirvana's stall. Julie was sitting on a bucket in the corner, studying a piece of paper.

"Will you need us for anything during the next fifteen minutes?" Abby asked her.

"No, thanks. I need to memorize my pattern now."

"How does it look?" Kira asked. She went into the stall and Julie handed her the paper. Nirvana came over and sniffed her pockets, looking for a treat.

"Nothing we haven't done before," Julie said. Her voice had a confident, optimistic note. She had practiced for this class all year. Of course, Nirvana had come very well trained from Abby, but Julie had done more than her share of the preparation.

"You'll do great." Kira gave her back the paper, and then she took a peppermint out of her pocket and gave it to Nirvana. "I'm proud of both of you."

"Thanks, Mom. Are you going somewhere?"

"I'm taking your mom on the roller coaster," Abby said. "She doesn't get sick on rides, does she?"

"Not usually," Julie said with a smile. "She might squeeze your hand to pieces, though."

"Well, my wrist is already in pieces, so I guess I'll be fine. We'll be back before your class."

They walked down the brightly decorated aisle. Each county's 4-H team had banners and matching nameplates outside the horses' stalls, and most of the riders were wearing jackets or T-shirts with their county logos. Posters illustrating everything from riding safety to parts of the horse's hoof decorated the walls, with various ribbons and awards taped on them. Julie had spent hours on her Horses of the World display, with its map and drawings of different breeds of horses and their countries of origin. Kira pointed out the poster to Abby as they walked by.

Even on a weekday morning, there were clusters of people in line at most of the rides. Abby bought them each a handful of tickets.

"Can I interest you in a deep-fried stick of butter?" she asked. "I owe you for last night's dinner."

"Ugh," Kira said with a grimace. "I'll definitely get sick on you during the ride if you feed me one of those first."

Abby made a show of hurrying Kira past the busy food stand. "That was a close one. Thanks for the warning."

"You're welcome." Kira stopped by a booth with a sign for earthquake burgers. A guy came away from the counter with a burger with the circumference of a large dinner plate. "Say, I could eat one of those first, though. We didn't have much for breakfast."

Abby gave her a look of mock horror. "This ride with you is getting more terrifying by the minute. Let's go before I lose my nerve."

Kira relaxed as they got to the near-empty twisting queue designed to keep the peak hour crowds in order. "I'll race you," she said, starting to run toward the narrow opening before she finished her sentence. She heard Abby's gasp behind her.

"Cheater!"

Kira grabbed the railing and used it to pull herself along as she ran through the serpentine path, but Abby grabbed her around the waist with her good hand at the second turn and pushed ahead. Kira followed for several yards, but since she didn't have room to pass, she ducked under the railing and cut across two more lanes. She came to a stop when she reached the end of the line of people and caught her breath while Abby slowly caught up to her.

"And you cheated again," Abby said. "Twice in one short race. That must be a record."

Kira shrugged. "Nowhere in the rules did it state that I had to stay in the lanes."

"I don't know what rule book you were using, but the universal line rules are clear about no cuts."

Kira grinned. Julie would have been embarrassed beyond belief to see her mother acting like a child, but something about Abby brought out her sillier side. She wasn't sure why, since Abby was one of the most by-the-book people she'd ever met. Her life was devoted to mending broken rules, but somehow she made Kira feel carefree. She'd gone through one of the most traumatic experiences of her life this weekend, but she'd also laughed with Abby more than she had in months. She'd need to think more about the dichotomy another time. Right now, Abby was standing close behind her, with her left hand resting lightly on Kira's hip. All other thoughts faded away, and Kira focused on the spot of contact between them. Abby's touch aroused her. There wasn't any ambiguity in that area.

She handed her strip of tickets to the bored-looking attendant, and Abby tugged her toward the last row. Kira liked sitting in the back seat, too, where she could feel the whip of the turns more than in the front. She loved modern roller coasters with their loops and sleek metal tracks, like the one she and Julie had been on where she had flown in a harness like Superman, but the sound and feel of an old-fashioned wooden coaster couldn't be beat.

"Built in 1935," Abby read off the plaque hanging over the boarding area. "Makes you think, doesn't it."

"Makes you think what?" Kira asked. Abby had kept contact with her since the end of their race, always some part touching, whether hand or arm or torso, and Kira's body grew taut as Abby's contact with her continually shifted from place to place. She didn't know where to expect the next jolt from Abby's touch, and the not-knowing had her skin tingling with anticipation.

"About how far we've come since then with materials and engineering. I'm surprised we don't have to sign a release to go on the ride." Abby leaned close to Kira's ear as she spoke, and Kira felt Abby's thigh rub against the back of hers when she moved.

"Don't even bother trying to scare me," she said. "It won't work." She wasn't lying. The ride didn't scare her at all. Her reaction to Abby's closeness? It terrified her because she was beginning to realize her body alone wasn't yearning for Abby. Her heart was getting involved as well.

A rusted and dented train of orange cars screeched to a stop in front of them. Kira and Abby got in the last car, and a carnival worker snapped the bar in place over their knees. Abby rested her bandaged wrist on her lap, and she had her other hand on the seat between them, against—and slightly under—Kira's thigh.

Kira pulled on the bar to make sure it was locked in place. "I'm surprised we don't have to wear seat belts," she said as the rest of the cars in their train were filled.

"I thought you weren't scared," Abby said, inching her hand until it was tucked under Kira's leg, just below her ass.

"I'm not," Kira said. "I'm merely being safety conscious."

Abby laughed, and the sound was swallowed up as they started to ascend the first hill. Slowly, with the steady click of a pulley system. Kira felt their weight threaten to pull them back as the protesting chain hauled them upward. The steep vantage point offered a great view of the fairgrounds, but Kira couldn't extend her awareness beyond the feel of Abby's insistent hand. When they reached the top of the hill, Kira gave in to the pressure and shifted her weight to her left hip, allowing Abby freer access. Abby leaned toward her, close enough so Kira could hear her quick breaths, and she curved her hand under Kira's thigh until her palm rested against Kira's crotch.

The first hill was a tease, only a short drop before the car's momentum brought it up to the second crest, but it dragged a sound somewhere between a gasp and a shout from Kira. The next plunge came faster, giving Kira the feeling of free fall. Abby's grip tightened, and Kira knew how wet she must feel. The thought of Abby's hand on her, damp with the moisture soaking through her jeans, made her ache for a deeper touch. She wanted her clothes off and Abby's fingers pushed inside her, but the restriction of touch and limited movement were more erotic than she had thought possible. Her body had never responded this way before, going insane for a touch that had less skin contact than holding someone's hand.

Kira was thrown against Abby as they rocketed into the first curve, and Abby's touch stilled while Kira's weight was on her. The car came out of the turn and plummeted down the steepest hill without a pause for breath. Kira was flung away from Abby as they straightened and dropped simultaneously, and Abby took the opportunity to tighten her grip, flexing her fingers against Kira. Kira gripped the safety bar to keep from crawling right out of her skin, and she ground down onto Abby's hand with an almost frenzied movement.

A hard turn to the left pinned Kira against the side of the car while Abby found a rhythm that matched the beat of the metal wheels as they spun over the joins in the track. The series of shorter but more rapid hills on the far side of the coaster built the pressure inside Kira. Space was in motion, but her consciousness was grounded on Abby, in Abby. She heard Abby's voice call her name as they whipped around the final, steep curve and dropped into the tunnel with a burst of energy. The sudden, firm pressure from Abby's fingers was timed perfectly with the last stomach-dropping descent, and Kira climaxed with a shocked gasp. The car jolted to a stop, and suddenly the world around her sprang to life again. People were climbing out of the car, laughing and talking. Abby was helping her to her feet and toward the exit. As soon as they were off the wooden platform, Kira stopped to rest with one hand against the fence surrounding the ride.

"That was fun," Abby said, in her nonchalant way.

Kira gave a strangled laugh and shook her head. "Fun? You're insane."

Abby looked at her with a furrowed brow. Not quite a frown,

but maybe an expression of concern. "I couldn't stop," she said. "I touched you, and you were so hot, so wet. The feel of you pulsing against my palm…I…" She stopped and shook her head. "Should I apologize for what I did?"

"God, no," Kira said. "Don't say you're sorry. Maybe we rushed into this, and maybe I'll have second thoughts later, but I didn't want you to stop."

They started back toward the 4-H barn. Kira smoothed her hair and retied her ponytail. She must look flushed and a little bewildered, but so did most of the people getting off rides. Abby was quiet as they walked, and Kira didn't know if she was having regrets.

"I was tied down this weekend," she said. "Locked in a trunk. I felt scared and trapped. I guess I needed a wild and freeing experience, and you gave me one. It was good for me."

Abby smiled at her. "It was damned good for me, too."

Kira was about to respond when Abby's brother stepped in front of them. They both jerked to a stop.

"Well, well. What a pair you two make. An accomplice to murder and a self-righteous bitch. She must be a damned good lay to make you compromise your sacred morals, little sis."

Abby stepped in front of Kira, just like she'd done when Dale had accosted her. "Shut up, Rick, and leave us alone. She had nothing to do with Milford's shooting."

He leaned around Abby and pointed at Kira. "Don't think his death means you get to save your precious swamp. I'll build on it, even if I have to pour the cement myself."

"I said leave her alone." Abby's voice was low and threatening. Kira wasn't surprised when Rick took a step back. She wanted to as well.

"Tad had the names of all your fanatic environmentalist friends. As soon as I find out which one killed him, I'll make them pay."

Rick walked away, leaving Abby and Kira in the center of a ring of people who had stopped to gawk at the argument. They slowly dissipated until Kira and Abby were alone again.

"What did he mean, Kira?" she asked. "What names?"

"I have no idea." Kira couldn't get past his accusations. Did he think one of her volunteers shot Milford and then left her tied to the chair? "My people care about wetlands, but not enough to kill for them."

"Kira, I know. But we need to find out what information Milford had before Rick gets to it."

"How?"

"We have to get Milford's files."

CHAPTER TWENTY

Abby paced the hallway in the police station near the visitor's entrance while she waited for Kira to arrive. She had been moving on autopilot since Rick had accosted them on the midway the day before. Somehow, she'd managed to hold herself together for the competition, and she'd cheered as Julie and Nirvana had left the ring with another reserve champion ribbon in Showmanship and a fourth place ribbon for Stock Seat. The 4-H riders and horses were required to leave as soon as the championship classes were finished, so the stalls could be prepared for another group of competitors that would be arriving the next day. Abby had offered to help them take Nirvana back to her home barn, but she was relieved when Kira said no. Abby wouldn't have been much help with her right wrist out of commission. Even less useful was her mental state. She was furious with Rick. She had experienced various strong emotions over the years when dealing with her family—disgust, contempt, anger—but never the white-hot rage she'd felt when he publicly attacked Kira. Abby was nearly frozen by her own response, and by the growing attachment to Kira that had provoked it. Abby had gone from ecstasy to distress in a matter of seconds, and even now, she was still reeling from the confrontation with Rick.

Her body was still hypersensitive after touching Kira. But something deeper had been touched at dinner the previous evening. She had accepted the invitation because she'd wanted to make sure Kira was safe and hadn't been followed to her home yet again. But the evening had turned out to be unexpectedly beneficial to *her*. Nutritious food, fun company. Abby had felt herself slipping into the family unit even as part of her hung back and watched from the sidelines. Kira's kiss had drawn her in completely, though, and if Abby hadn't been nearly asleep on her feet, she'd have wanted to immerse every part of her into Kira. As it was, she had needed all her remaining strength to keep from going back into the living room where Kira slept.

Abby saw Kira walking across the lobby. She made Abby lose control, her perspective. Now she was dealing with life—Rick, her desire for Kira—in a gut-level, reactionary way. She needed distance to help her regain her composure, her calculating assessment of the world around her and her role in it. Kira made her stomach drop more wrenchingly than the roller coaster. The feeling was an exciting one, no doubt, but it challenged Abby's comfort zone too much.

"Hey," Abby said when Kira came through the glass door. She stepped close to Kira and spoke in a low voice. The intimacy of having Kira in her personal space was overwhelming to Abby, but she didn't move away. Kira gave her the same feeling as taking a deep, cleansing breath. Her tight muscles relaxed and the world became still, even as her body responded to Kira's in a shockingly electric way.

"I was thinking about you last night," Abby said. "Did you get Nirvana home safely?"

"Yes," Kira said. "I think she was glad to be back in her own stall."

"I'm sure she was." Abby frowned. She needed to take a breath without feeling Kira everywhere inside. "Bryan Carter is waiting for us, but do you mind if we talk first? Just for a few minutes."

Kira nodded, and they walked in silence to Abby's office. She shut the door behind them and sat across from Kira. "About yesterday—"

Kira held up her hand and stopped Abby. "Please don't apologize again. It was amazing. But I don't think I'm ready for anything more."

Abby picked up a pen and slid it through her fingers, end over end. She had to keep her hands occupied or she'd reach for Kira. She had been determined to be resolute and follow her common sense instead of the tantalizing memory of how it felt to touch Kira.

Kira faltered. She was staring at the pen in Abby's hand, but she swallowed visibly and looked away before she continued. "I just…I can't be with someone who will always try to take charge. You took over when Dale was bothering me, without giving me a chance to take care of myself. And even after I asked you not to do it again, you did the same thing yesterday."

How could Kira have expected her to do anything *but* defend her? She knew Abby devoted her life to helping the people her brother hurt. Besides, he had been attacking Abby as well yesterday. "Rick is my brother. I know him. It's only natural that I'd be the one to confront him."

"Yes, it's only natural," Kira said. "Abby, you will always step in to rescue me. It's who you are. I don't want to be rescued."

Kira's argument sounded weak to her, but it was said with conviction. Abby wondered if Kira was searching for an excuse to break things off because she was afraid, just like Abby was.

"Abby, you're too complex, too wrapped up in your family's misdeeds, too involved in the world of violence and danger. Too, too much." Kira shook her head and closed her eyes. "I need someone calm and moderate. My emotions have been on a roller coaster long enough."

"You're right," Abby said, her voice sounding as expressionless as her face felt. Suddenly, she wasn't the same woman who had laughed and played with Kira at the fair or at dinner. She felt drained—but it was what she wanted, wasn't it? To let go of the passion and keep the rationality? She wasn't convinced, because the sense of loss left her too hollow and empty. "It's who I am. It's what I expect from a relationship. I protect when necessary, and I'm protected in turn."

Abby stood up. She wasn't going to argue with Kira or try to change her mind. She should be relieved that Kira had been the one to shut the door on a romantic relationship since she had considered doing the same thing, but she didn't feel relieved. All she could feel was Kira's warmth on her hand and the waves of Kira's laughter sliding over and through her.

"Carter is waiting for us," she said. "We should get to work. I won't recognize the names of your associates like you will, but if I see anything related to wetlands, I'll show you. This shouldn't take long since all we need to do is skim through his notes."

Abby locked the office behind them and took Kira to the same conference room she had been in before. There were boxes stacked around the room and on the table. Carter was rearranging a wobbly pile of plastic bins in the corner of the room. Abby could see notebooks and accordion files through the clear plastic. She groaned. She had been wrong—this was going to be a long day.

"This is the last of it," Carter said. "We've started going through the files, but we haven't found anything significant yet. I was glad when Lieutenant Hargrove called yesterday and said you'd be willing to help with this part of the investigation, Ms. Lovell, even though Tad Milford caused you so much pain. Anything you can find that might help us catch a killer will be appreciated."

"I'll do what I can," Kira said.

He handed her a paper to sign. "We're listing you as an expert witness since in your professional capacity you should be able to identify notes relating to Milford's properties and whatever legal or personal trouble he might have been having in regard to them."

Kira signed her name and sat down at the table. Abby sat next to her, reached for one of the boxes, and started to sift through the papers inside.

"It'll take months to go through all this," Abby said as she pulled a wad of handwritten notes out of a box. "Hadn't this guy heard of a computer?"

"Yeah, how crazy does someone have to be to have all these files stored in their office?"

Kira gave her an exaggerated look of disgust and Abby had to laugh, thinking of Kira's reaction when she'd first seen Abby's own room full of files. "It's not crazy. It's a sign of genius," she said.

Kira shook her head. "Hardly," she said, but she was smiling.

Abby turned to her stack of notes and slowly began to decipher Tad's messy handwriting. She felt the world right itself again when her sense of camaraderie with Kira returned. They settled to work in silence, punctuated by the occasional rustle of papers. Carter sat at one end of the table with what looked like account books. Kira and Abby took over the other end and soon had it covered with the piles of notes and lists they'd sorted.

After an hour of squinting at Tad's writing, Abby volunteered to go to the break room to get coffee for everyone. She was on her way back—slowly, since she was dreading her return to the tedious and seemingly useless task of organizing Milford's mess—when Rick's duty partner came around the corner and nearly knocked the paper tray of coffee down the front of her shirt. She used her bandaged right hand to straighten one of the cups and winced at the movement.

"Lieutenant," he said.

"Anderson." She was happy with the bare-minimum exchange, but he seemed to have more on his mind.

"You've got to cut him some slack, Lieutenant."

"Excuse me?" Abby asked. She'd never really liked Anderson. Mostly because of his association with her brother, but also because he seemed morally ambivalent to her. Supporting and idolizing Rick, but not actively involved. On the fence.

"Rick. I heard he said some things that got out of hand yesterday. He's broken up about losing his friend, and he needs his family to understand. You're helping the woman who might be responsible for Tad's death, and Rick was upset about it, that's all. For good reason."

Abby didn't know which part of his little speech to address first. She stared at him without speaking until he shifted away from her an inch or so. "For one thing, do not talk to me about my family or my obligations to them again. More important—and I want you to really hear what I'm saying—Kira was not to blame for Milford's death. She was a victim of his greed and cowardice. If I hear any more rumors around here that she somehow played a part in his shooting, I will hold you personally responsible. Do we understand each other?"

He took another step back and nodded before he turned and walked toward the locker room. *Coward.*

She was glad Kira hadn't been there to hear her defending her yet again. Was Rick's grief just for show, to deflect attention because he had killed his business partner himself? Even if Rick truly was as broken up as Anderson said, he didn't have the right to accuse Kira or to criticize Abby for spending time with her. It was his fault she'd met Kira in the first place. He seemed to see her actions as a family betrayal when she hadn't felt like part of her own family for years. She got to the conference room and paused outside. Just how angry was Rick with her? Angry enough to give her horse a stimulant and cause an accident? She stared down at her wrist. She had broken it against a wooden beam, but who was the real cause of her injury? She sighed. Maybe the answer was in one of Tad's boxes. Or maybe it was completely unconnected to Kira and Milford. She had too many questions and not enough answers. She had to focus on the task at hand and keep going through these scattered notes and disorganized files. Maybe some clue here would lead to the answers she needed—it would be fitting if the answers to this convoluted case would be hidden in the chaos of Tad's paperwork. She bumped the door open with her hip and set the tray of coffee on the table.

Kira and Bryan mumbled their thanks without looking up from the papers they were reading. They worked for the next hour without saying much. Abby and Kira were close enough that every once in a while they'd bump elbows or knees when one or the other reached for another stack of paperwork. Abby tried to ignore the tingling sensation she felt each time they touched and concentrate instead on what she was reading. Tad had collected copious notes on every city official and every zoning law in the county. He had maps of every Tacoma neighborhood with information about home owners and land-use restrictions. He had been a despicable man, but admittedly thorough in his job.

She noticed immediately when Kira went still beside her.

One moment she was relaxed and flicking the corner of a piece of paper while she read, and the next she froze as if made of stone. Abby looked at her and saw the emotions flashing across her face. Whatever Kira was reading disturbed her, and she glanced at Carter and then at the door. She seemed to be considering her chances if she fled with the evidence.

"Kira," Abby said softly. "What is it?"

"Did you find something?" Bryan asked from the other end of the table.

"No…I…well, yes." She hesitated before she pushed the notebook in front of Abby.

Bryan stood over her shoulder and read along with her. Abby felt her blood pressure rise as she turned the pages and saw the personal notes about Kira. There was detailed information about Julie, including her school, her teachers, and her friends. Kira's past attempts to protect wetland areas were analyzed, with explicit information about why she'd won or lost cases and where she'd made compromises with developers. Her volunteers were similarly analyzed, with marks next to each indicating whether they were committed to her cause or able to be dissuaded.

"Look at this," Carter said. He traced his finger along the lines as he read about Keith's arrest for assault during a college protest, when he'd still been a juvenile. Two other volunteers had similar episodes in their pasts. Abby guessed this was the information Rick had been after. Bryan scribbled in his notebook as he read.

"Is all of this public knowledge, Ms. Lovell?" he asked.

"Some of it."

"Then do you have any idea where—"

"Dale," Abby said. Kira nodded. Abby remembered her saying that Dale had been interested in hearing all about her work, all the details. Apparently Tad had been interested, too.

"Dale?" Carter asked.

"Dale Burke, Milford's stepsister," Abby said. Kira was pale and silent. "She and Kira used to date."

"Ah. I'm sorry."

Abby flipped through the pages again. She was bothered by the contrast between the scrupulous details listed in the notebook and Tad's brutish treatment of Kira. "If he had all this information, why did he stoop to kidnapping? Why not use it to fight you legally and with less personal risk?"

Kira shrugged. "I'm better now. I'm smarter than I was back then when I was learning the best ways to work with the county. I'm less emotional and more realistic." She gave a sarcastic snort of laughter and Abby guessed that Kira felt anything but detached right now. Her ability to fight within the system might be more rational, but her reactions to the events of the past week were probably more emotional than she could handle.

Carter cleared his throat. "We can stop for the day." He sounded eager to get moving as he took the notebook from Abby. He'd caught the scent of a possible lead and wanted to follow through with it. "This has been a great help. I hope I can call on you if we need more information."

Kira nodded shortly, and Abby hurried her out of the room.

"She was using me the whole time," Kira said, her voice flat. "No wonder I never met Tad or even heard about him. I'll bet she went to the Earth Day celebration just to meet me, to protect his investments in wetlands."

"I don't know, Kira," Abby said. "Remember what you said about Rick being opportunistic? Maybe he met Dale the night he came to your house and saw a way to use her. No arrest in exchange for information."

"That doesn't make it any better," Kira said.

"No. I guess it doesn't."

"And Keith, what will happen to him?"

"He'll be questioned," Abby said. She'd be surprised if he was the killer. He was idealistic and devoted to Kira and her work. He'd have untied her and not left her there all night. "It's better that the detectives get to him first, and not Rick."

Rick. What was his role in this? He seemed to be everywhere, in every corner of the investigation. If he had shot Tad, he'd have been happy enough to leave Kira behind.

"I need to go," Kira said. She started toward the exit.

"Kira, wait," Abby called after her. Kira paused but didn't turn around. "If there's anything I can do…"

Kira nodded, and walked away.

Chapter Twenty-one

Abby was in the parking lot when Rick arrived for his duty shift. She grabbed his shirt with her left hand and spun him against the car door.

"Really?" he asked with a laugh. "One blow to your wrist and you'd be on your knees and in tears."

"Try it," she said, her voice coming out as a deep growl. She had too much adrenaline in her to care what he did to her hand. She had a momentary flashback to childhood wrestling matches. She'd won those, more often than not. "Besides, you're the one who got me hurt in the first place, aren't you? What's a little more pain among family."

"You're crazy." He gave her a shove with open palms, using only enough force to get some space between them. "What do you want, little sis?"

"Back off with Kira," Abby said. "No more rumors, no more threats. Leave her alone."

"Or else what?"

"Or else I take everything I've learned about our family enterprises to IA. I might not have solid evidence for everything you've done, but I have enough suspicious material to keep you under investigation for years. One more hint that she's involved in Milford's shooting or one step in her direction, and I'll turn over all the files I've collected on you."

He laughed. "Blackmail? I see you carry the Hargrove genes

after all. Don't worry about your girlfriend. I'll beat her at the county hearing when I'm ready to build on my property."

"I'd like to see you try," Abby said. "And one other thing. If you were the one who killed Milford, I will arrest you myself. It'll be a pleasure."

Abby went to her car. Her hands were shaking. She'd spoken more words to her brother over the past week than over the past few years. She'd avoided contact with him as much as possible, until Kira. Abby rubbed her palm, where her bandage ended, as she realized what that meant. She'd do anything for Kira. Contact her family or turn her private shame into public accusations. Anything.

A sharp rap of knuckles on her window made Abby jump. Rick was standing next to her car with a cell phone in his hand.

She started the ignition and lowered the window halfway.

"I said I'd leave your girlfriend alone, and I meant it. But she's trespassing on my property right now. If I find her there, I won't hesitate to shoot her."

"What? She's at your house?" Abby frowned, confused.

He waved his phone. "A friend of mine saw her on Milford's swamp. It's mine, now. You tell her to get lost, or I'll do it myself." He turned and strode toward the station.

Abby tried calling Kira as she drove, but she wasn't answering her cell. She knew the location of the wetland, and she sped toward it. Why had Kira gone directly there? Abby knew she'd been upset about the notebook she'd found, but that didn't explain her actions. Maybe she, like Abby, handled stress by working, and she'd gone to do some research. Unauthorized, trespassing research.

Abby called her again and waited for the voice mail message. "Kira, stay put when you get this message. I'm coming to Milford's property to find you. Be there in ten."

Abby parked her car on the street next to one of the entrances to the acreage. Since she'd been investigating Milford's death, she'd read enough about wetlands in general—and this one in particular— to be an expert. It covered three city blocks and was bounded on all sides by residential and commercial buildings. The land itself was covered with cottonwoods and Garry oaks, with a seasonal lake in the center. A thin strand of wire marked the border, insufficient for keeping out vagrants or curious kids, in a weak attempt to protect the landowner from attractive nuisance lawsuits. Abby stepped over the fence and followed a worn path past the tree line. Once she was inside, she felt as isolated from the rest of the city as she had at Snake Lake. The area was peaceful and sounds were muffled. Maybe Kira had come here for some solitude. A place to think. Abby wouldn't want to interrupt, but Kira was better off being found by her and not by Rick.

She took out her phone again. She was awkward with her left hand, and dropped it when she tried to check for a message from Kira. She bent down to retrieve it and heard something sail over her back with a low whistle. She dropped to all fours just as a carbon arrow thudded into the trunk of an oak right in front of her. She scurried for cover behind the tree, and another arrow whipped past her ear. This one arced through the air until it embedded itself in a rotting stump several yards away.

What the hell. Was Robin Hood after her? More likely her brother coming after Kira. He and her father had been bow hunting together since Rick's tenth birthday. He had won his share of archery competitions, and she didn't care to have him hunting her like a deer.

"Rick, knock it off," she yelled. "It's me, Abby."

The woods were still and quiet. She moved slightly, and another arrow skimmed past her elbow where it had been exposed. Damn. Was he after *her*?

This last one had come with more velocity and force, so whoever was after her was on the move and heading her way. She couldn't go back toward her car, but the property wasn't huge. She would just have to run toward one of the other three sides.

She scanned the sparse trees in front of her, looking for the best route. The vacant lot had seemed dense and natural when she first walked in, but now that she was at risk of being skewered, she could see the advantage was clearly with the hunter and not the prey. She took a deep breath and bolted toward a stand of cottonwoods, veering to the right at the last minute and diving behind a mound of dirt and broken tree limbs. The arrow meant for her landed harmlessly in one of the cottonwood trunks.

Abby paused only a moment to catch her breath before she sprinted forward again. She could see the glimmer of sunlight on a car just beyond the trees in front of her, but a noise to her right sent her off on a tangent again just before an arrow sliced through the space she had occupied only seconds before. She dived through a thick patch of undergrowth, crying out involuntarily when she landed on her right wrist. She scrabbled for purchase as the branches caught on her clothes and hair, and she finally clawed her way free and ran to a tree that offered more protection.

She held her hand tightly against her rib cage, but her shallow, rapid breaths sent flickers of pain through her wrist. She inched her way around the tree and realized it was the same one she'd been behind only moments before. Whoever was shooting—was it really Rick?—was toying with her, keeping her from the safety of the property's edges and in the dangerous center. The bow had seemed like a silly weapon to her at first, but she was starting to see its effectiveness. No sound would travel out to the street beyond the property. No one would come to her rescue.

Another whistle and a thwack as an arrow landed next to her, forcing her to inch around the trunk. If she could just make it back to where she had dropped her cell phone…but the expanse of open space between it and her was too deadly to cross. She had one more option. Aim toward the thickest part of the property and out the other side—a path that would take her right through the small lake. She didn't know how deep it was, but she'd have to take her chance and run as fast as she could, hoping an arrow didn't catch her in the thigh or back.

She was about to make her move when she heard a voice calling her name. Kira. She was coming from the direction of Abby's car, directly into the path of the shooter.

"Kira, get down!" she called, coming around the trunk and waving her arms. She had to draw the arrows to herself, give Kira enough time to run, but Kira saw her and came toward her instead of away. Abby moved quickly into the open area between them. She tripped over an exposed root, but got back to her feet and continued to run. Any thought of protecting herself fled as she rushed to get to Kira. Protect her. Give her cover and get her out of danger. She expected the stab of pain to hit her any moment—what would it feel like to be shot by an arrow?—or, much worse, to see one slicing through Kira's skin.

They met in the center of the small clearing, close to Abby's cell phone, where everything had started. She stumbled forward and into Kira's arms. The next arrow never came, and the woods around them fell silent.

CHAPTER TWENTY-TWO

A bby didn't want to move. She wanted to stay where she was forever, huddled on the damp ground and wrapped in Kira's arms as the birds resumed their chirping in the trees, but she had to find out who had been shooting at her. She got to her feet and pulled Kira along with her.

"What the hell is going on, Abby? I got your message about meeting me here, and then you came running out and screaming. What's wrong?"

Abby scanned the trees around them, alert for any sign that the attack would resume. "Did you see anyone else here?"

"No. Our cars are the only ones on this side of the property. Abby, tell me what's happening."

"Wait," Abby said. She retrieved her phone and called dispatch to report her location. When she ended the call, she pointed toward the deadly black arrows in the oak tree. "Someone was shooting at me. We need to get you back to your car so I can find out who it was."

She watched Kira's face turn pale as she stared at the arrows. "I'm coming with you," she said.

Abby was going to protest, but she trusted her instincts when they told her the danger was over, for now. Someone—Rick?— wanted to hurt her or scare her off the case. Kira didn't seem to be the target. Peace settled over the wooded area, so Abby kept Kira's hand in hers as they crisscrossed the property. Abby was careful to lead them around any footprints they saw, but apparently the lot was used as a shortcut, and there was too much foot traffic to make any particular tracks stand out. She hoped one of the detectives would be able to determine where the shooter had been standing so they could isolate the suspect's prints.

As they walked, Abby told Kira about Rick's threats. "Were you here earlier today?" she asked.

"No. I went home after I left the station. I was…well, I didn't want to answer my phone. But when I listened to your message I came right over. Do you think your brother would do this to you?"

Abby sighed and sat on the ground when they got back to the clearing. She looked at the arrow that had nearly shattered her elbow when she had moved beyond the tree's protection. "It's possible. He's a great shot, and whoever did this was deadly accurate. I don't know how long I would have been able to outmaneuver the shooter."

"But why? Does he really want to kill you?"

"I don't think so," Abby said. *I hope not.* "He's used to getting his own way, and to finding any means to do so. Maybe he's just warning me to stay away from you and to back off the Milford case. Drugging Legs, hunting me with a bow and arrows. It won't work, though."

Kira cupped Abby's cheek in her warm hand. Abby leaned into the contact before she turned her head and kissed Kira's palm. "I can't stay away from you, Kira," she admitted.

"I…I can't stay away from you, either." Kira's voice was quiet, but full of conviction. She pulled Abby's face toward hers and kissed her with a lingering caress of her lips.

"This is your emergency, Lieutenant?" Rachel's voice startled Abby, and she broke contact with Kira. "I rush over here, expecting you to be dead or at least maimed, but instead I find you having a make-out session in the woods."

Abby had to laugh at Rachel's exaggeratedly put-out tone, but she heard the concern behind her teasing words.

"How'd you get here so fast, Bryce?" Abby took the hand Kira offered and stood up. "I thought we had a few more minutes before anyone arrived."

"Yeah, I could see that," Rachel said.

"Hey, I rescued her from a mad shooter," Kira said. "I deserved a little kiss for a reward."

Everyone smiling, everyone joking, but Abby heard the worry rippling under the surface of their voices.

"I was at Point Defiance, getting more feed from the police stables, when I heard the call on the radio," Rachel said. "What happened, boss?"

Abby was describing the attack when several patrol cars arrived on the scene. She paused in the middle of her story, and then repeated the whole thing when the detectives were there to listen. She kept Kira close by her side, ignoring the surreptitious glances from the officers. She didn't care what anyone thought. She was relieved to be safe, even more relieved to have Kira safe.

While they started searching the wetland for clues about the shooter, Abby walked Kira to her car. Kira leaned back against the driver's side door, and Abby stood in front of her with her left hand braced on the car by Kira's shoulder.

"I had a nice, quiet life before you walked into it," Kira said. She trailed her fingers over the buttons on Abby's shirt. "Nirvana dragged me down the barn aisle to you, and then all hell broke loose."

Abby shifted so her legs came into contact with Kira's. "My life isn't usually so full of intrigue, either. Mostly, I sit at a desk and do paperwork."

"But your family…"

Abby shook her head, still confused by the events of the past week. "We usually keep to ourselves. Away from each other, out of the public eye. I've never liked Rick's way of doing things, whether he turns out to be crooked or honest, but at least I used to understand it. Greed, a hunger for power. He wasn't a paragon by any means, but he was consistent and predictable. Now this"—Abby gestured with her broken arm—"none of this makes sense to me. The only thing that does is you."

Abby moved to kiss her again, but Kira tilted her head in the direction of the wetland. "We have company," she said.

"Sorry to interrupt. Again," Rachel said. "The detectives want you to walk us through one more time, to see if there's anything we missed."

"I'll go," Kira said. "You'll keep me updated?"

"Of course. Just be careful, please. I'll call you."

Kira nodded and got in her car. Abby hated to see her go. Kira was about to drive away, beyond Abby's ability to protect her. Abby was torn between doing her job and taking care of someone who had become even more valuable to her than career or reputation.

"How do you do it, Rachel?" she asked as she watched until Kira's car turned a corner and went out of sight.

"Do what?"

Abby turned away from the street and walked down the path again. "How do you manage to have your personal life and your professional one coexist? How do you keep priorities straight?"

"Easy. Cal is my priority. You know what this job means to me, and how much I believe in what we do. But Cal means more."

Abby stopped. "So you'd put her before your duties as an officer?"

Rachel shrugged and grinned at her. "Are you asking if I'd break laws for her? Yes, if I had to. And no, not as a favor or for convenience."

Abby shook her head. She understood what Rachel was saying, and she knew without a doubt that she'd do the same to protect Kira. But lines were getting hazy, and Abby still didn't know how to clarify them in her mind. "I've tried so hard to keep work impersonal, to stay detached. I don't—"

Rachel's snort of laughter made her stop talking.

"Are you amused by something I said, Sergeant?"

"Well, yes." Rachel didn't even try to hide her smile. "You make your job more personal than anyone I've ever met. Your grandfather, your dad, Rick. Your entire career is based on what's personal to you." Abby stood still with her mouth open as Rachel walked away. "Come on, Lieutenant. They're waiting."

Abby jogged to catch up, her mind spinning. She didn't know how much Rachel knew or had guessed about her involvement in her family's mishandled cases, but she realized her attempts to atone for their sins weren't as secret as she had thought. Rachel was correct, and Abby didn't know why she hadn't seen it before. She had tried not to make connections at work—had prided herself on keeping separate, not making friends in the workplace—but her relationship with her family was entirely personal. Yes, she was trying to make the lives of the people they'd harmed better, but why? Because her version of right and wrong was outraged by their actions. Because she herself had never healed from the hurt her father caused when he used dirty money to buy her a goddamned saddle. Because she hated the way other officers said the name Hargrove. All personal reasons.

Abby moved like a sleepwalker as she retraced her movements through the woods. She pointed to hiding spots and described the arc of arrows, but most of her was trying to reconcile this new view of her life with her long-held belief that she was somehow disconnected from her job. She had fought her attraction to Kira because she thought it would make her weaker, morally and emotionally. But Kira made her stronger.

She placed her hand on the oak tree and felt the rough bark against her skin. She slid her finger into the smooth gouge left behind after the detectives had removed one of the arrows. She had been approaching this case wrong. Abby moved in a slow circle, tracing the movements of the archer based on the arrows' final positions, as if watching a shadow move through the trees. She needed to understand this person if she wanted to keep Kira safe. She had been pushing her feelings for Kira away, even though they burst out whenever she felt Kira was being attacked. Her goal had been to solve the case and to regain her emotional distance, but now everything shifted. Her priority was to protect Kira—not so she could be free to get away from her once the threat was removed, but because she wanted to be with her. Purely selfish motivation, and it felt damned good.

Chapter Twenty-three

I'm ready when you are," Abby said when she came out of the police barn and over to the bench where Kira and Julie were sitting.

Kira felt a twinge of anticipation at the thought of finally being alone with Abby. Since Rachel had arrived at the wetland, they hadn't had a moment to themselves. She'd been sorting through the events of the day—the culmination of a harrowing, but sometimes thrilling, two weeks—in the privacy of her own mind, but she wanted to share her conclusions with Abby.

"Okay, Abby. Julie, you'll call Sergeant Bryce if you see anyone suspicious, won't you?"

"Of course, Mom. I'll be fine." Julie smiled with a somewhat shaky bravado. "What about you and Abby? What if someone tries to kill her again?"

"We'll call Bryce, too," Abby said with a shake of her head. "I'm sure she'll manage to rescue all three of us while single-handedly patrolling the fairgrounds."

Kira grinned at Abby's overt irritation. Rachel and the other members of her team had been glued to her side since her run-in with the archer this afternoon, and Abby clearly chafed under their attention. Kira knew how independent Abby was accustomed to being, and she felt the warmth of Abby's affection for her when she had learned Abby had asked for Rachel's help in keeping tabs on Julie this evening.

Kira gave her daughter a hug. "Text or call anytime you want, honey. Have a fun time with your friends, and I'll see you when you get home."

Julie nodded. "Take care of each other," she said, giving Abby a quick hug as well before she ran off to join Angie and the other kids from her 4-H group.

Kira had to laugh at Abby's adorable expression of both pleasure and awkward embarrassment at Julie's display of affection for her. Abby punched her playfully in the arm.

"Maybe we should stay," Abby said. "We could follow her far enough behind so she doesn't notice."

Kira had considered doing the same thing. Or telling Julie to cancel the plans she and her club had made weeks ago. Julie had been looking forward to the evening spent going on rides and goofing off with her friends after the competition was finished, but she wouldn't have hesitated to leave with Kira and Abby instead. Kira had been tempted, but she didn't want Julie to live in fear. To give up her plans and stay locked inside her house or her heart because of the meanness of others.

Of course, it helped to know that the entire Tacoma Mounted Police Unit would be her bodyguards.

"We can't embarrass her," Kira said. She put her hand on Abby's lower back and pushed her toward the exit gate. "Your unit will take care of her tonight."

She was acting brave, but she wouldn't have let Julie stay here without her if it hadn't been for Rachel's promise to keep Julie in sight of the mounted unit at all times. The walkie-talkie she'd given Julie helped alleviate Kira's concerns, too. As had Billie's offer to drive Julie to Kira's on her way home. They were all banding together to protect one of their own, and Kira—who had fought against anyone having a possessive attitude toward her since Dale—felt the difference between their loving concern for her and Abby, and Dale's need to control her. Today she had watched Abby make the same realization about her team, finally letting them into her life even though she'd spent years keeping everyone out.

Kira and Abby joined a throng of people crossing the road from the fair to one of the main parking lots. When Abby had called her, asking to see her this evening, Kira had already been on her way to the fairgrounds with Julie. Rachel had brought Abby here to meet them. They were gradually getting closer to being alone. They got in Kira's car and she slowly inched forward behind a line of cars waiting to exit the lot. She reached over and took Abby's left hand in hers, entwining their fingers and holding her tightly.

Something had snapped inside her when she had watched Abby running across the clearing toward her. Disregarding her own safety just to ensure Kira's. She had been angry with Abby for stepping in to rescue her before, but this was different, and she had suddenly realized why. Abby wasn't trying to prove her superiority or trying to put Kira in a subordinate position. Rather, she was risking her own life to protect Kira's. Kira had mistakenly seen Abby as taking something away from her, but instead she was giving Kira everything she had. Her own life, if necessary. Kira was awed by what Abby had done, and surprised, as well. Not because Abby had put her own life in danger by running across the archer's path, but because of the way she'd felt once she learned why Abby had been racing toward her. Abby hadn't taken her power away, but she'd offered herself to Kira in a way that made her feel strong and cherished.

And loved.

"Do you mind if we make a stop on the way home?" Kira asked. She wasn't sure to which home she was referring. Was she taking Abby to her big, empty Victorian, and then spending a lonely night on her own until Julie got home? Or was she going to be brave enough to ask Abby to come with her. To share a night together, and the hope of many more to come, like she'd been too nervous to do after their dinner together?

"Not at all," Abby said. She gave Kira's hand a squeeze. "I'll go anywhere you want."

Kira bit her lip to keep from grinning like a fool. Abby's voice, low and suggestive, had just given her the option to choose the direction they went tonight. Kira had been hesitant to get close before, to get too physical with Abby in the too emotional atmosphere of her house, but now she wanted to do something even more intimate. Make herself even more vulnerable to Abby and prove—to both of them—how much she trusted her.

Kira turned off River Road and drove across the Puyallup River Valley. She slowed when they reached a deserted stretch between fields of tall corn stalks and low, thick rows of lettuce and searched for a barely discernable dirt path.

"This looks like an ideal place to dump a body," Abby said, looking out her side window. "Should I be concerned?"

"It's a little late to be asking," Kira said with a laugh. Her headlights lit up the cement berm between them and a small, meandering stream. Patches of brush encroached on the rarely traveled road, occasionally scratching the side of her car with an eerie, shrill sound. She came to a break in the berm and stopped the car. No need to pull to the side and park since no one else should be out here for days.

Kira smiled at Abby and turned off the ignition, plunging them into blackness. The blanket of dark lasted only a few moments, until Kira's eyes adjusted and allowed the light of the moon to illuminate them. She saw Abby watching her with a heartbreaking look of longing.

Kira got out of the car and scrambled up the cracked side of the berm. She had come out here to make herself vulnerable to Abby, but the expression she'd just witnessed was tender and revealing. She wasn't the only vulnerable one here, and with the knowledge came a sense of power and gratitude. Dale's method of controlling had made Kira feel like nothing. Abby's desire to protect her made her feel like Abby's *everything*.

She reached out and grabbed Abby's right elbow to help her climb the low wall. Abby sat beside her, and they looked at the slow-moving stream in silence. A full moon, with craters and valleys shown in deep relief on the clear night, was mirrored in a rippling image on the water. Solid black silhouettes of trees made the sky turn shades of dark purple and navy in comparison. Crickets chirped lazily in the distance and mosquitoes buzzed, but otherwise there was no sound except for breath and heartbeat. A clump of cattails, remnants of the wetland that used to be here and a symbol of what was to come, reached almost to Kira's shoulder.

"It's a beautiful place," Abby said. "Except for the cement and all the garbage floating over there."

Abby gestured toward a pile of debris in the shallows, caught in the trailing branches of a willow. Kira would have to come back in the light of day and do yet another cleanup in the area.

"Don't see what's here," Kira said. "Try to imagine what it will be."

Abby looked at her and not at the scenery. "Tell me what to see."

Kira felt Abby's focus on her, but as she spoke she lost herself in the fantasy she saw in her mind. "The whole valley used to be filled with a series of wetlands, but in the early nineteen hundreds, people channeled the streams and covered the marshy land with fill and drainage tiles to turn it into farmland. But if the berms are removed, allowing the stream to flow on its natural course, the area can be restored."

Kira pointed toward the bank opposite them. "Take away the Scotch broom and those clumps of thistles. Replace them with snowberry and salmonberry plants. Instead of the mucky scum along the edge of the stream, imagine sedges and bulrushes lining the banks." She waved her hand as if painting trees one by one. "Willow, red alder, black cottonwood. Filled with singing birds and giving the stream shade."

Abby watched Kira and saw the new ecosystem come to life through her words and gestures. The beauty of the dream was reflected on her face. "Who will make this happen? You?"

Kira smiled at her with a mix of pride and shy humility. "I'll help. Sometimes when we can't stop a developer from building on a wetland, for whatever reason, we can at least get them to create a mitigation site to replace it. This is one of our victories. It'll be restored with native plants and the groundwater will be allowed to pool naturally again. Someday it will be beautiful and full of life."

Abby brushed Kira's hair off her cheek. "Because of you." She understood why Kira had brought her here. She was sharing part of herself with Abby—as meaningful as trusting Abby and her team to take care of Julie, and just as personal. A gift.

Kira turned toward her and leaned forward to kiss her. Abby felt only Kira's desire. No hesitation or connection to old memories. Present, and looking forward. Abby relaxed against her and let the growing intensity of Kira's kiss set their pace.

Abby willingly lay back on the rough cement when Kira pushed against her shoulders. The contrast between Kira's softness on top of her and the unyielding coldness of concrete beneath her head and spine intensified both feelings until Abby's entire body felt like one quivering nerve ending. Kira kissed her neck, her throat, the skin revealed by the open neck of her polo shirt. Abby twisted the fingers of her left hand in Kira's hair, holding her tightly but not directing or guiding. Abby felt the exhaustion she'd been storing up since her accident, since Kira's abduction, since she first learned about her family secrets, slowly leach out of her body and into the rock below. It was replaced by the healing warmth of Kira's skin and of Kira's tongue moving slowly over her belly. Abby closed her eyes and let Kira take control.

Abby gasped when she felt Kira's fingers slowly open her jeans, and her mouth following the slow progression downward. She raised her hips to allow Kira better access, and denim skimmed along skin electric with arousal. Kira's fingers spread her lips, and the briefest flick of a tongue threatened to send Abby over the edge. Kira wasn't about to let her off so easily, though, and her intermittent touches and licks made Abby strain against the confining denim around her thighs. Finally, thankfully, magically, Kira took Abby fully into her mouth and brought her to a climax that she knew must have sent tremors into the earth around them.

Abby shivered, and Kira moved up to lie next to her and hold her close. Abby rested against Kira's chest and felt a racing heartbeat matching her own.

"I love you, Abby," Kira whispered, her breath ruffling Abby's hair.

"I love you, too," Abby answered without hesitation. She knew it with as much certainty as she knew she'd do *anything* to keep Kira safe. Suddenly her breath caught.

But Kira *was* safe. The shooting in the wetland had stopped as soon as she had arrived. Because now there were two targets and more risk of getting caught, or because the archer didn't want to hurt Kira? And she had been left relatively unharmed when Tad Milford was shot—only being left blindfolded and tied because she would be able to identify the killer on sight. Abby stopped breathing and stood still. Someone else had the same goal she did—to keep Kira safe.

Abby nearly rolled Kira off the cement shelf when she pushed herself to her feet and yanked up her jeans.

"What's wrong?" Kira asked with a frown.

"Nothing, nothing," Abby said, her mind racing. "Just let me call and check on Julie, then I'll be right back."

Abby scrambled off the berm and jogged over to the car. She got her cell off the passenger seat.

"Rachel, it's Abby. How's Julie?"

"She's great," Rachel said, with the midway sounds loud in the background. "She and her friends seem to be having a great time."

"Good. Thank you again for watching her. Say, who's on guard duty with the horses tomorrow night?"

"Billie. Why?"

"I'll take her place," Abby said. "Let her know. In fact, let everyone you can think of know."

Rachel was silent for a moment. "You know something. Are you planning to use yourself as bait?"

"That's exactly what I'm doing. Meeting this person on my terms."

"I don't think—"

"I gave you an order, Sergeant," Abby said. Her voice left no room for argument. She ended the call and tossed her phone in the car before returning to Kira. This had just gotten personal.

CHAPTER TWENTY-FOUR

Kira stepped under the yellow police tape and walked down the empty barn aisle. Legs was still at the vet, and there was a cot and sleeping bag in her stall. The other three horses were doing their second demonstration. Abby was probably in the audience, watching and wishing she could ride regardless of her wrist.

Kira paused in front of a chalkboard the unit had been using to list practice times and stall cleaning or feeding duties. A large note written in Abby's handwriting announced that she was on guard duty tonight. She wasn't surprised by the information—Abby had called her earlier and said she was sleeping in the barns to give her officers a break—but she wasn't sure why Abby was advertising the fact that she'd be here alone all night.

No, not alone. Kira smiled and ducked under the tape again on her way out. She had her own plans, hastily made after Abby's phone call. She had brought Julie here to meet some 4-H friends who were showing alpacas, and Julie had already been planning on staying with Angie overnight. Kira had decided to organize a slumber party of her own. For two.

Kira had wanted to see Abby again tonight and she'd been disappointed when she heard about the duty shift. She wanted to feel Abby's touch, her kiss. To quietly whisper words of love she couldn't keep inside any longer since she'd acknowledged them herself. She'd hoped for a quiet evening alone with Abby, sitting on the bench in her backyard. A repeat of the night she'd first realized how smoothly Abby fit into her and Julie's world. Then, she had been scared by the evolving intimacy between them. This time, however, she wouldn't hesitate to be with Abby, wholeheartedly and unreservedly. No way would they have gone to separate rooms when they went to bed.

Kira walked quickly around the barns and back to the busier section of the fair. She felt a shiver of excitement as she thought about the night ahead. She'd hide somewhere—there must be plenty of nooks and crannies where she could disappear until the fair was closed—and then she'd sneak back to the horse barn. Open the door and walk across the stall. Slide into the sleeping bag and into Abby's arms...

She imagined the surprised look on Abby's face and couldn't contain her smile. Luckily, there were too many people around for anyone to notice the heated blush she could feel creeping up her neck as her mind wandered forward in time.

Kira looked at her watch. Still a few hours to go. She bought a bag of popcorn and ate it while she searched for a hiding place. The horse barns would be ideal, but she worried the mounted unit would check them before they left for the evening. She didn't want Don or Rachel to discover her lurking in one of the empty stalls. She considered the other animal barns, but she'd rather not bring the smell of livestock to her tryst with Abby.

She wandered into the agricultural building. The granges from across the state each had a large display, like huge shadow boxes placed in two rows, back-to-back, displaying the produce and other goods from their region. Some were simple with neat rows of corn and berries and tomatoes, but others were more elaborate. A horse and buggy, the logo of the Seattle Mariners, complete with autographed baseball bats. Kira was admiring the variety of winter squashes in one of them when she noticed the gap between the two rows. It was just big enough for her to squeeze through, and the dark corridor inside looked relatively clean and roomy. Who'd bother checking inside there every night?

Kira grinned and went outside the building again. She'd wander around the fair until it got dark and the crowds thinned out. Then she'd come back to her chosen spot and slip between the rows when no one was looking. And once the fair was closed and empty, she'd go to Abby.

❖

Kira shifted and brought her legs underneath her until she was in a kneeling position. Her plan had sounded so romantic in her mind, but the reality was less comfortable than she had expected. She'd been sitting on the cold concrete floor for two hours now, having made the mistake of hiding away as soon as she had the chance instead of waiting until it was almost time for the fair to shut down. She'd spent her time wondering how many rats would be attracted to the building full of produce and grains where she was hiding.

The occasional sound of a person passing by kept her on edge, and once the lights had been turned out, she waited where she was instead of jumping up and running to Abby. The place was creepy as hell when emptied of fairgoers, and she wished she had taken her chances with an empty horse stall closer to Abby. She hadn't anticipated the return of her memory of being kidnapped, and her nerves were frayed and raw by the time she felt it was safe to leave.

Finally, she crawled out from behind the grange exhibits and stood in the quiet darkness. The abandoned carts and information tables cast mysterious and bulky shadows on the walls. She had spent an hour searching for a place to hide, and now the building seemed full of secret spots. She stretched her cramped legs and shivered in the cold. A nice brisk jog over to the police barns would do her good. Or a mad dash. She was on her way out the door when the sound of a display falling over made her spin around. Her heart was thumping against her ribs, and the unexpected beam of a flashlight made her squint and cover her eyes.

A guard. They must have night watchmen patrolling the fair. Hopefully, whoever it was would kindly escort her to Abby. She was about to identify herself and explain her embarrassing predicament when a voice stopped her.

"Waiting to meet your girlfriend? How romantic."

Dale.

Kira felt her blood turn to ice, sluggish in her veins. Run? Cower? She couldn't decide how to respond, but she snapped back to full awareness when she heard a faint click coming from the direction of Dale and her flashlight. The same click she'd heard right before Tad's brains were spattered all over her. She couldn't identify the gun from the sound, of course, but all the pieces fell into place in her mind and she *knew*.

"You. You killed Milford?"

Dale laughed and moved closer. "I was only trying to save you, baby. That idiot stepbrother of mine was going to hurt you. You have no idea how much."

Kira had a very good idea of how much Tad had wanted to hurt her. She had felt it running through his fingers and into her soul. She inched back toward the door behind her. Toward Abby and safety.

"Then why didn't you untie me? You left me there all night next to him."

"You were safe. I couldn't let you see my face, or I'd have had to kill you, too. I don't want to do that, Kira."

The disembodied flashlight moved with Kira. She didn't want to risk a look backward to see how far she had to go. Could she make it in time? Get to the doorway and out into the dark, empty fair before the bullet reached her?

"Why?" Kira asked. She wasn't sure specifically what she was asking, but she needed answers.

"I love you, Kira. I always have. You've been so good over the past year. No dates, nothing to make me upset. But this week you've disappointed me. She's no good for you, Kira, and I'll prove it to you."

"You're the one who poisoned her horse and who shot at her." Kira stopped her painstakingly slow backward progress and stared into the flashlight's beam. Abby's injuries were because of her. She had been attributing the events of the past week to money or Abby's disreputable connections, but Kira had brought danger into Abby's life, not the other way around.

"You belong to me, not her. I was going to take care of her once and for all tonight, but luckily I saw you by the barns. You might have gotten in the way, but instead you'll get to watch while I prove how much I love you."

Kira was going to be sick. She had to get to Abby and warn her. She turned and bolted for the door, but Dale tackled her from behind before she made it far. The cold pressure of the gun at her temple put an end to her escape attempt.

Chapter Twenty-five

Abby paced back and forth along the dark aisle. The three police horses had watched her with pricked ears at first, but soon they'd lost interest and returned to munching their hay. Abby stopped every few feet and listened for the sound of approaching footsteps, for a change in the air that meant company. Anything. She had given Dale the chance she wanted, and Abby was here alone to confront her, but so far she was disappointed. She wanted a fight, was itching for one. The thought of that woman ever touching Kira in the past or the future made her want to retch. She'd hurt Abby already, but the pain was minor compared to the worry about what Dale might do if she got back into Kira's life.

She whipped around and had her gun aimed at the door at the first sound of shoes on pavement, but Bandit's shrill whinny made her shake her head and lower her weapon.

"What the hell are you doing here, Rachel?"

"I could ask you the same thing." Rachel appeared in the doorway, lit by the soft glow of the nightlight plugged in by the tack room. Her features were shadowed and hard to read, but Abby could guess what Rachel's expression would be. One of concern. And stubbornness.

"You know why I'm here," Abby said. "Guard duty. Where's the rest of your posse?"

"I'm right here," Cal said from behind Rachel. "Don and Billie are on recon."

Abby rolled her eyes at Cal's television-inspired police lingo. "Why don't you all go home and have a beer. I got this."

"Why don't you tell me exactly what's going on," Rachel offered instead. She sat on a bale of hay and leaned against Bandit's stall. Cal sat close beside her and crossed her arms over her chest. Abby sighed. They weren't going anywhere.

She propped her shoulder against the wall near the hay and told them about her suspicions. Why Kira had been kept safe from Tad and the flying arrows. Why Abby herself had been singled out with increasingly lethal intent. Why she needed to confront Dale and put an end to her tyranny over Kira.

Rachel nodded when she was finished. "Your suspicions make sense," she said. "The only flaw is your foolish attempt to fight her on your own. You have a better chance of defeating her if we're working together. Five of us will be more able to keep Kira out of danger than you alone."

Abby couldn't argue with Rachel's last statement. She wanted to, but Kira's life was more important than her need to fight every battle on her own. This time, she'd have to accept help.

"Okay," she said. "You're here, so you might as well stay. Can you watch the horses while I walk around the barns and check for any sign of her?"

"Will do, boss. Keep one of these walkie-talkies with you and promise you'll call me at the first sign of trouble."

"Will do, boss," Abby mimicked, but she took the walkie-talkie from Rachel and snapped it at her hip. She went out into the cool night and stopped for a moment, staring up at the stars. She wasn't sure what to feel now that she had backup, friends on her side. Relief? Yes, a little. And some discomfort as well, with the unaccustomed sense of connection. But they were all working for Kira. She was the one who mattered.

Abby walked down the aisles and checked each stall with her flashlight, but she felt the emptiness of the space around her without needing to look. She trusted her instincts, and they told her to widen her range, to look beyond the barn. She had expected Dale to come to her, knowing she'd be alone with the horses, but she found herself wandering through the nearby structures as well. Cows and pigs turned their heads to watch her as she walked. She was about to head back when she saw the beam of a flashlight cut across a window in the agricultural building. Don and Billie. She went over to meet them.

A sharp blow to her injured wrist made her drop the flashlight she'd had cradled against her side. She doubled over in pain and loosened her grip on her gun just enough for Dale to kick it out of her hand. It clattered over the concrete and came to rest under a display of vegetables. Her right hand was wrenched behind her back and Dale forced her to walk deeper into the building.

"We were just going to come looking for you," Dale said. She propped her flashlight on its end so it lit the room enough for Abby to see Kira where she stood in an awkward position next to a Mariners pennant. Her hands were behind her back and her eyes were wide and frightened. Abby tried desperately to reach the walkie-talkie with her left hand, but Dale grabbed it first and tossed it aside.

"Who were you planning to call?" she demanded. "Who else is here?"

"I don't know," Abby lied. "We use the radios to communicate with other officers on the grounds. I was hoping one might still be here."

Dale laughed. "No such luck, I'm afraid. Well, there was a night watchman on duty, but he's, shall we say, indisposed."

"Kira, are you all right?" Abby called. Kira nodded, but Dale jostled Abby's arm in punishment. Abby gritted her teeth and fought to stay conscious. She couldn't let Dale's brutal treatment of her injury make her faint, or she and Kira would never have a chance of getting away.

"I didn't want to do it this way," Dale said. Her voice had shifted from demanding and abrasive to whiny. "I tried to make Tad stop hurting her, and to make you stay away from her, but no one would listen to me." Her voice turned raspy with anger and she shook Abby's wrist. "No one listened!"

Abby saw bright spots in front of her eyes. She wasn't going to be able to fight the pain, to save Kira. A dim part of her mind saw

Kira moving against the rough boards of the grange exhibits. What was she doing? Abby struggled to make sense of something she knew she should comprehend, but her head was swimming. Kira's hands were tied. Was she trying to get free? Yes, she was loose. What was she reaching for?

Abby inhaled when the meaning behind Kira's actions seeped through the confusion of pain and fear and she looked at the door behind Dale. "Don, thank God! We're over here," she called to the empty doorway. Dale turned to look, distracted only momentarily, but long enough for Kira to cross the distance between them and swing the baseball bat she held in her hands.

❖

Abby's vision swam back into focus and she saw Kira's face close to hers. She shifted and winced as an aftershock of pain rippled through her arm. She was lying on the concrete, her head cradled in Kira's lap. The memories seeped back into her consciousness.

"Where's Dale?" she asked, struggling to sit up.

"Rachel's here," Kira assured her. "She's got Dale in handcuffs."

Abby finally noticed the motion around them. Her team, Cal. Some other officers she didn't recognize. "You rescued me," she said, reaching up with her good hand to stroke Kira's cheek. "You hit her with something, didn't you?"

"A baseball bat," Kira said with a smug-looking smile. "It felt good, too."

Abby laughed weakly. "Remind me to stay on your good side. What were you doing here tonight?"

"Long story," Kira said. "I'll tell you after we get you to the hospital to have your wrist checked."

Abby sighed. She needed some painkillers and a good night's sleep. But even more, she needed Kira by her side.

"You won't leave me, will you?" she asked.

Kira lowered her head and kissed her softly on the mouth. "Never," she promised.

Chapter Twenty-six

"Move it a little to the left. No, not so much. Back to the right an inch."

Abby groaned and stood up from her crouched position next to the floral-patterned love seat. "Broken wrist here, remember?"

"You've been riding for two weeks with that wrist. You just don't want to move furniture anymore, but I guess it'll be okay where it is," Kira said. She sat in a burgundy wing chair with her bare feet propped on a matching ottoman and made a grand gesture encompassing the entire room. "What do you think?"

Abby turned in a slow circle. She barely recognized her house since Kira had appointed herself chief decorator and had hauled Abby on a series of shopping sprees. The result was fantastic and well worth the hours spent trying one chair or couch after the other like a pair of jumping beans in a furniture store. Kira had suggested tones of reds, tans, and golds for this particular space, and Abby had agreed hesitatingly. She would never have chosen the bold colors and patterns for herself, but now that she saw them in the living room she knew Kira had been right—as usual. The furnishings suited the grand old Victorian, and the house was slowly beginning to feel like a home.

"It's gorgeous," Abby said. She sat on the ottoman and lifted Kira's feet onto her lap. The real reason Abby felt like she had a home was Kira herself. She didn't need more than a card table and an air mattress as long as Kira and Julie were with her. Before they'd come to live with her, she'd used the house as a way station. Eat, sleep, reread old case files. If she wanted to relax, she had to go outside, on the back porch. Now, room after room was being made ready for her new family. In here there was a desk for Julie's homework and Kira's wetland books. Comfortable chairs for reading or playing games. Abby had never before seen such potential in a room, as if hints of all the family evenings to come were echoing off the walls.

She massaged Kira's insteps with her thumbs. "What room next?" she asked. They'd finished Julie's bedroom first, followed swiftly by their own. "The kitchen?"

"Or the guest bedroom," Kira said. She leaned back and closed her eyes. "Oooh, I needed this. Your hands feel so good."

"Your poor feet must be exhausted after watching me move furniture for hours."

Kira laughed and playfully kicked at her. "You're forgetting I moved the ottoman without any help."

"I would have offered to carry one end for you, but I had a two-ton couch strapped to my back at the time." Abby grabbed Kira's feet again and lowered them to the floor. "Come upstairs with me. I have a surprise for you."

"Yum. Is this surprise in the bedroom, I hope?"

Abby stopped outside her office door. She wrapped her arms around Kira's waist and nuzzled her neck. Even the mention of their bed or bedroom made her drip with desire. "That'll come later, darling," she said. She gave Kira a kiss and stood back, motioning at the closed door. "Look inside."

Kira hesitated before reaching for the doorknob. She hadn't been back in Abby's lair since they'd researched Rick's and Tad's schemes to trick people out of their land and develop it. This was Abby's domain, where she handled her family issues in her own way. Kira had been determined to give Abby her space and not nag at her to give up her fruitless and exhausting search for absolute justice.

Abby nudged her arm, and Kira opened the door. She stepped inside the room and stared at the transformation Abby had made. Framed botanical prints lined the walls where the timeline illustrating Albert Hargrove's corruption had once hung. A massive oak rolltop desk and matching bookshelves took the place of the old, utilitarian desk and locked metal file cabinets. Kira's field guides and massive binders were neatly stacked on the shelves, and a brand-new plant press sat on a worktable.

Kira walked over to the desk and ran her hand over the smooth wood. A bouquet of sunflowers sat on top, catching the light from the window. The effort Abby must have put into this project overwhelmed her and made her eyes sting with sudden tears. Not only had Abby moved everything in here in secret, but she'd also painted the walls a pale green and had installed a cushy carpet. "I love it, Abby. It's perfect—every part of it."

More significantly than the changes in decor, Abby had removed the case files and charts that had haunted her for too many years. Kira understood what a difficult step it must have been for Abby to pack up those memories. Abby had let Kira into her home and her heart, but installing Kira in this room meant Abby was inviting her to settle in her soul. She went to Abby and kissed her.

"What does this mean?" she asked, her hands cupping Abby's cheeks. "Are you through trying to singlehandedly fight for justice? Or did you just move everything to a different room?"

Abby covered Kira's hands with her own. "I needed to stop, Kira. I let my grandfather's sins take over my world, but I won't let him do the same to you or Julie. I'll find another way to help people, something less destructive to our lives. An action I can take instead of living my life as a reaction to his."

Kira flung herself into Abby's arms. She'd been proud of Abby before and had admired her bravery and sense of justice, but never had those feelings been as intense as they were now. She didn't know how to express how much she cherished not only the study, but Abby's words about her new plan for life. Kira wanted to help her with the process of letting go. She pulled back a little and tugged on the front of Abby's green shirt.

"I have an idea," she said. She popped the buttons open one at a time. "We should christen this room together."

Abby looked at the walls, then back at Kira. "Christen? Or exorcise?"

"What I have in mind ought to take care of both," Kira said. She lowered her head and kissed her way along the edge of Abby's bra, dipping her tongue in the hollow between her breasts. When she heard Abby's soft gasp, she put her hands on Abby's hips and pushed her back until she bumped into the desk. She leaned into Abby and kissed her hard on her mouth, fumbling to get Abby's shirt and bra off her body and onto the floor. She was drowning—in Abby's love, in her generosity, in the beauty of their future together. She moaned against Abby's lips and kissed her with more passion than she'd ever believed she'd be capable of feeling.

Abby scooted back until she was sitting on the edge of the desk. She broke away from Kira's kisses just long enough to pull her T-shirt over her head. She'd made love to Kira in plenty of ways since they'd been together. Fast and hot, or slow and erotic. She'd never felt Kira's urgency like this before. She'd never been so completely *comprehended* before. Kira had absorbed her, taken her in and examined her. And she accepted and loved the Abby she knew so well.

Abby braced her hands behind her on the desk and arched her back when Kira moved from her mouth, achingly along her breastbone. She took one of Abby's nipples in her mouth and held it in place with her teeth while her tongue skimmed across, over and over until Abby was unable to remain still. She tangled one hand in Kira's hair and grasped the curved side of the desk with her other. She felt so wet she worried she'd slide right off the polished oak.

Abby closed her eyes tightly as memories from this room threatened to distance her from Kira and the wonderful things she was doing with her mouth. She struggled to stay afloat, to keep from sinking into the past. She'd packed up the physical reminders of her Hargrove pain, but would she always carry the guilt in her heart? She had wanted to prove her love for Kira by stripping this room of its power over her, and she knew Kira understood the importance of the gesture, maybe more than Abby herself, but was she—

"Where are you?" Kira whispered in her ear. "Where did you go?"

Quiet questions. Kira loved her. Wanted her. It was up to Abby to decide. She'd seen her path as inevitable, but freedom was only a choice away. "I'm here, with you," Abby said. Her sentence ended with a moan as Kira unzipped her pants and tugged them over Abby's hips.

Abby gasped as Kira licked her ear before whispering in it. Hot breath on damp skin sent a shiver of goose bumps over Abby's exposed skin. "Look at me," Kira insisted.

Abby slowly opened her eyes, expecting to see ghosts in the room. But there was only Kira. A green room, pictures of plants, books. Kira. Touching her. Sliding deep into her wetness and releasing the last of Abby's bonds.

Kira held Abby against her chest as she shuddered from her orgasm. Kira had felt her slipping away, back to the familiar world of self-protective barriers and endless atonement, but in a single moment she had changed. She'd turned away from her past and come back to Kira.

She yelped in surprise when Abby spun her around and deposited her on the desk.

"My turn to christen," Abby said with her wicked grin. Kira dropped her head back when Abby kissed her throat, opening herself, heart and soul, to the woman she loved.

About the Author

Karis Walsh is the author of the Rainbow Award–winning romances *Harmony* and *Sea Glass Inn*, as well as a romantic intrigue series about a mounted police unit that begins with *Mounting Danger*. A Pacific Northwest native, she recently relocated herself and her goats to Texas, where she lives with her partner and their four-legged kids. When she isn't writing, she's playing with her animals, cooking, reading, playing the violin or viola, or hiking through the state park.

Books Available From Bold Strokes Books

Making a Comeback by Julie Blair. Music and love take center stage when jazz pianist Liz Randall tries to make a comeback with the help of her reclusive, blind neighbor, Jac Winters. (978-1-62639-357-8)

Soul Unique by Gun Brooke. Self-proclaimed cynic Greer Landon falls for Hayden Rowe's paintings and the young woman shortly after, but will Hayden, who lives with Asperger syndrome, trust her and reciprocate her feelings? (978-1-62639-358-5)

The Price of Honor by Radclyffe. Honor and duty are not always black and white—and when self-styled patriots take up arms against the government, the price of honor may be a life. (978-1-62639-359-2)

Mounting Evidence by Karis Walsh. Lieutenant Abigail Hargrove and her mounted police unit need to solve a murder and protect wetland biologist Kira Lovell during the Washington State Fair. (978-1-62639-343-1)

Threads of the Heart by Jeannie Levig. Maggie and Addison Rae-McInnis share a love and a life, but are the threads that bind them together strong enough to withstand Addison's restlessness and the seductive Victoria Fontaine? (978-1-62639-410-0)

Sheltered Love by MJ Williamz. Boone Fairway and Grey Dawson—two women touched by abuse—overcome their pasts to find happiness in each other. (978-1-62639-362-2)

Searching for Celia by Elizabeth Ridley. As American spy novelist Dayle Salvesen investigates the mysterious disappearance of her ex-lover, Celia, in London, she begins questioning how well she knew Celia—and how well she knows herself. (978-1-62639-356-1).

Hardwired by C.P. Rowlands. Award-winning teacher Clary Stone and Leefe Ellis, manager of the homeless shelter for small children, stand together in a part of Clary's hometown that she never knew existed. (978-1-62639-351-6)

The Muse by Meghan O'Brien. Erotica author Kate McMannis struggles with writer's block until a gorgeous muse entices her into a world of fantasy sex and inadvertent romance. (978-1-62639-223-6)

No Good Reason by Cari Hunter. A violent kidnapping in a Peak District village pushes Detective Sanne Jensen and lifelong friend Dr. Meg Fielding closer, just as it threatens to tear everything apart. (978-1-62639-352-3)

Romance by the Book by Jo Victor. If Cam didn't keep disrupting her life, maybe Alex could uncover the secret of a century-old love story, and solve the greatest mystery of all—her own heart. (978-1-62639-353-0)

Death's Doorway by Crin Claxton. Helping the dead can be deadly: Tony may be listening to the dead, but she needs to learn to listen to the living. (978-1-62639-354-7)

The 45th Parallel by Lisa Girolami. Burying her mother isn't the worst thing that can happen to Val Montague when she returns to the woodsy but peculiar town of Hemlock, Oregon. (978-1-62639-342-4)

A Royal Romance by Jenny Frame. In a country where class still divides, can love topple the last social taboo and allow Queen Georgina and Beatrice Elliot, a working-class girl, their happy ever after? (978-1-62639-360-8)

Bouncing by Jaime Maddox. Basketball coach Alex Dalton has been bouncing from woman to woman because no one ever held her interest, until she meets her new assistant, Britain Dodge. (978-1-62639-344-8)

Same Time Next Week by Emily Smith. A chance encounter between Alex Harris and the beautiful Michelle Masters leads to a whirlwind friendship and causes Alex to question everything she's ever known—including her own marriage. (978-1-62639-345-5)

All Things Rise by Missouri Vaun. Cole rescues a striking pilot who crash-lands near her family's farm, setting in motion a chain of events that will forever alter the course of her life. (978-1-62639-346-2)